VICTOR

BOOK 2 - THE EDEN EAST NOVELS

SACHA BLACK

COPYRIGHT

*For mum and dad. Thank you for giving me an imagination
filled with a thousand worlds and a million stories.*

CONTENTS

ONE

> *There is only light and dark. Balance and Imbalance. Right and wrong. There are only two sides to every war* - Balance Proverb

When I kill someone, I expect them to stay dead. It's only polite, after all. But Victor didn't stay dead even after I stabbed a poisoned knife through his heart. When he gate-crashed my Coronation Ceremony two months ago, Victor was very much alive. No one's seen him since, but I know he's out there...watching and waiting.

Steam rolls through the station, giant billowing clouds broken only by the occasional nervous Keeper wandering through the steam looking for luggage and friendly faces. My stomach twinges as I step off Trey's train and onto Stratera's platform.

Trey steps down behind me and passes me my suitcase.

"Are you ready?" he says, bending to kiss me.

I close my eyes, leaning into him, inhaling the scent of his warm skin barely covered by his string vest. I look up and say, "Ish. Mostly I'm swinging between feeling sick with nerves and feeling sick with excitement."

He laughs as he touches his forehead to mine, "I can't believe I'm finally here, and with you."

He picks me up, swings me around, and then pops me back on the floor, a grin spreading across his face lighting up his sparkling blue eyes.

"Neither can I." I wrap my arms around his neck and slide my lips over his. When I disentangle myself, I spot a hand waving at me behind him: Bo. She and Kato traveled on the public train as they met Bo's parents early this morning for breakfast.

Trey looks over his shoulder. "Go," he says. "I'll take our bags and meet all of you outside the station."

"Okay."

He kisses me on the forehead before walking away. Staring after him as his figure disappears into the shroud of smoke, my chest tightens. I still struggle to accept that he's mine. I spent my whole life thinking I was fated to Victor, and now I'm with Trey it all feels *too* good, too dreamy. Part of me is terrified it's all a giant mistake. That I'll wake up any second and the First Fallon or Victor will have taken everything away from me.

"What's that face for?" Bo says as she reaches me.

"Nothing," I say, pasting on a smile. "I'm fine."

She shrugs and then wriggles her hips at me, "Do I look okay?"

It takes everything for me not to roll my eyes. Of course she looks okay. Bo is the most flawless person I know. Her skin is always smooth and creamy-white like a perfect doll. She's wearing fitted beige shorts to the knee, a corseted type top, which is now maroon instead of her usual black, something I suspect is to represent Kato - her Siren Balancer, as well as her usual fur cloak – an essential for any Northern Shifter. Where her right calf used to be is a prosthetic leg Titus and Lance made her. The cogs and brass tubing are shinier than normal; she must have polished it especially for today. Staring at her leg reminds me of Evelyn, and my chest tightens another notch. Evelyn is Trey's old Balancer – she tore Bo's leg off during the battle with Victor.

"You look stunning. Been shopping, have we?" I say, trying to distract myself.

"Kato treated me for the start of term. Guilt buys, I think." She pulls her bright red lips into a smile but doesn't look at me. Instead she pats her hair as if to check her bun is still immaculate, which of course, it is.

"And you clearly accepted. So, I take it things are better?"

She pouts. "Well, I wasn't going to say no to this beauty, was I?" she says, pointing to her corset. "We're... Better, I guess. But it's infuriating. I can't stay away from him for long because our Binding pulls me back. I mean, I love him, but I'm still going to make him suffer a bit for what he did."

Before the fight with Victor, Kato compelled Bo to give me some of her blood - blood that helped to end her brother's life.

We exit the platform to find Trey and Kato hovering with their suitcases on the other side of the street looking up at the academy campus, which is set at the top of a hill over-looking Siren City.

Within seconds of leaving the station, a sticky sheen clings to my skin as the humid Southern sun bears down all hot and angry onto the street.

It takes us ten minutes to reach the top of the hill. This high, you can see over the South and West State lines and it's stunning. I look west, and in the distance right on the horizon is the skyline of Luna City's network of thatched bungalows. Between us is the Trutinor coastline and the glittering Blood Ocean. I turn and scan the southern side and the valley that's home to Siren City. Regal mansions made of marble and shimmering creams skim the skyline. We arrive at the front entrance, and after a few minutes of pulling maps out on our CogTrackers, we find our way around to the rear entrance where we're due to meet the principal.

I take a deep breath as we near a set of wrought iron gates. The four of us: me, Trey, Bo, and Kato, take tentative steps as we approach the towering black gates. Filigree twists decorate the tips of the iron poles, and in the center, where the round handles hang, a plaque reads:

WITH KNOWLEDGE SHALL WE JUDGE

The academy's motto is a stark reminder of what we're here to do: weigh the Balance of fate, and ensure the fate of humans and Keepers alike is carried out.

"I'm nervous," Bo says, glancing at the sign, "my stomach is all knotted with butterflies."

"Me too," I say, slipping my hand into Trey's. "I'm dreading being head girl."

"At least you have a handsome head boy to accompany you," Trey grins.

"I heard it's a lot of governors' board meetings and administration," Bo says, shrugging.

As we rest our cases on the floor, I glance over to her, unsure of what that comment meant. We're a little early, but already, the street is crawling with students from our year group at Keepers School as well as a myriad of faces I don't recognize from other realms.

I peer through the gate, into a flowering courtyard. It's long and thin with a row of flower beds on either side. Down the center is a walkway and in the middle, a fountain that froths and bubbles as it showers its basin with watery spray. At the far end is a set of arches, and if I strain, through the arches is another courtyard which, I think, leads to the entrance.

A tall female appears; she's wearing fitted maroon trousers that hug her curves and a flowing white blouse. Her hair is short and flops in loose curls around her face, and her eyes are piercing blue. She's a Siren.

"Is that the head teacher?" I ask.

"Yeah," Kato says, raising an eyebrow, "damn fine Siren too."

Bo digs her elbow into his ribs.

"Er, highly skilled Siren. I meant highly skilled, obviously."

"Course you did," she growls.

I suppress a grin as the head teacher reaches the gates and unlocks them.

"Welcome to Stratera Academy," she says, pulling the

gates wide open and gesturing for us to enter. "My name is Professor Astra."

She leads the now sizable group of Keepers through the first courtyard, under the arches, and into the second courtyard. This one is similar to the first but without the fountain.

Standing on the opposite side of the courtyard is the academy building. It's comprised of a bulbous square made of dark red bricks in the middle – the main building, according to my CogTracker map, is home to our lecture halls, theory classes, and the academy's library. And on either side of it are white circular towers: practical simulators, fighting arenas, gyms, and testing zones.

Professor Astra stops near a large oak door in the middle of the central brick building.

"Welcome to Stratera Academy," she starts. "It is both a great honor and testament to your dedicated studies that you have made it to the academy. But it is my duty to remind you of the great burden you bear as Keepers and Fallons in bringing to pass the judgment of fate. You are no longer apprentices. Here you will train both in the simulators and in the field alike, but unlike Keepers School, your field training is live, as will your exams be. And they'll take place on Earth. As the humans say, you're not in Kansas anymore."

She places her hand on the door, and as if under their own power, the doors swing open into a spacious foyer. The black and white checkered flooring clacks underfoot as I wander behind Professor Astra. Corridors shoot off at intermittent points down each side of the room two of which lead to the practice towers. In the corners of the room, two staircases spiral up to other floors. Then I notice an enormous door three times as tall as me, standing alone in the middle of the foyer, and I pull to a sudden stop. Trey, Bo, and Kato all career into my back.

"What the hell?" Kato says, brushing himself down. I grab his chin and point his face toward the door.

"Woah," he breathes.

The arched door frame is made of milky colored marble with a web of maroon veins spidering over it. The door itself is made of polished silver, or maybe it's glass because as I circle the door, my face and the faces of my future classmates, all wearing the same bemused expression, are reflecting back at me. The most interesting part about the door is that there's no handle. No way to open it.

When our group settles, Professor Astra quietens us and says, "This is the Door of Fates. It is said that once, long ago, it bore a single lock, which when opened would allow certain souls to return from Obex. Of course, it's shrouded in myth; it's stood for two hundred years in this very foyer, and no lock has ever appeared. Now, in the room on the left, you can pick up your dormitory keys." She points at a door in the corner of the foyer. "The rest of the day and the weekend are free for exploring. Monday morning after induction, you'll have a formal tour, and then classes will commence."

She stands a little straighter, a glint in her eye, "Welcome to the toughest three years of your life."

TWO

'After the lands and magics were created but the soil was still young, the First Fallon tore the land in two and banished her sister to Obex.

Rueben, the eldest child of the First Fallon, decreed that Darique, the eldest child of the Last Fallon and first-born anomaly, should abdicate and renounce his claim on the Trutinor throne because his mother was shamed in defeat.

But Darique, as the first-born of all the children and true heir to Trutinor, refused to renounce his claim; a brutal and bloody war raped the lands of Trutinor, pillaging life and Balance from the people and the earth. Rueben lost and as punishment Darique created a law determining his lineage as rulers of

Trutinor for all eternity. And so, the fifth law became: the First Family of the East shall rule Trutinor.'

Excerpt from the History of Trutinor Vol. 1

Our luggage cases rattle over the cobbles as Trey, Kato, Bo, and I exit Stratera Academy and cross the road toward the dormitories. A long marble mansion nestled on the street opposite Stratera is our term-time home for the next three years.

A few days ago, after some not entirely legitimate CogTracker work, Kato brandished his Tracker at us. The academy system was displayed on it, and showed that our dorm rooms were all conveniently located on the same floor. In. The. Same. Apartment.

"We're roomies, baby," he had pronounced as he thrust the Tracker in our direction.

Once again, Kato pulls out his Tracker with the same smug look as before and gestures to the top set of windows.

"Penthouse," he says, "obviously."

"If I don't ask, I can keep assuming that this is all a pleasant coincidence, and no one did anything illegal," Trey says, glaring at his brother.

"Totally one hundred percent legal, non-hacking, happy coincidence."

Grinning, I push through the cream-colored doors and into the dormitory foyer. There's a bustling as students pull pieces of paper from bags and crane heads to view floor names as they try to figure out where their new room is.

The foyer floor, like the academy building, is checkered

black and white, and in the middle is a twinset spiral staircase, twisting around each other as they ascend through the roof into the next floor.

I glance down at my bulky suitcase. "Lift?" I ask.

Bo nods and leads us round to a lift hiding behind the stairs.

When we reach the top floor, it opens into short a corridor with a single door labeled PENTHOUSE. Kato pushes a key into the lock, and it springs open into an enormous shared living room with sky lights, sofas, and a huge CogTV on the wall. At the far end of the living room is the door to the shared kitchen. On my left and right are room doors with little gold numbers: 103 and 104.

"We're 103," Kato says, "you're on the right." He throws Trey a set of keys, and we split from them. As we walk across the living room toward our door, my feet sink into the plush carpet. Trey places our CogKey over the lock; there's an electronic click and the door whooshes open.

I take a step, but Trey grabs my arm. "Wait," he says, and drops the bags. He sweeps me off my feet, holding me in his arms.

"What are you doing?" I say, gripping his neck so I don't fall.

"It's tradition," he says, his blue eyes sparkling at me.

"Yeah, if you're human and just married, of which we are neither."

"Don't be boring. I'm carrying you over the threshold, then I'm putting you on the bed, and I'm going to kiss you until you moan."

"Trey," I say, giggling, and crane over his shoulder to make sure Kato and Bo aren't in the corridor.

He laughs and grabs our suitcase handles with one

hand, dragging them into our room, kicking the door shut behind him.

For all the emotions Sirens can control, none of them seem to have mastered modesty. Our room is enormous and a strange fusion of South and West decor. A four-poster bed made of red mahogany and royal green drapes sits proudly on one side of the room, and at the end of the bed is a moss colored sofa. There's a second sofa area on the other side of the room. Next to that are two large mahogany desks, one for each of us. Hanging over the desk is a CogTV screen. In the furthest corner is a door hanging open to what I think is a walk-in closet. Last, to my right, is another door to what must be the bathroom.

"My kind of bed," Trey says, dropping my suitcase and carrying me across the carpet to the four poster.

He slides me down onto the silky sheets. He pulls off his string vest and pushes me further up the mattress till my head rests on the pillows. Then he's on top of me, his hand slipping behind my head and tangling through locks of my hair. His lips brush mine, and I smile into his kiss. My fingers trace the curves and bumps of his abs, and it makes my skin heat. I bite my lip as my eyes run over his muscled torso. His hand cups my cheek as he pulls me up to kiss him, the hot trickle of his breath flowing over my skin.

His hand drops, his gentle touch moving over my chest and down toward my trousers. As his fingers hover over my button, I tense. He freezes, pulling his lips away from mine.

I didn't mean to tense. I want this. I do. I feel stupid for even thinking about her. But we've not talked about his and Evelyn's relationship. I'm not an idiot, I know they had sex, and thank God I never had to sleep with Victor, but that means he's experienced and I'm not. What if I'm not good enough?

"I'm sorry," he says, "we don't have to..."

"No, it's fine, I just..."

There's a crackle, and the CogTV hanging above the mahogany desk flickers to life.

"What the...?" I say, silently grateful for the distraction and scramble down from the bed to find the off switch.

I'm half way across the floor when static flashes across the screen and a face appears. I halt, the blood pumping through my veins. Both mine and Trey's discarded CogTrackers in the middle of the floor flare to life simultaneously. Trey gets off the bed, picks his Tracker up, and moves over to stand with me. We stare up at the CogTV, silent, horrified, as Victor's pale face fills every screen in my room. The same maroon vein that tracked down his temple at the Coronation Ceremony throbs on the side of his face.

There's a series of muffled screams from the floor below, followed by doors banging, and the thud, thud, thud of feet running through the corridors. My blood turns ice cold; he must have hacked the entire network.

"Good morning, Trutinor," he says, calm and straight-faced, as if it's normal for him, a dead Shifter, to come back to life and take over our comms channels.

His head snaps backward at a strange angle, making me flinch. When he rights himself, his face is contorted, sharper, maroon filling his eyes. His voice isn't his usual whine but a gravely rasp I've only heard once before.

"Oh, Cecilia," Victor says, his eyes narrowing at the screen. "Be a dear, lift my banishment, won't you?"

I turn to Trey; any normal Keeper listening might think it's Victor threatening the First Fallon, that he's the one banished. But it's not. It's Rozalyn: the Last Fallon.

"I'm coming back whether you like it or not. If you assist me, I'll negotiate terms. If you don't or you try to stop me,

I'll consider it an act of war, and I'll destroy the Balance. For good."

Victor's face stretches into a strangled expression and then slackens. As the screen fades to black, he mouths two words. I frown; I must have read his lips wrong.

"Did he just...?" I ask Trey.

"...say 'Eden, help'?" Trey says, nodding, "yeah, he did."

THREE

---

*'Darique, while proud and ruthless, was
driven by reason and fairness. After the
war with Rueben and the banishment of
his mother, he established the first
Council of Trutinor comprising each of
the First children: Darique, Rueben,
Aurora, Karva, and Clarissa.'*

Excerpt from the History of Trutinor Vol. 1

Kato and Bo appear in the doorway their breathing rapid.

"What in the name of actual fuckery just happened?"
Kato asks, striding through my doorway. He raises his
eyebrow at Trey, who is still topless so he takes the hint and
gets himself dressed. Kato picks up my abandoned
CogTracker, gesturing with it as he speaks. "Victor hacked
the entire network. It was a work of art. Fifty CogTV channels, the entire satellite system, CogTracker networks, even
steam radio. The point," Kato says, flipping open my

Tracker and tapping it, "is that even I couldn't do that, and I'm a god damn genius. So... I say again, people... What the actual fuck just happened?"

Bo rolls her eyes at Kato and takes a seat in one of the green arm chairs in the sofa area. "Remind me why we're Bound again?" she says.

"Oh please, Beatrice, you know it turns you on," Kato says, flashing a grin at her.

"I think you're missing the big picture here. One, Victor is meant to be dead. Two, it wasn't actually him speaking and three, did you blank out the part where the Last Fallon declared war on Trutinor?"

"Well, there was that," Kato says, sticking his bottom lip out, "but I still want to know how he hacked the system."

My CogTracker beeps, so Kato throws it across the room at me.

I catch it and flip to the message screen. "It's Nyx," I say, grimacing. "She's in Stratera foyer waiting for me. Titus has my train in Stratera station ready to collect us for Council tonight."

Bo sits a little straighter on the sofa, "I'll call my parents. Victor hadn't made contact with them the last time I asked, but you never know. I'll also put The Six on standby. You two can CogMail us any Council developments. I'm sure they're all freaking out and on high alert now."

I hesitate; neither Trey nor I want to go to another Council inquisition, but maybe given Victor's public appearance, we won't have to endure another truth trial.

"It's fine," Kato says, "we've got this. I'll try tracing the source of Victor's hack and see if I can locate him. You guys go."

"Okay," I say, "CogMail us any updates you have. We'll be back Sunday morning at the latest."

"Good luck," Kato says, giving Trey's shoulder a squeeze. Then he pulls me in for a hug. "Don't let them break you," he whispers in my ear.

"I'll try," I say, then Trey and I leave our dorm.

When we reach the academy foyer, I place my hands on the oak doors, and just like they did with Professor Astra, the doors swing open of their own accord. The foyer, although still busy, is quieter than earlier because most of the students are where I should be: settling into their dorms and finding out who lives in their block.

The students still hovering in the foyer have huddled in small groups. The mumbles quieten as we enter, a hushed whisper circles around the foyer, and every pair of eyes in the room fall on Trey and I. My eyes glance up at the massive screen hanging on one side of the foyer. *Perfect.*

"Is there anyone in Trutinor who didn't see his broadcast?" I growl at Trey under my breath.

I spot Nyx in the center of the room. She's the only one not pouring over a CogTracker. She has a strange expression on her face. Her hand is raised, hovering millimeters above the Door of Fates' frame, and her face is twitching, like a cat catching the scent of catnip. Something must startle her because she recoils, her hair all spiky and stiff, as though her cat-hackles are bristling.

"You okay?" I say as I reach her.

"Huh? Oh, yes, I'm fine. Sorry. Strange old door, isn't it?"

"I guess." I brace as she puts her arms around me squeezing me far too hard as usual.

"Anyway," she says, letting go and straightening herself out, "shall we leave? There's a lot to discuss on route."

"Did you see the broadcast?" I ask, looking from Trey to Nyx.

"I did. Very troubling. But hopefully, the First Fallon will leave you alone now there is unequivocal proof of his return." She blinks at me, long slow cat blinks with her green cat-eyes and vertical pupils.

"Are you sure you're alright?"

"I'm fine. We just have a lot to talk about, and Titus has to do some stops on route so it will be late evening by the time we get to the Ancient Forest."

"Okay," I say, and we leave, the students' eyes following us as we exit the foyer.

It's a short walk back down the hill toward Stratera station. Titus and I decided to retire my parents' train. I couldn't face using it, walking the corridors, and still smelling their perfume. It hurt too much. So he spent the rest of the summer refurbishing our reserve train. It's sat in Stratera station, docked, shiny, and ready for us to board. Except for the brass tubing that traces the lines of the exterior, my train is long and sleek, like the sky scrapers in the East.

Titus steps out of the engine cabin, his blond dreads drawn up in a loose knot. His navy Steampunk Transporter uniform is tight over his stomach, the gold buttons straining over his port belly. He waves, the nubbin of his thumb in the air making a surge of guilt roll through my chest. During the summer, I lost control of the Imbalance that's resident inside my head and accidentally burned Titus' hand. The Dryad doctors fixed him, but he still lost the tip of his thumb.

"Hello, trouble," he says, pulling me into a hug, "it's

been a while. Magnus has been greedy and kept you all to himself."

"I missed you," I say, squeezing him.

"Are you okay?" he says, putting me at arm's length so he can see me. "I saw the..."

"I'm okay. Kato is trying to trace the source; I'm sure the Council are all over it."

"Good," he says, and shakes Trey's hand.

"Let's go see what the Council have to say, shall we?" He places a kiss on the top of my head and clambers back up into the engine cabin.

Trey, Nyx, and I board the train and climb the stairs to my private quarters on the second floor. I've only been on this train a couple of times since Titus finished it, and this is the first-time Trey's been aboard. Which makes me smile to myself as I enter the glass-roofed private quarters. The sun sets in here, and the view is mind-blowing.

I push open the door. There's a bar immediately on the right as we enter. On the left is a seating area comprised of sandy colored square sofas and after that, a door to sleeping quarters.

Nyx drops behind the bar as the train shudders, and we pull out of the station. The carriage judders at first until the train gathers enough speed to find its rhythm. Billows of steam roll past the window, and the carriage falls into a lulled rocking. There's the crack of a lid flicking off of a bottle, and her head reappears with a small glass of milk, or maybe it's cream.

"Want one?" she says.

"Umm, I'm good thanks."

"Suit yourself. Trey?"

He shakes his head.

"Fine. Take a seat, you two," she says, "we need to talk East business."

"Okay," I say, bracing myself as I take a seat on the larger sofa, so there's room for Trey. He swings his arm around me as Nyx pulls open her CogTracker, and a stream of notes fly across the screen.

"Eden..." Nyx starts, her expression stiff.

"Don't," I say, raising my hand, knowing exactly what she's about to say, "I'm not ready to come home yet."

"When are you going to be, honey? We can't have a State without a Fallon. I know you're at Stratera, but that's not really an excuse. You're going to have to come home soon. Your people need to see you lead."

My jaw tightens, my fingers rubbing the throbbing pressure building behind my forehead.

"I'll be with you," Trey says. "I can make it easier..."

"I know," I say. "But I don't want you compelling the pain away. I *will* go home. I just need time to prepare."

"There's a long weekend break from studies in a couple of weeks. What about then?"

"Will it get the pair of you off my back?"

Nyx nods, Trey shrugs agreement.

"Fine. I'll think about it. That's the best you're getting."

Nyx smiles, the lunchtime sun streaming through the glass roof and speckling her face. I narrow my eyes; her birthmark looks dark, almost brown instead of the pale orange it normally is. She slides a black envelope across the table, which has a white label on the front with the word REPORT typed in big font.

"What's that?" I say, curious.

"It's, umm. Well, you need to sign it... It's the official inquest into your parents' death. The Guild's asked me to get you to sign the death records as suicide."

I look up at her, tears pricking the backs of my eyes.

"I see," I say. I pull out the sheet and scrawl a signature, shoving the packet away as fast as I can, and try to push the lump in my throat away.

"I'm sorry," she says, but I shake my head.

"Can we move on?"

Trey squeezes my hand, but the softness in his touch makes the lump even harder to swallow.

"Of course we can," Nyx says, pressing buttons on her CogTracker, and a map of the East State appears. She zooms in. "There are outbreaks of civil unrest and a variety of Shifter attacks right along the Northern border."

"Any intelligence on the attacks?"

"Some. A couple of water Elementals on the ground are suggesting the most recent attacks are from the Third House in the North."

"Third?" I stare out the window, trying to rack my mind for the names of Bo's six elite generals. I've only met a couple of them. Then it comes to me. "Delphine?" I say, unsurprised. "Delphine Delacrois."

"Correct," Nyx says. "Israel is claiming no knowledge of it. He's also said Delphine herself has no part in it. But nonetheless, he's given her an official warning about any of her house breaking the treaty. Especially so soon after it was signed."

I nod, unsatisfied, but also unsure of what steps to take next. Israel and Maddison were furious with me when Victor died. There was an incident outside the Council Chamber. Understandably, Israel blamed me for Victor's death but he also blamed me for Bo losing her leg. So when he saw me for the first time in the Council foyer, he saw red and tried to choke me, and he would have done if it wasn't for Trey who had to compel him to stop. After a few weeks, and I suspect a strong word from Arden, Israel came to me and suggested we have a Siren mediate a session between us. Those sessions are what led to the treaty being signed. I can't help but wonder what my father would have done in this situation. I know he would have been proud the day the treaty was signed. Despite the tensions on our borders, and their differing opinions on politics, he and Israel were in the same year at school. Children don't care about politics and power. They saw through the hate they were supposed to feel because they knew each other before Trutinor's system corrupted them. That's why as adults, when they were forced to bend and obey as Councilors, their friendship lasted through their differing opinions. I decide Father would have wanted me to take the most diplomatic stance possible. I can almost hear him saying, 'protect the treaty at all costs, Eden.'

"What about the Siren peace keepers?" I ask Trey.

"They're patrolling, twenty-four hours a day. But they're not trained as peace keepers, so pockets of violence are still breaking out. I'm going to negotiate some training with Bo. The Six can give the squad of Sirens the basics, and hopefully, that will make them more efficient."

As the sun sets, I yawn and tell Nyx I can't discuss any more skyscraper bridge constructions, proposals for East State Council members or state dinners and retire, with Trey, to the train's bedroom quarters. We lie on the bed, me in his arms, both of us staring up at the sky streaking past in a blur.

"Told you it was spectacular," I say, leaning into him, my eyes already heavy.

"It really is," he says, kissing my forehead.

Above us, baby blues turn to deep pink, and then to slate gray. The sky darkens as evening arrives and the twinkling sparkle of stars blinking to life fills the cabin. I close my eyes, telling myself I'm just resting them, it's not bedtime, and it won't be much longer before we arrive. But I'm lying to myself. My breathing slows, and I drift into sleep.

I am alone on the peak of a mountain somewhere deep in the Eris region of the North State. It's freezing; snow covers the mountain tops like whips of ice cream. Swathes of white smother the ground leaving only sparse patches of rocky boulders. The air whisks a chill around me; a few gray rocks crunch under my feet as I shiver and pull my jacket tight. The mountains are dull somehow like everything is tainted with age. Something splatters against the snow behind me. I spin around, and the mountains vanish. I'm standing in the middle of Maddison and Israel's castle courtyard; the same courtyard I killed Victor in. Only this time, the walls are crumbling. The doors are splintered and hanging off their hinges. Under the arches where the snow hasn't reached, photographs, papers, and ornaments litter the area, abandoned remnants from the lives that used to fill the castle. Snow covers the rest of the stone square, hiding the names of the residents that were once etched into the concrete slabs. The turrets that used to impale the clouds are broken. As I crane my neck up, a few black tiles crumble and fall from the sky only to be swallowed by the snow. Everywhere I look there's decay; Trutinor is dying.

The splattering was blood. Red droplets speckle the snow in an arc, like a sword that's sliced open a body. A figure stands a few feet away from me; it's motionless. Another appears next to him, then another.

One by one, the Shifters, Elementals, and Sorcerers who fought with and against me in the battle with Victor, materialize in the courtyard. They replay the same battle but in slow sweeping moves, like I'm standing in the middle of a slow-motion video game. I shout at them to stop; we don't need to fight anymore, it's over. But they can't hear me.

Wisps of Evelyn's green magic shoot past my head and collide with a giant bear's paw; the bear spins and hits the ground in his Shifter form. Dead. In the corner of the courtyard next to a row of stone pillars, Trey stumbles, gripping his chest. His life is connected to Victor's. His chest bleeds where I stabbed Victor. I run, reaching out to staunch the bleeding, but the harder I run, the faster he shrinks away.

Suddenly, there is a hand around my throat. Victor's eyes glint as the sun beams through the clouds and illuminates the square. He wants to kill me. Any moment now, he will try and suffocate me, so I die and he survives our broken Binding. A strange knife shaped like a key appears in my hand; it's tipped with a smudge of dried red: Bo's blood. I know what I'm meant to do; I have to pierce Victor's heart.

But Trey is in Victor's place, and as I glance at the knife in my hand, a cold chill trickles down my spine. I'm no longer me. I am Victor.

Trey's voice echoes around me. "I love you, Eden," he says, over and over. Three little words that give me the energy to fight on.

The shadowy figures around me stop fighting and circle us: Trey and me in Victor's body. Panic flickers in my eyes. Trey's hand grips my throat tighter, and in response, Victor grips the knife harder. The rest of the courtyard is silent and empty. Even the blood on sheet-white snow has gone. The real me is flung outside the circle. Excluded.

This is all wrong. Victor stands in the center, in my place, and Trey stands where Victor was. No one is in the right place. Panic drives me forward; I know how this ends, and Trey isn't supposed to die. I pull at the bodies, desperate to get inside and stop the Victor version of me from killing Trey. But the bodies are immovable and solid like ancient statues fossilized in the ground. Tears streak my cheeks. Trey's words echo around me again, and just like the first time this happened, the last shred of my Binding disintegrates from my arm and evaporates into the air. I watch Victor take my last breath. He rips Trey's hand from his throat and plunges the knife straight into his heart. Trey's body twitches then slumps to the ground. Gone.

I scream and blink. I'm standing over Trey; blood covers my hands and drips rhythmically to the stone. Victor has vanished.

Trey is dead, and I killed him.

I wake, sweat pooling on my forehead, heart pumping. Every time I've fallen asleep since Trey and I were Bound, I've had nightmares. Mostly of me, or Victor, killing him. But other dreams are of bizarre twisted versions of Trutinor. Sometimes the land is bleached of color, other times it's ravaged by war and any life left is decaying or broken, and the faces in my dreams are hollow and shadowy like their souls are lost.

"Are you okay?" Trey asks, brushing sweaty curls away from my face.

I shudder as the dream fades and lie on Trey's chest; his

arms wrap around me, safe, warm, protected. My hand slides up and over his heart. A silly ritual that makes me feel better. I wait. His heart beats: once, twice, three times, then I know I'm awake, and he's safe.

"I am now," I say.

Each dream is different, but they all end the same way: Trey dead and Trutinor in ruins. I don't know what it means, or why they keep happening. But what I do know, is that I'd give up my life for both of them.

FOUR

---

*'**From chaos comes Balance.**'*
Teachings of the Last Fallon.

We arrived in the Ancient Forest late in the evening. All four of us spent the rest of the night on the train, discussing State politics, the Northern border, and my homecoming ball that Nyx has somehow decided is happening.

As we finish breakfast the next morning, my CogTracker pings an alert from Hermia. I pick it up and walk to the bathroom, locking the door behind me. Hermia is the First Fallon's messenger, but she also runs a tracker business and she's a personal friend of Trey's.

From: Hermilda.Endlesquire@TrackerServices.com
Subject: Lost & Found??
To: Eden.East@FallonCogMail.com

Good news and bad news.

I've not found either Lani or Victor, yet. But I am making progress, with Victor at least. However, Eden, I must insist that you tell Trey what you're doing. Given my history with him and the severity of who you're asking me to find, I don't think it's fair you're putting me in this position. Have you considered just asking Cassian where Lani is? I am sure he would gladly take you to her place.

I have, at least, worked out why I am having problems tracking her. I can't say over CogMail though. I want you to come to the shop as soon as you can – Kato says he can modify all our CogTrackers so they're encrypted. I won't disclose details over CogMail until he has. We don't know who's listening, especially after Victor's little public appearance.

Tell Trey.

That's all.

I'm off for a drink.

P.S. T.E.L.L T.R.E.Y.

H x

　　　I close my CogTracker and return to the breakfast table, distracted and wondering how I should tell Trey what I've done.
　　　We leave Nyx and Titus on the train to wait for us and walk across the Ancient Forest's main platform. A

mesh of thick branches and leaves weave a tunnel over the tracks, blocking out most of the morning light. I shiver and pull on an oversized sweater I found in the train's wardrobe; it used to be my father's. If I lift the collar of his sweater up, I can still smell his aftershave. My chest twinges as the scent of autumn rain fills my nose; it's fresh and warm, all in the same breath, just like his essence - water. I hesitate but take another sniff because today the memory of him feels more like a comfort than the devastating pain of weeks gone by. Trey slips his hand into mine, and we walk through the canopied darkness of the Ancient Forest.

The center of Trutinor isn't much further, but I slow my pace anyway; I'm enjoying the alone time with Trey too much. I glance up at him, just to reassure myself he's real and still mine.

As we near the center of the forest, rays of light spear through the canopy and shower us with warmth. I hold him back.

"Everything alright?" he says, turning to me.

I grin, wrap my arms around his neck, and pull him down so I can slide my lips over his. Pushing a kiss deep into his mouth, he picks me up, and I wrap my legs around his waist. He staggers toward a tree trunk and leans me against it. I break the kiss and stroke his bristly cheek. "I love you," I say.

"I love you too," he says, leaning in and kissing my neck. His familiar frankincense smell washes over me, as does his breath, and with it, a throb of magic. He keeps his Siren powers under such strict control, sometimes I wonder if he's afraid of them.

"Are you sure you're okay?" he asks, scanning my face.

"I'm fine," I say, brushing my lips against his, "I'm

happy. Right here, with you. In this moment. I don't want any of this to change."

He places the softest kiss on my lips as if savoring the taste and then puts me down on the floor, "Nothing's going to change, Eden. We're Bound. No more Eve, no more Victor."

My stomach twists. I hate when he calls her Eve instead of Evelyn.

"I know that," I say, and trail off trying to decide what it is I'm feeling. I guess when you finally get the thing you've wanted for so long, you realize how fragile happiness can be. It teeters, like the trapeze artist on the thinnest of wires, and even the lightest of breezes could send her tumbling into oblivion.

We continue toward the center of the forest. Within a minute, the tree line breaks, and we step into a circular clearing. Hot summer rays blare down on us, a warm contrast to the shade under the forest covering. Dozens of Keepers, Council members, and school children mill around, some doing business, others using it as a meeting point, and the children, I assume, on school visits. In the middle of the clearing, the five wooden root-towers of Trutinor Council soar into the air. Each tower is bent and gnarled like a witch's finger, prehistoric roots that entwine hundreds of feet in the air and then burst apart again to form points. Where the roots meet the earth, archways maw open in their bases: five arches for the five States.

Trey pulls me around, swinging me into his arms, "I'll see you in two. I'm going in through the Siren entrance. Don't forget me."

"Don't take my memories then."

"Ouch," he says, sucking the air, "one-nil to Eden."

I laugh and blow a cocky kiss at him, then head toward

the East State's door. I might be joking about him taking my memories now, but when I discovered what he'd done, it nearly tore us apart. On the night of my sixteenth birthday - almost two years ago - I was going to break it off with him. We'd been meeting in secret because we were meant to be Bound to other people, or so we thought. Victor was going to be named my Potential the following day, and Trey was already Bound to Evelyn. I guess Trey thought he was protecting me by taking my memories of him away. In his mind, that way, being apart from each other wouldn't hurt. It did, of course, and when I found out what he'd done, I was furious.

Like all the arches, the East State entrance is door-less. It's meant to be a symbol of the openness and connectivity of all Keepers: united in our mission to bring Balance to the realms. For the first few feet, the tunnel is dark, but as I pass through a layer of hanging vines representing the earth element, the tunnel gets lighter. Two types of lantern hang from the wall, one pulsating electricity representing the air element, the other, fire: two more of the elements we control. Together they throw a strange orangey-violet hue over the earthy corridor. It takes about five minutes to walk the length of the tunnel, deep enough into the belly of Trutinor that my ears pop when I reach the end. I pass through a watery door, a mirage representing the final element, and down a set of steps into Trutinor's Council foyer.

The chamber is a vast underground cavern with walls made of the same twisted tree roots that stretch into the sky overground. Around the edges are several doors and tunnels leading off to chambers, offices, and Council areas. The five tunnel archways leading from the State entrances are spread evenly around the perimeter of the room. Except for the South and West, where there's a gap.

Although there was never a door in the wall, if you squint at the floor, you can just make out the shadow of an arch – the remains of the sixth State none of us talk about. That tunnel leads to the sea and Aurora's Mermaids. Across the rest of the floor, carved in gold, are our State symbols.

Trey smiles and waves as he enters through the South State entrance on the opposite side of the cavern.

"I don't see why we need to give evidence again," I say as I reach him. We walk through the foyer to the main Council Chamber. "I'm hoping we won't have to given Victor's rather public appearance yesterday."

Trey snorts, "Give over, this is Cecilia we're talking about. Torturing us is sport."

"I just wish the Council was awake enough to see what's going on."

"They'll see. Eventually. But we need to pick our battles like Arden says." He lowers his voice, "The Libra Legion informal meet and greet is in a few days. Hopefully, we'll know more then. But for now, we just need to stick to the plan and survive the trial."

The Libra Legion is the army that Arden founded when he discovered mine and Trey's prophecy cog. My parents were part of it, and I'm going to attend a few meetings out of respect for them. In my heart, I know they'd want me to join.

"Mmm," I say, "I know the Legion is trying to do the right thing, and I really do love Arden, but it feels like we're rolling over and letting her get away with poisoning Trutinor."

"I get that, but no one ever said war was easy to end.

Especially not when there's an immortal, all-powerful being on either side of the battle."

"I guess," I say, and change the subject. "So it's been weeks..."

"I already dislike where this is going."

I ignore him because Hermia's right, I do need to tell him I commissioned her to track his mother down. "So, umm...We still haven't agreed about your mother."

Trey halts. "Eden, I told you. What difference does it make if she is alive? I don't want to know her. She left me to fend for myself and my little brother when I was twelve..." he cocks his head and pinches his mouth, pretending to think. "Yeah. I'm good without knowing that mother, thanks."

I take him by the shoulders, "You can't avoid this forever. I won't let you. And you're missing the point. What if she did those things for a reason? What if there's something bigger we're missing? We're still part of a prophecy, Trey. Don't you think you should at least give her the chance to explain?"

"Explain why she inflicted the torture of Inheritance on her flesh and blood for no reason?" His voice drops to a growl, "Did I mention that she left a kid in charge of an entire Trutinor State? Or that she gave up her Fallon magic, and for what? To look after Maddison's Unbound baby? No, Eden. No, I really don't care why she did it." A flicker of red flashes across his blue eyes.

"Fine. I'll drop it," I say, "but only because this isn't the place, and you need to control yourself unless you want to create a crack in the vault..." *and because I know you're lying, and the fact you're angry tells me you do need to deal with this, which is exactly why I asked Hermia to track her down in the first place. But I don't add that* aloud because cracking his vault is just as bad as cracking mine.

The vault is a by-product of the Inheritance we both experienced. When our parents died, we Inherited their power, making both of us Imbalanced. Something the Council thinks we got rid of when we were Bound to our Potentials. We didn't. We just learned to hide it better by stowing it away in a kind of mental prison that we call the vault; it's better locked shut because when it opens, bad things happen.

"Consider it dropped." *For now.*

"Thank you," he says, cupping my neck and placing a stiff kiss on my mouth.

I wrap my arms around his back, and slide them into his skinny jeans pockets, pulling him into my body. He grins at me, his body relaxing.

"You're infuriating, you know that?" he says.

"A special, lovable kind of infuriating, you mean."

He rolls his eyes and leans in, millimeters from my lips. He must lower the barrier on his Siren powers because my eyes shut, and I suck in a breath as tingles and heat blend together. His mouth moves over mine, his tongue slipping into my mouth.

"Ahem," a strained cough from behind makes us jump apart. "You're late," Nivvy Pushton says, brushing her untamable blond hair behind her ears. She flattens her green tunic and floor-length skirt, then moves behind us hustling us through a corridor toward the Council Chamber. Nivvy is a Sorcerer and the Council's secretary; she's also a ball of nervous energy.

We walk through another corridor moving deeper underground where the scent of wood and wet earth grows stronger. The tunnel eventually opens into the Council

Chamber, another hollow cavern with the same root-walls as the foyer. There's a long table at the front of the chamber with two dozen throne-like chairs behind it. Some are alight with fire or electricity; others are made of tree or animal furs, each one representing a part of Trutinor. A little way behind the Council table are five colored drapes hanging from the ceiling with our State symbols emblazoned on them. In front of the drapes, on a raised platform, is a pure white throne, the back of which is carved into white flames. A cold chill runs down my spine as my eyes meet Cecilia's. The First Fallon's milk-white skin and lilac eyes stiffen, and she sits a little higher in her throne, her lips tightening into a smile as she watches us, her pray, enter the chamber.

Trey and I bow to her as we pass, her face blank except for her eyes following us through the room, like a haunted painting. It makes me shiver, so I drag my gaze away. Curved around the other side of the room are rows of knitted roots protruding from the earth to form benched seating areas for Council members.

Israel Dark, the deputy head of the Council, nods to me as I enter. He's been acting as head of the Council since my father died and will do for the next couple of months until my eighteenth birthday when, much to both of our annoyances, I will take over. Israel is far more suited to Council life than me; I'd rather be in the trenches of the front line, fixing Imbalances and protecting Trutinor. But thanks to an ancient law, neither of us are going to get our way.

Once Trey and I have taken seats at the top table, the room fills fast, and the last Council members take their seats, each one stopping to bow to the First Fallon.

Israel, already at the Council table, stands. The black leather from his uniform creaks as he rises. He pushes his fur cape behind his shoulder and signals for silence, "Welcome, your Majesty, Keepers, Fallons, and Council members. Given recent ahh, events... Today's agenda is a lengthy one, so I ask for your patience as we make our way through the items of business."

Arden, my father's best friend, is sat opposite me, his green-robed rotund belly resting on the edge of the table. He rubs his hand over his gray handlebar beard and smiles at me. He looks tired: rich plum colored bags hang from his eyes, and as I scan him, I notice an air of the disheveled about him. Nothing's quite as pressed and neat as it should be. I wonder if all the additional Libra Legion work is taking its toll or if he's just been drinking too much again.

Israel, the First Fallon, and a few of the older Council members start talking about rebels and attacks in the forest, so I tune out.

I open my CogTracker and flip across the tabs to my CogMail messages. There are already half a dozen from Nyx. How she can have sent that many since I left the train I don't know. I open the first one, read the first line:

Don't even think about ignoring this Eden...

And promptly close it. The next one is from Bo. I skim it; there's no news from Kato yet, he's not managed to trace the source of Victor's network hack yet, and she's having a clothing dilemma deciding what to wear on Monday for the first day of lessons. I'm not dealing with any of that now. I reach to close my CogTracker, but another mail pings in from Trey. I glance up at him, and his lips twitch.

From: Trey.Luchelli@FallonCogMail.com
Subject: Urgent

To: Eden.East@FallonCogMail.com

How can I possibly be angry with you when you're sat there all lilac eyed with your gorgeous curls... It makes me want to rip your clothes off and ravish you on the Council table...

My eyes bug wide, and I stifle a cough.

"Everything okay, Fallon East?" Israel says, his serious expression boring into me. My gaze flicks up to the First Fallon. Her eyes narrow. Trey's playing a dangerous game. As far as I can tell, the First Fallon is tolerating our Binding in public but only because she doesn't want news of the prophecy getting out. She wants the masses controlled, suppressed, and brainwashed. Flirting with him under her nose is going to wind her up. There's a muffled creak of wood as the entire Council Chamber shifts to look at me. Heat paints a layer of pink over my cheeks, "I... Umm. Yes, sorry. As you were saying." I wave my hand at him dismissing the comment and glare at Trey, who isn't even attempting to hide his grin. His sparkling blue eyes crease with laughter as he shrugs innocence at me and signals that it's 'one-all.'

Right. I tap out a reply.

From: Eden.East@FallonCogMail.com
Subject: RE: Urgent
To: Trey.Luchelli@FallonCogMail.com

Much as I'd love that, I'm slightly off-put by the green thing you've got hanging off your chin...

He flicks open the CogMail, and his face falls. Sitting up straight, he wipes his chin. I lean back against the bench, my shoulders rocking silently. When he realizes I was joking, he blinks at me, and I give him a smug look as I gesture 'two-one.' He smiles a look at me that screams 'game-on,' and I know I've lost. He shuffles to the edge of his chair until his leg touches mine.

Don't you dare, Trey Luchelli, I think as I fire a filthy look at him. But it's too late; where his thigh touches mine, Siren compulsion washes over me. My eyes close as warmth and golden waves of lust trickle into my system. I want him. I don't care if we're in the Council. Or if the First Fallon is watching. The sensation flows through my legs until it reaches my groin, and my eyes snap open.

"That's enough," I gasp, and Trey removes his leg.

Israel stops speaking and turns to me. "Fallon East?" he says, scratching his blond top knot.

It takes me a moment to compose myself. "Excuse me," I say, trying to recall what the Council was talking about.

"Winner," Trey mouths at me.

I glare at him; this isn't over.

The air cools, making goosebumps pock my arms and neck. The First Fallon glides out of her throne, moving to the front of the raised platform, her eyes glinting.

"No, Eden. I think you're right. That *is* enough."

"Of course, Your Majesty," Israel says through gritted teeth.

"Your Majesty, given yesterday's broadcast..." I start. But the First Fallon raises her delicate hand to signal my silence.

"That's quite enough from you," she says. "Yesterday's broadcast is meaningless. CogTracker trickery. Council members, you can be assured of both yours and Trutinor's safety," her words are silky, filled with hypnotic Siren charm. My mind wobbles, wanting to fall under her spell, to accept her words. But I won't. I know better now. I shake my head making the trance fall away and steal myself for whatever comes next.

"My sister is banished to Obex. I personally ensured there was no possible way she could return. The Balance and your wellbeing is, as it always will be, my highest concern. Therefore, I must insist that we submit Fallon East and Luchelli to a truth trial once more. We must get to the bottom of these serious and disturbing accusations before they unsettle our Keepers and damage the Balance." She smiles, soft, serene, full of hypnotic beauty.

I glance at Trey. *She can't be serious.* I scan the room; the Council Chamber is enthralled, doe eyes and slack expressions all nodding at her words. I can't believe I ever fell for this. Arden and Israel exchange worried looks across the table, but Arden shakes his head. This is not a battle he wants to pick, and he grimaces an apology at me. My hand forms a fist under the table. This is not okay; the Libra Legion needs to step up. Sometimes I wonder why my parents were even part of it. How is this fighting a war?

"Councillor Bertrum, if you please," the First Fallon says, returning to her seat. She leans back and crosses her legs as if getting ready to watch a movie.

Councillor Bertrum, a Siren elder, stands. Despite being ancient, he's retained his Siren good looks. His hair is short and white against his tanned skin, which despite his age, is taut. The only wrinkles he's developed are laughter lines around his mouth, which make him look permanently happy. But buried deep beneath the curve of his eyes, is another story; he carries a weariness that comes from always knowing the truth. I guess the truth is a prison as much as it sets you free.

"Fallon East, do you willingly submit to compulsion?" he says, standing. I look at the First Fallon, her sneer mocking me, then at Arden, his expression furrowed, pleading, and I sigh.

"I do," I say. But I'm not doing it for the Libra Legion; I'm doing it for Arden because I can't stand the guilty knot his face is creating in my chest.

I get up and walk to a lectern booth on the right-hand side of the Council table. It's made of woven branches that are sanded smooth. The tree knots speckling the lectern are like freckles sprawling across its skin.

Bertrum enters the booth with me, clasps my hand, and my third truth-trial begins.

FIVE

---

*'Do nothing secretly; for Time sees and
hears all things, and discloses all.'*
Sophocles - Human philosopher

Nivvy stops taking meeting minutes and carries a pair of
brass goggles over to the lectern. She slips them over my
head and onto my eyes making the room go dark. Cogs click
and whirr in my ears like crickets. She adjusts the leather
frames to my face, and a few seconds later the noise softens
as it settles into the rhythm of my brain waves. Bertrum
turns me around, so I'm facing the Keepers in the Council
Chamber: my jurors. Behind me, a screen will be lowered
from the ceiling to project the memories Bertrum's about to
make me re-live.

His touch is warm against my hand as he starts to speak.
"Fallon East," he says, his words smooth and creamy with
hypnotic compulsion. "I want to you go back to your first
coronation. Begin recalling the events of the day as you

climbed the stage stairs in Element Square. And, Eden...
You must tell the truth."

I suck air through my teeth as the warmth from his hand
disappears and is replaced with a cold slimy sensation that
crawls through my veins, up my shoulder, and into my neck.
The thick goo coagulates around my voice box, tightening,
suffocating, until it chokes the secrets out of me.

If I fight, it will hurt even more. But I don't because I
have nothing to hide; the First Fallon might be able to force
me into taking a truth trial, but that doesn't mean I'm giving
her the satisfaction of watching me in pain.

I let the words flow, and the images of my memories
crystalize inside the goggles.

"I'm standing on stage, Trey's next to me," I say,
"Arden's at the front with the CogMic in his hand, about to
announce us. It's bright, the desert sun is burning hot, and it
makes me squint. Arden starts speaking, welcoming us all,
but something passes over the sun and casts a shadow over
the crowded square. I look up but see nothing. Arden can't
have seen it either because he continues with his welcome.
A moment later the shadow drifts over the crowd again."

There's an audible murmur in the Council Chamber; it
breaks my concentration, and the memories in the goggles
flicker.

"Concentrate, please," Bertrum says, pumping a pulse
of ice so cold into my throat it burns. I swallow hard and
force myself on, even though the pain from the icy strangle
hold is making me sweat and my knees weak.

"I can't see at first," I say, and my hand rises in front of
my goggles, mimicking the movement I made on the day to
block out the sun.

"Huge scaly wings beat the air. They're creating gusts
of wind that wash over the crowd. I narrow my eyes and

scan the sky to get a better view. But the sun is so hot I can't look in the creature's direction for long. I remember thinking it must be Maddison. Her Dragon Shifter wings are black like that."

I falter. I don't want to say the next words. If Israel is here, Maddison is probably in the Council Chamber somewhere too.

Bertrum senses my hesitation and says, "The whole truth, Eden."

His grip on my voice tightens; sharp icicles that taste bitter dig into my throat making me gasp.

"I... I decide it's Maddison because I killed Victor. But as soon as I think it, the creature passes in front of the sun and stays there, blocking the rays out and coming into focus. I'm wrong, it's not Maddison."

There's louder murmuring in the chamber, and the air around me grows chilly as if the First Fallon has stepped closer. But I'm too deep into my memories for it to distract me.

"I'm certain the creature is a Shifter. But Shifters can't shoot enormous balls of fire and green magic across the square. No one can do that except the First and Last Fallon. But he is. Even though it's impossible, he's wielding magic from more than one State. I stumble back, my legs weak as I realize who the creature is. While its body remains in dragon form, its head shifts in an out of its Keeper form as if to taunt me. His greasy blond hair and dark eyes give him away."

As my memory crystallizes on his face, there are shouts and jeers in the audience. They don't believe me. They didn't believe me the last two times I did the truth trial either. Yet he's on screen for them to see with their own eyes.

"Eden, you must tell the truth," Bertrum says.

"I am."

"Liar," the First Fallon spits.

There's a hiss from the chamber, and then someone yells from the audience, "Force the truth, Bertrum."

"She is under compulsion," Bertrum says, and raises our clasped hands as if to prove it.

It's a smattering at first, then the chorus of voices crescendo into a rhythm. I can imagine the First Fallon waving her fingers at the audience like a musical conductor, brainwashing them into their chant.

"Truth. Truth. Truth."

"I'm sorry," Bertrum whispers under his breath.

I cry out as the icy compulsion tightens like a noose around my throat. Sharp splinters dig into my shoulders and up the back of my skull making black and white spots fill my vision.

"I swear it's the truth," I plead, "it was Victor Dark."

"Continue," Bertrum says, his voice straining with the exertion of controlling a Fallon so much stronger than him.

I stop speaking. They don't believe me anyway so the rest of the memory can play out on screen minus my narration.

Victor dips and swoops then pauses to hover above the crowd. Thousands of Keepers stand like soldiers in Element Square, each one wearing an identical expression: slack jaw, wide eyes, and ghost-gray skin.

A piercing scream rings out through the crowd. There's a pause, long enough for a single heartbeat. Then an explosion of screams, frantic running, and panic erupting through the square. Keepers flee, scrabbling and climbing over each other. People are pushed and shoved out of the way. There's a crush by the two main exits. Balls of fire and electricity are launched into the air toward Victor. He rolls and flaps out of the way. The acrid scent of ash fills the air, and a plume of smoke rises in the far corner of the square.

"Trey. Control them. Now," I shout, pulling him to the front of the stage. I push out a wave of air and hold it in place like a barrier. It blocks the path of a large group of Keepers running to join the crush at the exit.

Trey's head shakes as if to wipe away the shock, then he launches into action, throwing his arms out wide and pushing a pulse of Siren compulsion into the crowd. It's so strong I swear I see the air wobble. Deep red flashes across his eyes. My shoulders tense. But he blinks, and the red is gone. *Thank Balance*, I think.

When the crowd is motionless, frozen in place by compulsion, everything quietens. There's only the crackle of a few stray pieces of rubbish burning in the square and the flap, flap of Victor's wings beating above us.

He descends towards the stage. My breath roars loud in my ears compared to the now silent crowd. I don't understand how this is happening. I stabbed him in the heart. He died in front of me.

When he was alive, Victor was a Fallon Shifter, which meant he could shift into any creature he liked. But what's hovering in front of me is something different. When he used to shift into dragon form, his wings were skin colored. Now they're midnight black, stretching out twice the length of his body with spiny bones hooked out of the joints. He looks like a demon.

Where the crowd panicked and ran, a gap has formed in the center of Element Square, and there's a clear path to us on stage. Victor's wings crumple and fold into an arrow shape as he plunges into the space like a hawk diving for its prey. And like the mouse it's hunting, I'm paralyzed by fear.

Trey steps closer to me, his fingers slipping into mine, "How is this possible?"

Words won't form, so I shake my head because I have no idea. I grip his hand so hard my knuckles turn white.

I killed Victor. I broke our Binding by putting a blade tipped with the same poison that killed my parents through his heart. There is no way he can be alive.

Victor pulls up several feet short of the ground; he opens his enormous wings, flapping them in slow, steady beats. Sand and dust whip up with every flap, and the breeze he creates washes over me. Time seems to stall as I'm mesmerized by this demon creature in front of me.

He floats down to the ground shifting to his normal self, landing one foot then the other. He's elegant like a swan, but when he smiles at me, it makes my mouth go dry. He takes controlled, purposeful steps forward. His smart maroon-red brogue shoes clap against the concrete stones. As he gets closer, each clap echoes around the square or maybe it's my heart ringing in my ears. He's wearing a black suit with a shirt the same red as his shoes. His blond hair is scooped back into a top knot, and the sides look freshly shaved. On one side of his face, starting at his temple, and spider webbing down his cheek, neck, and disappearing into his shirt collar, is a scar, or a mark, or something. It, too, is maroon-red, and I wonder how he got it in Obex after he died. The mark pulses, like it's alive, and it makes me shift on the spot.

When he reaches the front of the stage, his feet slide together against the stone as he draws to a stop. Victor looks at Trey, then to me. I open my mouth to speak, but he draws a finger up to his lips and with a shake of his head, silences me.

His dark eyes drill into mine creating a shudder of goose

flesh that slithers down my back. Now he's closer, I examine the red scar. But it's not a scar so much as a vein, pulsing like a heartbeat. "Where there is Balance, there must be Imbalance," he says.

My brows knit together as I turn to Trey, who's wearing the same expression. That's what the Last Fallon said to us when we found her in Obex a few weeks ago.

Victor steps closer and leans into me, whispering so quietly the Council Chamber can't hear his words. But I remember the chill it filled me with.

"I am not your enemy," he breathes into my ear, and just like in the changing rooms before our Binding Ceremony, he sucks my ear lobe. Then he retreats and smiles, displaying yellowed teeth, "And, Eden...?"

I glance at him.

"The Imbalance is coming," he says, then his wings spread wide before wrapping around his body and collapsing in on himself, making him vanish from sight.

The goggles go black; the memory is over.

Bertrum releases my hand, and I pull off the goggles. He's pale, sweaty, and unsteady on his feet. He must have exhausted all his energy trying to force the truth out of me. It makes my blood boil. The Council have seen this bloody memory three times. I can handle the First Fallon berating me, but why put Bertrum through this? He'll have to do the same to Trey in a minute, and he can't even hold his own weight up. I wipe the sweat off my forehead and glance across the room. Though her face is blank, the First Fallon's eyes are smiling. Something snaps inside me. I grit my teeth and guide Bertrum back to his seat. I reach for a glass of water on the table and help him sip it. When he's done, I turn to the silent Council Chamber.

"Do you see?" I say, my voice hard, raised. I scan the seats, making sure I lock eyes with the First Fallon. I don't care how dangerous it is to be this defiant in public.

"Do you see what you're doing?" I shout at the crowd. "This is over. I will not submit me, or Trey, OR BERTRUM, TO THIS AGAIN."

I pause, take a deep breath and lower my tone, suddenly aware of how hard the First Fallon's face has become. "You've seen the same memory repeatedly from both myself and Fallon Luchelli. And each time, it's identical. The evidence is clear. A judgment will be made today. So I ask her Majesty and the Council, do you accept these memories as a true account of the events in Element Square?"

At first, there is only silence in the chamber. I glance over my shoulder at the head Council members and Fallons, and even they are quiet. Trey's face is pale, his eyes wide, skirting between me and the First Fallon. My heart pumps harder; I shouldn't have overreacted. I've pushed too far. I'm going to get thrown into Datch Prison for this. The chair behind me scrapes along the floor, slicing through the silence. Bertrum is trying, haphazardly, to stand. I reach to grab him, but he holds his hand up and continues by himself.

When he's stable, he extends his palm out flat. A silvery-white infinity symbol appears – his essence: the ability to extract the truth. It's dim; it must be the exhaustion. I've seen his essence once before, and it's so bright it's almost blinding. He nudges it, coaxing it until it floats upward.

"I accept," he says.

"I accept," says another voice from the Council Chamber: Arden's. Then several more 'I accept's ring through the room. I face the Council. Each member is standing, displaying their essence, a sworn oath. A declaration; a judgment. Relief makes my shoulders sag, and I let out the breath I'd been holding.

With a face of thunder, the First Fallon extends her hand and joins them. Then she disappears in a puff of navy smoke; the last part of her to disappear are her lingering eyes glaring at me. I turn to the Council Chamber, relief making my body sag.

"That's what I thought."

SIX

'*In a world of Balance, there are few things of permanence. Like the osmosis of mother to child in the womb, Trutinor and Earth, ebb and flow in a constant shifting correction of Balance and Imbalance. The weather, however, is Trutinor's symbol of stability, separating North from South and East from West. It is etched into the fabric of each State.*'

Excerpt - *The Balance Scriptures*

"Try not to look too smug, will you," Trey says as I waltz out of the chamber. "You could have been done for treason. That was a huge risk you took."

"Yeah but come on. They'd heard the evidence three times already."

"Eden..." he says.

"Yes," I say, stopping and turning to him. "I get it. Less smugness, more humility."

He turns to me, "This isn't a game. You don't understand how dangerous she is. There's a prophecy basically naming us as her future murderers. The only reason she's not killed us already is because without an heir in the East, the Balance would suffer untold damage. There would be a public rebellion, and she'd lose all her loyal brainwashed subjects."

"Okay, I hear you: don't underestimate the First Fallon," I say, lacing my fingers through his again.

A few of the Council members push past us tutting, so Trey pulls me out of the corridor and back into the Council foyer where we step to the side, moving out of everyone's way. But as a group of Council members passes us, I catch their conversation.

"Well I'm just saying, it could have been Lani Luchelli all those years ago, you know what she was like..."

Trey's face curls into a pained expression.

"Are you okay?" I ask, pulling him close.

"Fine."

"Trey," I say, touching his cheek, "we're not supposed to be keeping things from each other."

"I know. It's just... She died seven years ago. Can't everyone drop it?"

I shift on the spot, a cocktail of confused emotions bubbling inside me: guilt for asking Hermia to track Lani down, frustration that Trey won't confront this.

"I really think..." I start, but Trey interrupts me.

"I meant what I said earlier about my mother," he says. Where his palm holds mine, there's a cold void. A vacant nothingness that I've come to loathe. It means the strain across his eyes is present because he's holding back his emotions. Again.

I let go of his hand, "Don't do that, Trey."

"Do what?"

"One, don't pretend we both don't know what you're doing. And two, hold out on me. I thought we got past that when we were Bound? You promised me, no more memory stealing, no more gatekeeping your emotions. We're Bound. *For life.*" I lower my voice, glancing around us to make sure there are no Council members eavesdropping. "We're meant to share the load of Balance and Imbalance together."

He stands upright, arms folded, "Are you finished?"

"Are you going to share?"

His jaw flexes just once; the impact is like a cannon exploding into my chest. I gasp, stumble back against the root-wall, and look up at him as I struggle to catch my breath.

He grabs my arm to steady me as the tears from his twelve-year-old-self flow down my cheeks. His hurt rolls around my ribs as if it were my own; he was so afraid and alone, but it's not the isolation or abandonment that's making the tears run down my face. It's the anger threading through my veins like acid. He hates her for what she did. As he places his hand on my back, a cooling worm slides around my chest, pulling his pain out of me and back into him. But the tears remain, only now, they're mine.

"You see?" he says, "you see why I wasn't sharing? Some things don't need to be shared. They need to be left alone. That is one of them."

"My parents are gone, Trey. They aren't here to love, let alone hate."

He swallows, no longer able to look at me and stares off into the foyer.

"We should go," he says.

We stand there in silence for a moment, both of us too stubborn to back down. Then he reaches for my hand, "I'm sorry. You know I didn't mean it like that."

He leans down and kisses me on the forehead. "But I'm done with this conversation. It's over. I forbid you to bring it up again, and that goes for Kato too. He doesn't need this ruining his life any more than it already has."

Fury bursts into flames in my throat. My teeth clench shut; it's all I can do to prevent myself from spitting fire at him. How dare he forbid me to do anything! I give him a tight smile and turn on my heel marching up the East State exit, leaving him to find his own way out.

Storming through the dim corridor, I bounce a ball of fire in my hand. The Keepers weaving through the corridor lean into the walls as we pass each other as if I'm infectious or something. Or perhaps it's the white-hot ball of fire, *literally* burning in my eyes that's concerning them.

As I exit the Council tower, the last thing I think before a deafening crack explodes in front of me and I'm lifted into the air, is that Trey must have lost his mind if he believes I'm dropping this. Then I'm flung against the North State entrance door frame, and everything goes black.

Screams punctuate the smoke undulating through the clearing. Groaning, I pull myself upright and rub the back of my head where the frame caught it. It's wet. There's a small patch of blood on my fingers. Keepers dart around each other with panicked expressions, arms lunging for loved ones. The fresh greens of the glade and the forest canopy are washed with smoky grays and wisps of green Sorcerer

magic. Parents and children visiting the Council dash across
the grass and into the forest for safety. Keepers fling magic
through the air. A pair of hands grabs for a child with a mop
of jet-black hair. The child scrabbles out of her parent's
hands and back to the ground where she summons water
and launches it into the smoke. *She'll make an amazing
Keeper,* I think. A scream to my right snaps me out of my
daze and makes my stomach turn.

Where's Trey?

I'm alert, panic tingling my spine. I push my sleeves up,
my Fallon training kicking in. I summon wind and blow a
gust over the clearing. Some of the smoke nearest me
dispels, drifting up to join the natural clouds. But most of it
refuses to budge, keeping the clearing in a thick layer of fog.

I can't see Trey anywhere. I'm running. Shouting.
Dodging Keepers as they sprint into the forest for cover. My
heart pounds my chest as I bellow Trey's name. I've lost too
many people. I can't lose him too. Arden collides into me.

"Council members are forming a protective perimeter
around the entrance. Go," he shouts, pushing me back
toward the Council.

"But..."

"Eden, GO."

I do as he says, checking every random Keeper I can as I
make my way back toward the entrance towers. I have to
find Trey. A hand grabs me from behind.

"Trey. Thank God you're okay." I fling my arms around
his neck before dragging both of us to the circle of Keepers
forming around the entrance towers.

"When I couldn't find you, I panicked. I thought you'd
been hurt," I say.

"I'm fine. Are you okay?" he says, pushing hair away
from my face to kiss me. He jolts back, pulling his hand

away from my head. "You're bleeding." His face is stricken as he pulls me this way and that to search for the source of the blood.

I pull his hands down, "It's fine. It looks worse than it is. It's not oozing blood."

His eyes probe my face as if to check I'm telling the truth.

"I'm fine. Really," I say, giving him a smile.

"Okay," he nods, his face relaxing, "I don't think anyone else has been hurt seriously either. It's some kind of smoke bomb."

"Weird smoke," I say, putting my back to the root towers. "Look." I push a more powerful gust of wind out into the clearing. Another reluctant cluster of smoke dislodges and floats skyward, but it's not enough to give us a clear view. A lone figure wearing a strange white mask stumbles through the smoke aiming a wand straight at us.

I move on instinct. My conscious brain shuts down, and the vault cracks. A tiny sliver of Imbalance slips out and weaves through my thoughts: whispering, controlling, tempting me to dismember whoever the masked attacker is.

"Trey, out the way," I say, my voice distant, disjointed. My body jumps in front of him, pushing him back. Part of my brain shouts at me to slow down. Assess the threat. To stun not kill. But the Imbalance screams louder. *The masked attacker is going to kill Trey*, it whispers. My arms rise like robots. Two bolts of electricity shoot simultaneously, one to the heart, the other to the brain - whichever one the attacker deflects, the other will kill him. But a hand grabs my shoulder as I fire and pumps ice into my blood, shocking me back to reality. I turn to the attacker; he dodged the head shot, but the heart shot smacks into him, dropping him like stone to the floor.

Trey releases my shoulder, both of us breathing heavily. "Your eyes," he says, glancing around us.

I slam them shut and wage a silent war on the Imbalance, coaxing it like the Pied Piper back into its vault so I can lock it away.

"Is it gone?" I say to Trey as I peel them back open.

He glances into my eyes, checking for shadows and remnants of our secret.

"It's gone."

I glance at the body, still twitching as I step into the perimeter line. I pray to the Balance that Trey drained enough power out of the pulse to enable the attacker to live. Dead enemies are useless. Living ones tell stories, stories I'll be happy to extract.

A chorus of voices echoes around us. Then, as fast as it appeared, the smoke evaporates. Trey was right; there are a couple of Sorcerers limping and a Shifter holding his head, but there are no bodies, except the one in front of us. The smell of charred skin floats through the air. I swallow hard, a knot of guilt forming.

Arden runs toward us, joining the growing ring of Keepers protecting the Council.

"DEFENSIVE POSITIONS," he shouts.

The ring of fifty or so Keepers changes stance, brandishing wands, element balls or shifting into whatever their essence animal is, ready to fight.

Silence falls over the glade; even the forest stills as if the plants and leaves are waiting to see what carcass this battle leaves behind. A second later the crackle of branches crunching underfoot comes from the tree line. A row of people all wearing the same mask as our attacker break through the forest edge and into the clearing. The mask is made of a haunting white texture; it looks like the First

Fallon, except with hollowed-out eyes. What's more unsettling, is that I can't see the eyes of the Keepers behind them; the masks must be enchanted. Seeing rows and rows of the same masked face that's meant to represent all that is right and Balanced in Trutinor, spirals the unease into anxiety. I shift on the spot. There must be fifty First Fallon faces staring at me. For any normal Keeper, it's a comforting view. But after the summer's events, I know different.

They chant, sing, and scream, "Break the Bindings, Break the Bindings."

Arden steps forward, his arm dropping to his side, his fingertips skimming his wand like it's a sword. A tall slim woman, opposite me, whose mask covers her entire head, twitches. Sensing the danger, she raises her hand, which is gripping a wand, and the sea of white faces fall silent.

"What do you seek?" Arden says.

Another lone figure, a male, I think, steps forward. He's taller even than the girl who silenced the attackers. Tufts of thick brown hair escape above his mask as his stocky body steps forward. I squint at his arm, turning my head to get a better look. His Binding scar is odd. Only one colored scar. The other is missing. I scan the rest of the group, some of them with normal Binding scars, others with broken ones like his.

"We do not seek a war with you. We seek only what is our right: justice..." he says, a calm confidence in his voice. I glance at Trey, both of us thinking the same: Siren. Which means this isn't a rebel group from one State because the girl used sorcery magic. This is an organized group, and they aren't part of the Libra Legion. So who the hell are they?

"I think Israel mentioned some attacks during the

Council meeting," Trey breathes, and I scald myself for not paying more attention.

"Justice?" Arden says, his fingers still quivering over the head of his wand.

"Justice..." the masked Siren says, "...Balance and freedom."

The girl who silenced the crowd steps forward. It must startle someone behind me because a fireball is launched toward her, and in that instant mayhem breaks out. Keepers protecting the Council charge the line of masked rebels who fire wisps of magic and element balls back at us. Explosions and clumps of grass and wood splinter the air.

One of my Elemental Keepers charges into the girl who stepped forward, his flaming fist colliding with her face. He bounces off her, a loop of green sorcery magic knotting around his throat as he drops to the floor.

I ignite my fists, which she sees and immediately releases the Elemental.

Her mask is hanging halfway off her face. Arden halts, his wand raised above his head, about to strike her. But instead, he sucks in a sharp breath, "Tilley?"

Tilley? Tilley died years ago.

A ball of fire skims past my ear. To my left, Trey is controlling a growing group of masked Keepers who are buckling to their knees, whimpering.

Something cracks above me. I glance up as one of the Council root towers shears off and crashes to the grass, splintering into a million broken pieces. There's an audible gasp that ripples through the glade as if the rebels attacking us are shocked too. I seize the lapse in concentration and pump electricity around the clearing. I siphon as much power as I can into the lines of fizzing lightning. The bolts stretch from my hands, all the way across the glade, forming a barrier between them and us. Deep inside my mind, the pressure from coercing so much electricity makes my vault shudder. A vault I have to keep bolted shut this time. If it bursts open while I'm wielding this much power, there would be enough force from the Imbalance to decimate the clearing and half the forest. Trey must sense my struggle; he releases the group of rebels and moves to stand next to me, close enough that a patch of his bare shoulder presses against mine. The relief is immediate. The pressure from the vault subsides, retreating into the darkness of my subconscious. I smile to myself at the reminder that with him I am stronger. And with me, he is also stronger: two equal parts of one soul.

"No one gets hurt. We all want the same thing," I say when everyone freezes. *I hope,* I add in my head, because I'm not entirely sure what the Libra Legion wants and I definitely don't know what these guys want. But it sounded right.

The girl hesitates, scanning the area around us. A dozen of her rebels are limping or injured. The clearing is full of moans, cries of pain, and splatters of blood. The rebel I hurt is groaning. I glance behind me; thankfully, there are fewer of us injured than our attackers, although one Keeper is lying uncomfortably still, their leg snapped to the side.

I think the girl is frowning, but I can only see one of her eyes. She shrugs at Arden, pulls the mask back over her face, and touches her wand to her throat, "We did not come for war." Her voice is altered, robotic almost, using magic to mask it. My eyes narrow. Why would you cover your voice unless you had something to hide?

She throws a tiny glass marble to the floor. Smoke plumes around her. I leap at her marble, fingers stretched out to grab it as dozens of other glass marbles are dropped.

Billows of smoke pop up faster than I can throw electricity loops to trap them. When the smoke clears, the masked group have vanished taking their injured with them. So have the remnants of the glass marbles, which means we have no way of using them to track the group.

I sit up on my knees. "Dammit," I say, pounding the grass before I stand up.

Arden is staring at the place the girl was standing, his wand still raised. I touch the back of his arm. "Are you okay?" I ask.

He flinches, then lowers his wand-arm. "I think so," he says, "sorry, I shouldn't have frozen, it's just...she looked so much like Tilley."

Tilley was Arden's wife. She died in a train accident with their eldest daughter years ago. The youngest daughter, Renzo, survived. I haven't seen her in years; she was troubled after the accident and kept away from the public eye. Rumor has it she was sent to a specialist school. Something about the girl's reaction made me wonder if it was her. "Are you sure it wasn't Renzo?"

"Ren? Don't be ridiculous; she would never... I mean, she's at boarding school anyway, so she couldn't," he says, snapping out of his daze and stalking off to help a Sorcerer clasping her arm. As he reaches her, he shouts an order to a group of Dryads leaving the forest, "The Council needs help with the root towers." They nod and rush to the Councillors picking up the pieces of the tower.

"Fine," I mumble after him, "it was just a suggestion."

Two more small gatherings of Dryads appear from the forest and rush to tend the wounded, their thin branch-like hair locks bouncing down their backs as they move. One Dryad disappears back into the tree line; I assume to hunt for flowers and herbs. Another Dryad sticks one of his hands into the ground and the other over the woman's arm that Arden's supporting. A golden haze of power glistens under his hand. The more he heals her, the more his strange bark-like skin looks wooden. Bark knots and ridges cover his arms as he sucks energy from Trutinor to heal her. Then he approaches me. "Your head," he says.

"I'm fine," I say, "help the others."

He ignores me, tuts, and reaches up behind me to touch the back of my scalp. Warmth and gold sparkles crest around my head as the taste of honey appears at the back of my throat.

"Thank you," I say once he's finished. He nods and disappears to help another injured Keeper.

I turn to Trey, "Are you okay?"

He nods, "Are you?"

"Healed. But annoyed I missed the smoke marbles. We could've used them to trace the attackers."

"How much do you love me?" he says, grinning.

I raise an eyebrow. "Really?" I ask, "time and place, Trey."

"Just answer the question."

"Fine. A lot."

He raises his fist, uncurling his palm. Rolling between his index finger and thumb is a glass marble.

SEVEN

Never shall the weather falter. If it falters, so too, shall we - Balance Proverb

---

The Guild of Investigations always smells of explosions and fish. The fishy waft is because the Guild is so close to the Blood Ocean. But I'm never sure if the aroma of burnt materials and ash is as a result of the Guild's experimental research or because Sorcerers, in general, have a thing for blowing stuff up. Someone's obviously been trigger happy today because as Trey and I exit the Guild, the acrid stench is spreading into the street.

Once the wounded were attended to in the glade, Arden asked us to come straight here to drop the marble off to the investigations team for analysis and deconstruction. Whoever those rebels are, and whatever they've used to create the smoke marbles, the Sorcerers will find out.

Trey grasps my hand as we walk down the path. "I don't

want to go back to Stratera yet," he says, veering right down another cobbled street that leads to the docks. "Come on."

We meander toward the docks, a growing unease weaving its way around my insides. Before the rebel attack, Trey forbid me from talking about his mother. But maybe the attack changed that? What if we'd died, and I never told him what I was trying to do? Who would have told Kato his mother is alive? He deserves to know what happened as much as Trey does. A knot of guilt slopes around my insides. I have to hope the attack changed his mind because when Hermia finds her, and I know she will, I'll have no choice but to tell him.

As we reach the docks, the afternoon sun crests the horizon, orange and yellow streaks pouring over the clouds. We sit on the dock front, Trey a foot away from the edge, ever careful not to get too close to the ocean. The Mermaids bite, and after they lost the war against the Sirens, they especially like to bite them. As an Elemental, I'm safe, so I kick off my shoes and let my feet skim the cool water. My toes wriggle in the surface of the ocean until something slimy brushes against my heel, and I yank my feet out. Maybe not as safe as I thought.

As the sun dies, the orange liquid changes, burning the blood red color that gives the ocean its name. I shudder, put my shoes back on, and slip my hand over the cobbles to Trey's. He pulls me closer, sliding his arm around my shoulders and resting his forehead on mine.

The last rays of sun wrap us in a fading blanket of warmth. I close my eyes, relaxing into his arms. My guard drops allowing my Elemental powers to drift into the wind, feeling it, sensing it, and coaxing some of the evening air back into my system. I open my eyes and frown, pulling away from him. The air is tight, the breeze too fresh, cut with an angry-sharpness that doesn't belong in the West. I stretch my senses out again, pushing and prodding the air until I find the anomaly. It's slight, a tiny hiccup in the Balance, but it's definitely there.

"What's wrong?" Trey says.

"I'm not sure. An anomaly in the wind." But as soon as I say it, it disappears. "Doesn't matter, it's already gone," I shrug. "It can't have been anything; it was tiny anyway."

"Okay," he says, winding his fingers through mine, "there's something I want to ask you."

"Oh?"

He lets go of my hand and checks around us as if making sure we're alone. Just as I'm about to ask him what's going on, he says, "There's an ancient Siren ritual. A kind of coronation of sorts for Siren Fallons and their Balancers. Not everyone takes the ceremony. My mother didn't. But it's important to me."

"Why?" I ask.

"Because of what we will control."

"Control? We already control two of the five Trutinor States as well as far more magic than most Keepers. What more could you want to control?"

"Pure power."

"Power?" I say, raising an eyebrow.

"I need to show you. But the only way to see is to go through with the Siren ritual."

I smile at him, bring his face down to mine, and push my mouth onto his, kissing him, slow, deep, and full of static electricity popping under my lips. He hitches back from the dock edge and pulls me closer. Careful not to fall into the water, I slide my legs over his until I'm sat on his lap. He grips his arms around my waist, his eyes glancing between me and the water.

"We're not going to fall," I grin, the glint of danger in my eye. Well, I'm like, ninety percent sure we won't. But I sort of like how the ten percent is making my stomach clench.

"You know I'd do anything for you, right?" I say.

His shoulders relax, "Is that a yes?"

"It's a yes."

He lifts me up, smiling and laughing. This time, I yelp with terror as my feet dangle precariously over the water. He brings me down, laying me on the dock and sliding down next to me. He leans over me so he can stroke my hair and shower my face with kisses.

"We'll do it tomorrow," he says between caresses. "Before Stratera starts on Monday."

"Okay," I say, relaxing under his touch. I close my eyes, giggling where his lips tickle me.

Images flash across my mind: Me. Victor. Trey. A knife. Trutinor in ruins. And blood. So. Much. Blood. My eyes snap open, and I gasp for breath.

"Stop," I say, hauling myself up. "Stop. I need a second."

"What's wrong?" he says, scanning my face.

"Another dream-flashback."

"That's it," he says, "I'm taking you to see someone." He pulls out his CogTracker before I can protest and starts tapping out a message.

"Come on," he grabs my hand and pulls me up, "we're going back to Stratera. I want you to meet someone."

I pat the cobble dust off my clothes and pull my hands over my face and through my hair trying to wipe the images away. But as we head toward Titus and Luna City's central station, I can't seem to shift the shadow of my dreams.

The train from Luna City in the West to Stratera on the South border is a couple of hours long. Under Trey's insistence, Titus used the private Steampunk line to get us back to the academy faster. Despite every ounce of me wanting to stay awake, as evening drew over the sky and the light faded, the train's rhythmic rocking lulled me into a doze.

I wake as the train pulls into Stratera. Sitting bolt upright, sweat nestled in the crook of my neck, I see Trey perched on the edge of the armchair right next to mine, holding a damp cloth.

"I wasn't sure what else to do," he says, a slight hint of pink on his cheeks. Trey never blushes, he's far too controlled.

"No, that's... It's really thoughtful. Thank you," I say, sitting back.

"Was it bad?" he says.

I nod, not wanting to vocalize the nightmare I just went through because it was more gruesome than normal. I take the cloth and pat the sweat off my face trying to rid myself of the image of me standing by the Pink Lake drawing a knife over Trey's olive skin. As the blade cut into the flesh of his throat, flecks of his blood splattered over my face; tiny hot dots of red that I couldn't rub away. Blood flowed in steady spurts, covering his neck and clothes and swirling into the water until the pink liquid turned poison red.

I manage to push the dream away, but I can't shake the sensation of his sticky blood on my face no matter how hard I rub the cloth over my cheeks.

We leave Nyx and Titus at the station. They both kiss me goodbye. Nyx squeezes far too tight as usual, and whispers, "I really am going to make plans for that grand ball on your return."

I keep my lips pressed shut, hoping it's a joke but

doubting it is, and Trey and I head for the station exit and out into Stratera.

The evening air is off. I close my eyes sending my essence out into the wind; the same prickle I felt in the West has tinged the air here too. Trey touches my back, jolting me alert.

"Everything alright?" he asks.

"Sort of." Like before the strangeness has disappeared again. "I keep feeling anomalies in the air. It's probably nothing, come on." But as I dismiss it, my gut kicks back.

Trey leads me toward Stratera Coffee, a coffee shop in the center of the main academy street. It's busy, probably because it's central and no one knows where anything else is yet.

"We're meeting her in here," he says, "grab a seat if you can, and I'll get the coffee."

He dances around some fellow students and heads for the enormous queue. I take a seat on a simple wooden chair in the corner and stare out the window at the dark night sky wondering what's causing the anomalies.

"Eden?" a Siren woman says, interrupting my thoughts.

I look up; she's wearing navy hot pants and a plain white t-shirt. Her brown hair is short and cropped like a pixie. I've no idea who she is, although the longer I stare at her, the more familiar she looks. She smiles and holds out a tanned hand, "Felicia Fensley."

I shake it, and she leans down and pulls me forward to air kiss both my cheeks.

"You probably don't remember me," she says, displaying a set of perfectly straight teeth. "I work for Trey. We met briefly in his bar over the summer, while I was working with Sheridan."

"Right, yes," I say. That was the night I burned Titus'

hands not long after my parents died. I was struggling to control the additional power I'd inherited, and he was trying to help me. "That's right; you were helping a Sorcerer with anxiety."

"That was Sheridan," she smiles, her blue eyes sparkling. "We... I mean she..." she stutters.

"Felicia, hey," Trey says, returning and placing three coffees down on the wooden table. He turns to face Felicia; she puts her hand out flat, and Trey does the same. They touch palms: a Siren greeting. The air around their hands wobbles as they conduct a kind of instantaneous power exchange, each of them controlling the other's emotions for an instant. I think it's weird and intense and unnecessary. I've told Trey it's the equivalent of dogs sniffing each other's butts, but he just grumbled something about Elementals being as emotionally barren as the desert we come from. Which frankly, given Trey's complete lack of confronting anything emotional, is a smidge ironic.

"I got us coffee," Trey says once their greeting is finished, "how's Sheridan doing?"

"Good actually. Since that night you saw us in the bar," she nods to me, "her recovery's been exponential. She's able to leave the house by herself now, although she tends to stick to the same few places. But we've taken a trip back to her hometown, and she's gone to open up the bar for me this evening."

"That's great news," I say, smiling, "so you two are working in the bar now?"

"They are," Trey says, "just while I'm at Stratera. What with Fallon duties, and study, I can't really run it anymore." I slip my hand under the table and reach for his. Our lives will never be our own; we're pulled in too many directions. Which makes a knot of guilt loop around my stomach as I think about how much slack Nyx is picking up for me. I'm going to have to say yes to that weekend she mentioned.

"Thanks for coming," Trey says, "I wanted to ask if Sheridan was working again?"

"Working? As in dream keeping?" Felicia leans back in her wooden chair, her penciled eyebrows rising as she sips her coffee. "Not really, but it depends who's asking."

"I am," Trey says.

"Then yes, she is."

"Good. We need your help," he says, and nudges me.

"I'm having a sort of reoccurring dream. The content is different each time, but the outcome is the same."

"I'll speak to Sheridan. We set up a dream room in our apartment, so she can keep working."

It takes me a minute to realize what she said. 'Our apartment.' Are they together? I glance at Trey, and he nods as if answering my question.

Felicia glances around before lowering her voice and leaning in to whisper, "Yours isn't the only Binding that didn't work."

I give Trey a knowing look. 'Potential' Balancers are announced at Keepers School a few years before we're Bound. Every so often, during a Binding Ceremony, a pair of Potentials will be Bound to other people. As if the Balance spontaneously changed its mind. It used to be a rare occurrence, but I'm hearing more and more rumors of Bindings being faulty. There was an Elemental girl in my year group, Rita, that went through it. She ended up being Bound to Trat Riplock, Victor's best friend, but I haven't seen her all summer.

Felicia chews her fingernail, before taking a huge gulp of coffee, "Petra, my Balancer, died in a Balance keeping mission not long after we were Bound. Sheridan's ran off when she became housebound a couple of years ago. She's not seen her since, but their Binding doesn't seem to be affected."

"Do you know where she went?" Trey says.

"No. But there are rumors..." her voice drops so low I have to turn my ear to hear her, "...of a rebel group with broken Bindings."

Trey looks at me, the same thought going through both our minds. "I wonder if it was the same rebel group that attacked us," he says.

I nod, "Some of the attackers had weird half-Binding scars like half their Binding was missing. Do you know anything else? Does Sheridan?" I ask.

"I don't," she says, but she doesn't look at me when she says it, instead swilling the last dregs of her coffee around the cup, "but Sheridan should be able to help with the dreams."

The coffee shop door tings as a group of our classmates walk in. Felicia puts her empty cup down, and Trey stands to walks her out. "I'll be back in a minute, bar business," he says. "I'll sort a date with them for the dream stuff too," and they disappear out of the coffee shop.

Digging in my pocket, I pull out my CogTracker. There's mail from Hermia. My heart misses a beat. I glance around me to make sure Trey isn't about to reappear and when I'm satisfied, open it.

Trey might have forbidden me from bringing up Lani, but that doesn't mean I've dropped it. His mother is alive. I don't care how angry he is; I'd kill to spend just one more hour with my mother. Besides, I want to know what she knows about the prophecy. There has to be more to it; I refuse to accept my parents died for a few lines scrawled on some ancient cog.

From: Hermilda.Endlesquire@TrackerServices.com
Subject: RE: Lost & Found??
To: Eden.East@FallonCogMail.com

Still no news on Lani. But more progress on Victor. There are hotspots. Or, more correctly, dark, Imbalanced spots popping up over Trutinor.

I look out at the sky, wondering if they're the same things I've been sensing in the air.

I'm convinced they're connected to Victor so I'm mapping them in the hope it shows a pattern of movement I can use to pinpoint his location.

H x

"Ready?" Trey says, making me jump out of my skin and slam my CogTracker shut.

"Everything alright?" he says, taking my hand and pulling me out of my chair to kiss me.

"Yes, fine," I lie, guilt already nestling into my chest.

"Good. We need an early night tonight. The Siren Ceremony is going to be intense tomorrow; I want us to enjoy it."

I fold my lips shut to prevent myself spilling my secret and smile, but it doesn't reach my eyes, so I pick up my CogTracker and take his hand, leading him out of Stratera Coffee.

I will tell him. Just not today.

EIGHT

'Custodes Cordis – Keepers of the Heart of Trutinor.'
    The Lost Scriptures

'The Heart Of Trutinor – The one true source of all Keeper power. The beating heart of Trutinor, the Balance, and existence.'
    The Lost Scriptures

"Morning, head girl," Trey says, leaning on the frame of our dormitory door. The sun beams from the window, pouring light over his glistening skin. He's holding a drawstring bag over his shoulder and is wearing shorts instead of trousers.

"Been to the gym, have we?" I say as he saunters across the room, his veins throbbing in his pumped arms.

He slides onto the bed, "It's going to be a long day; I wanted to get some exercise in first."

"Should I be nervous about this ceremony?"

"No," he puts his bag down and picks up my beeping CogTracker, handing it to me. He touches his forehead to mine and places a reassuring kiss on my lips. "It's going to be fine. Check your tracker; we've been asked to help with the induction session on Monday."

"Oh?" I say, taking my tracker, "I hadn't seen, I've not long been awake."

"More dreams?"

I nod and try to shake away the images of blood and his broken body. Victor was in my dream again last night; he pushed Trey off one of the tallest buildings in the East. When I peered over the parapet, the ground zoomed in. Trey's head was split open, a halo of blood pooling around his skull, and his limbs were all deformed.

I flip open my tracker and locate the message. Our first head boy and girl duty is to meet in the foyer half an hour before the induction and help direct students.

"Was it a bad one?" he says, stroking my hair.

I look up at him. I don't need to say anything; they're always bad.

"No one is going to hurt me, Eden. They're just dreams, and that's exactly what Sheridan will tell you a couple of nights from now."

"I know," I say, weakly.

"Go get ready," he says, and the excitement bubbling in his eyes makes the last of the dreams disappear.

"Okay," I say, and take myself into the bathroom to shower and get dressed.

A couple of hours later, after breakfast and coffee with Kato and Bo, we leave our penthouse apartment and take the public train back into the center of Siren City and to Trey's mansion.

Trey leads me down a mansion corridor I've not been through before. Even though I've spent most of the summer in the South, I still find corridors and rooms I've not been in. We walk down a set of marble stairs that spiral all the way into the basement. The walls in this corridor are dappled white marble that suck the heat out of the air. It's strange to feel cool in the South. Hanging on the walls are fire lanterns, which at least give the perception of warmth.

The floor is made of white marble too, and etched into the stone at regular intervals is the Siren symbol: a pair of hands controlling a heart. Instead of gold etching, like I usually see, the symbol is white. I stare at each passing symbol, a gnawing in my gut as I try to work out why they feel odd. Kneeling on the floor, I touch the marble. The etched symbols are cold and hard like a floor should be, but I'm sure the symbol is moving. Maybe it's the light from the flickering fires. I raise my hand, drawing on my element power to siphon a small orb of fire from the closest lantern. Once the fiery ball is at my eye level, I move it over the symbol. *It is* moving. Rippling almost, like it's not made of cream stone but liquid sprinkled with shimmering gold.

"What is that?" I say, pointing to the liquid running through the symbols.

I return the fire orb to the lantern and stand up.

"Power," Trey says, and continues walking.

As we move through the basement, a light thud beats around the hallway. It's musical almost, and the further we go, the louder it gets. It vibrates the walls, the floor, and as it crescendos, my chest too. I'm no longer sure if I'm hearing it in my ears or feeling it in my body.

"Where are you taking me?" I say.

"To the source."

"The source?"

"Yeah, to the source of all our power."

"What do you mean? I thought the First Fallon was the source of all our power?"

He stops and turns to me, "What I'm about to show you, only the most trusted of Siren elders know about. As a Fallon you swore an oath to the East and the elements; a Siren Fallon has another oath. One of protection, one of dedication, and utmost secrecy. The First Fallon isn't the source of all our power; she's just the first embodiment of it. She might be more powerful than us, but she's no more a god than you, or I."

"Why doesn't everyone know about this? How do you even know?"

"I know because of the time I spent with her after I Inherited, but as for everyone else... How many centuries has war governed the border between the East and the North?"

"For all of history," I say, shifting on the spot and wondering where this is going.

"Exactly. There have been wars over: power, who the most powerful Keepers are, who deserves to reign over Trutinor, and who came first, the Elementals or the Shifters. But do you not find it odd that we Sirens, who can control any Keeper we wish, have never contested that right?"

I cock my head at him. The Book of Balance says that the first Keepers to be created were the Elementals followed by the Shifters. I'd never considered that the Sirens might think of themselves as the most powerful.

"I suppose I'd never thought of it like that. So why haven't you contested it?"

"Because we don't need to. Our true purpose is to keep the source of all power safe. Even from the First Fallon. If a constructed state hierarchy has bred a centuries-old civil war between the East and the North, can you image what the possibility of harnessing power like this would do?"

"But what is it you're protecting? What is the source of all power?"

"The Heart of Trutinor," he says.

I stare at the walls, my eyes bugging wide as I realize what he's saying. "The beating..." I say, "it's real?"

"It's real."

"A heart?"

He nods.

"So the liquid...?"

"Blood," he says, and continues walking.

I stare at the floor, looking at it in a new light, and make sure to pick my feet up off the symbols as if it might somehow hurt the heart.

"Why do you want to do this?" I say, a sudden nervousness attacking my insides. "You haven't spoken much about what happened between you and the First Fallon, but is this some kind of revenge plan? Gain enough power you can destroy her before the prophecy makes us?"

"No," he says, shaking his head. "Not revenge."

"Then why?" I say, relief washing over me.

"Because I don't want to fear her anymore."

I reach for his hand, wondering what awful things she did to him.

"If the prophecy is true, and war is coming, then yes, one day we're going to have to destroy her. And controlling both parts of the Heart of Trutinor will help us to do that.

But it's also a sacred Siren ritual, and it will connect us in ways even I can't imagine."

"Okay," I say, and continue to follow him.

We reach a set of iron gates, with three interlinked cogs attached to a lock. Trey puts the palm of his hand out flat and commands his essence to appear; a head, with a flurry of flashing images flying around its skull – memory – materializes, and the cogs twist and turn, grinding as the gates creak open. At the next set of black wrought gates, the same cog lock secures the gate but attached to them is a black spike. Trey presses his index finger to it, and a drop of blood rolls down the spike. The gates groan open, and we pass into the next corridor.

We pull to a stop outside a large black door. Engraved on the door are the words:

DEFENSOR CORDIS

"Keepers of the Heart," Trey says, nodding to the words. He takes my hands, "Are you sure you're ready for this? Once you pass this door, you swear a lifelong oath to protect the Heart of Trutinor."

"Trey, I am ready for anything as long as I get to spend the rest of my life with you."

He pulls me into his arms and kisses me, his lips moving over mine in slow, hungry circles. I kiss him back, pushing my body against his. I have a fleeting desire to skip the whole mystical Siren Ceremony and head straight to his room instead. But I think I'm starting to understand why he wants to do this.

He pulls away to look me in the eye. "I mean it, Eden, this will be..." he pauses and scratches the stubble across his jaw, "intense."

"We're already Bound. Our souls are literally connected for eternity. How much more intense can it get?"

He smiles, soft, wanting, his eyes glittering in the fire lanterns hanging above us, "That's the point, Eden. I want to give you everything. Every part of me. Always and forever. My parents never did this ritual together, so my mother was the only Keeper of the Heart. But I don't want any secrets between us. I want to give you all of me, and this is a part of me."

"Okay," I say, reaching up to kiss him again, "okay."

He brushes his lips over my jaw and neck occasionally kissing my skin. When he reaches my ear, he whispers, "Do you consent to compulsion?"

I pull back, "Why do you need to compel me if I'm willing to take the oath?"

"This isn't normal compulsion. They won't command you to do anything you don't want to, and I will also be under compulsion. The compulsion will only bring to the surface whatever is already in your heart."

"Then I consent," I say, and he smiles into my neck, picks me up, and pins me against the wall, kissing me hard, his hands roaming over my top, his fingers skimming the skin under my waistband. When he draws a breath, his eyes are fiery blue, and we're both breathing heavily.

"I love you," he says, then he puts me down and pushes the door open behind us.

The room is grand but simple. It reminds me a bit of Trey's bar, and I wonder if that's a subconscious choice on his part. The walls are split in half, the lower part made of soft maroon leather, with chesterfield buttons depressing the fabric at uniform intervals. The upper part is one long continuous mirror, looping around the room and framed in gold. I can't help but feel self-conscious as I see my face repeating infinite times in the mirror's reflection. The floor looks like black marble, but my feet sink into it as if it's plush tufts of carpet. Hanging from the mirror on the back wall is a large carving of the Siren State symbol. There's no furniture in this room. Except for a collection of cushions, a small circular table with a cup, knife, and ribbon on it, and in the center of the room, a marble fountain with the heart resting on a plinth in the center. It's gigantic, perhaps bigger even than a full-grown wolf. It beats, slow, rhythmic, and loud. The vibrations, or maybe it's the power in the air, make my head giddy as I make my way toward it. I walk around the fountain and take a sharp breath; the white heart is damaged. Cut in half. The other side is missing. The room smells like Trey: thick with frankincense and summer breeze and something else – the metallic tang of blood. As the heart pulses, it bleeds. Shimmering cream blood flows from the heart, pouring over the plinth and down into a circular hole in the floor surrounding it. It must be how the blood is flowing under the symbols in the corridor.

Glancing around the room, I realize we're not alone; there are two elder Sirens hovering in the corner. I only recognize one of them: Bertrum.

"Bertrum," Trey says, holding his palm up to greet him.

Bertrum bows deeply. "Fallon Luchelli," he says before putting his palm up to exchange a little power between them.

I shake his hand and frown. It's cold, icy almost, and the sensation travels up my arm and into my throat where it sticks. *Did he just compel me?*

He smiles, but he doesn't respond to my pinched expression.

"And this is Amori," Trey says, gesturing to the young

Siren woman on Bertrum's left. She is breathtaking, and it makes me feel even more self-conscious. Most Sirens are brunettes, all bearing the same year-round tan, locks of thick brown hair, and blue eyes. But she is different. Her hair is golden blond; it reminds me of Evelyn. Her skin is smooth and appears even more tanned against her golden waves and watery grey eyes.

"Bertrum and Amori are Siren elders. Both are rare and gifted Sirens wielding two of our most powerful abilities: truth and love."

"It's an honor to meet you," Amori says, her voice full of the familiar silk of compulsion tones. She lifts my hand to her mouth and curtsies as she places her lips on the back of my hand.

I suck in a breath. Where her lips meet my skin, a pulse of electricity squeezes through my hand and up my arm and into the same spot in my throat as Bertrum's icy compulsion. When she removes her lips, her eyes remain on me, a sly smile spreading across her mouth. There's a tingling in the imprint of her lips.

"What was that?" I ask, but she continues to smile and doesn't answer.

I blink, suddenly feeling woozy. The room throbs in time to the heart's beating. Even the walls and mirrors seem to wax and wane as if they aren't glass and stone but flimsy rubber.

In turn, they take Trey's hand and bow, kissing his skin like they did mine. His eyes gloss over. At least whatever compulsion they've placed on me, they've put on him too.

"What are we doing?" I say, but the words slur in my mouth as I speak. My legs weaken, so I lean on the edge of the marble fountain.

This close to the heart, the stench of iron and blood makes my nose wrinkle.

"How can half of it be missing and it still beat?" I say.

"We don't know," Trey says, coming to my side, "we also don't know where the other half is."

Standing this close to the heart, I notice that as it squeezes in and out, so too do six faint threads of essence: violet for the East, black for the North, green for the West, maroon for the South, blue for the Ancient Forest and silver.

"There's six, not five," I say, my words jumbled. Bertrum puts his arm around me, helping me down onto some cushions. The plinth the heart is resting on lowers in silence until it's at our level on the ground.

I sit next to Trey, and on the other side of the small coffee table, Amori sits. Bertrum takes the knife, cup, and ribbon and sits on the other side of the coffee table with her.

"Just because the First Fallon banished Aurora and her kind, doesn't mean Trutinor has forgotten her," Amori says.

"Their power still exists in Trutinor," Bertrum adds.

Oh, I think, my head thick and foggy. The walls pulse harder, and the vibrations from the heart beat inside my chest making it hard to breathe.

I grab Trey's shoulder to steady myself.

"Defensors Cordis, Keepers of the Heart," Bertrum starts, "do you swear to give your life, your essence, and your Binding to the protection of the Heart of Trutinor?" He turns to me first, indicating that I should place my palm out flat.

"I swear," I say, and he draws the knife over my palm. I wince, as warm red blood pools in my hand, then I'm giggling, and I'm not sure if it's the compulsion or the light-headedness from blood loss.

Bertrum passes Amori the knife. She speaks to Trey, "Defensor Cordis, Keepers of the Heart, do you swear to give your life, your essence, and your Binding to the protection of the Heart of Trutinor?"

"I swear," Trey says, and she draws the knife over his hand.

Amori and Bertrum tip our hands over the edge of the fountain, and droplets of our blood pour into the fountain of white. Steam sizzles up from the circular pool, forming smoky strands: one violet, one maroon. Amori takes a cup from the table, dips it in the fountain, and fills it.

"Drink," she commands.

"The blood?" I say, my face creasing.

"Don't think of it as blood but as the life source of Trutinor," she says, her voice smooth and comforting.

"Okay," I say, my words sounding more and more slurred.

I take the cup with my non-bloody hand and drink. It's hot, burning hot, and I cough as it slides down my throat. My vision brightens as if someone switched on a blaring spotlight. Everywhere I look there's color. It threads through the room, the walls, the floor, and the air, hovering around Bertrum and Amori. My mouth falls as I realize what I'm seeing: Trutinor's essence. It's in everything, reflected in the mirrors, flowing, pulsing through every atom like a rainbow of oxygen.

"Woah," I say, wobbling in my seat. Bertrum catches me and holds me upright.

"Now Trey," Amori says, taking the cup and handing it to him. He sips, and his face falls slack as he observes the same intoxicating mirage of color I do.

"Your hands," Bertrum says. I raise my good one, and he

smiles, "I know this is difficult, but try to stay conscious a little longer."

I giggle as my arms refuse to respond, but eventually, with a little aid, I manage to raise my bloody hand up to where Trey is holding his. He's grinning like an idiot, and I wonder if I look as silly as he does.

Bertrum holds our hands together. "Palm to palm, blood to blood, essence to essence," he says.

Amori picks up the maroon ribbon and wraps it around our wrists and hands. "Each of you must answer two questions of the soul. These answers will seal the oath. Bertrum...?"

"Our greatest strength lies in overcoming our greatest flaw and our deepest fears," he says, one of his hands gripping my wrist and the other, Trey's, "as Keepers of the Heart, we must share our greatest fears so that together we can overcome them to honor our oaths. What is your greatest fear?"

Trey doesn't speak. There's a cold tug in my throat, the nudge of compulsion. I answer because it's an easy answer. Losing my parents was one of the worst things that could happen to me. There's only one thing I fear more. "Losing everyone I love," I say, "losing Trey."

Trey's gaze falls on me, pain behind his eyes; he's lost as many people as I have. But I know that's not what plagues his heart.

"Losing control of my emotions," he says.

Amori dips her fingers in the cup of blood and dabs them on our free arms where our wrists meets our hands, "And what is your greatest desire?"

This answer is even easier.

"Trey," I say, blushing.

"Eden," Trey says, leaning toward me. "In this lifetime..."

"And all the lifetimes to come," I finish the sentence for him.

I lean the rest of the way in so I can kiss him, but Amori places her hand between us, "Not quite yet, you don't..."

She nods to Bertrum, and they speak together, "We Bind you with truth and love, blood and heart, essence and oath, to serve, protect, and keep the Heart of Trutinor with your life, your essence, and your Binding. You have taken an oath, which you must honor till death. This mark, is the promise you have made to Trutinor."

Where she dotted blood on my wrist, it heats up, a white scar appearing. It's shaped like the half-heart that beats before us.

"Will you honor this oath?" they ask.

"I will," Trey and I mumble.

I gasp as our words pop into existence. Like molten gold smoke, they hover in the air, the smoky words joining to form a thicker, singular 'I will.' They quiver and disintegrate into a thin strip of smoke that loops around our tied hands, splits in two, and burrows its way into our skin.

I yelp as heat floods my system. My head kicks back; a bright blue spark pulsates in my vision, spreading into my chest. Between the folds of my V-neck shirt, it beats in time with the Heart of Trutinor. When I look up at Trey, the same spark is nestled in his bare chest. Then it winks out and reappears in our wrists, turning the white scar momentarily blue.

"The oath is complete. You should rest here for a few hours. You can seal the Binding with that kiss if you wish," Amori says, grinning at us.

"With pleasure," Trey says, his eyes narrowing with lust.

We're both unsteady. With our hands still wrapped, we bring them between our chests. But I wobble and collapse on the floor bringing Trey with me. We lie on the cushions, side by side, our hands pressing against each other's chests, a blue spark pulsing in our eyes. The floor reverberates with the hum of Trutinor's Heart; it's almost as if the beats are singing a melody that only we can hear. I giggle, drunk on the power of Trutinor's blood. Above us, the heart thuds on, only now, I can hear the drumming in my soul, and the faint thudding beneath it is my permanent connection to the oath: our oath.

"I can feel you," I say, touching my forehead to his.

"I can feel you too," he says.

Somewhere above us, Amori and Bertrum pad out of the room. The light dims further, the red hue deepening. The flame lanterns burn low, the smell of blood and love and power drifting through the room. The door clicks shut. We're alone.

Trey kisses me, long, intense, and full of wanting. He's too inebriated to control his emotions so the barrier holding back his Siren powers falls, and his feelings wash over me making me gasp. Waves of warmth, tingly love, lust, and a longing that permeates both of us, fill my body. I push my kiss deeper, my free hand roaming over his skin, abs, and back. He stops kissing me, his body becoming heavy as his eyes close. Mine close too; the light dims, and I fall into a drunken sleep.

NINE

'With knowledge shall we judge, with experience shall we keep, and with love shall we choose.'

The full extended version Stratera Motto

At some point in the night, Trey must have carried me back to his bedroom because I wake to find myself in his room. For the first time since we were Bound, I didn't have a nightmare. Smiling, I roll closer to him, relieved he's there. Still alive. Still mine. Even though my sleep was dreamless, habit makes me put my hand on his chest, just to be sure. His ribs rise and fall in time with the soft snuffles coming from his nose. I snuggle in closer, leaning my head on his chest, listening to his heartbeat. I breathe in because I love the smell of him, the faint aroma of yesterday's aftershave, mixed with hot, sleepy skin. He mumbles, and rolls into me, kissing my head and then pulls my cheeks up to his face so he can kiss my lips.

"Another nightmare?" he asks.

For once, I can shake my head.

"Good," he says, and slides his arms around me, pulling us even closer. His hands slip under the covers, lust burning in his eyes. Part of me wants him. Wants him to take my night clothes off and do all the things my heart is telling me I want. But I'm not ready. Not yet. He must sense my hesitation because he kisses me on the lips and says, "We shouldn't hang around this morning, we need to get back to Stratera before the induction."

The moment's gone. I climb out of his bed and dig around in the overnight bag I leave here for some clothes. My fingers skim my arm, the heart-shaped scar still sitting in the middle of my wrist, but the blue spark has faded.

Pushing his deep red velvet curtains open, morning light pours into his room, making the sheets on his silky four poster bed shine. Trey's toned body is bathed in light, and I can't help but smile. But then something on his shoulder catches my eye: a white gash two inches wide; a scar. He fiddles with the curtain ropes, turning his entire back to me. I clasp my hand to my mouth, my smile falling as tears well in my eyes. His back is smothered in thick laceration scars. I walk over to touch his back, but he flinches under my touch.

"What the f..."

His shoulders sag, "They reappeared this morning."

My fingers brush over the scars; this time, he lets me.

"What are they? How did you get so many scars?"

He closes his eyes for a second as if stealing himself; then he turns to me.

"I had a feeling Bertrum's truth compulsion would override what was left of Eve's magic."

"What do you mean 'Eve's magic'? I don't understand. What happened to you?"

"After I Inherited, the First Fallon 'experimented' on me. Or that's what she called it anyway. She wanted to test my abilities, see what it did. Looking back, she must have been testing me to see if it would affect the prophecy cog. But back then, she said she was trying to make me stronger, help me control the Imbalance. The scars are what's left of her experiments. Evelyn used sorcery to cover them up. But now she's gone, her magic is fading. They would have reappeared by themselves anyway. I guess Bertrum's truth magic overrode Eve's."

Tears sting my eyes as my fingers trace the lines of dozens of striations, some deep and wide, others uniformed shapes. His back is covered. Heat sears through my chest: anger; outrage; jealousy. Jealousy that Eve not only helped him in ways I couldn't but knew things about him I didn't.

"I hate that she did this to you," I say, but I'm not sure if I mean the First Fallon or Eve.

"One day the First Fallon won't be able to hurt any of us anymore."

I wrap my arms around him, a couple of tears splashing onto his shoulders. "I know," I say, and let him go.

I pull on the only clean pair of khaki-colored pants I have. A coin digs into my thigh, and it makes a lump form in my throat. The hexagonal coin came from Earth. Father gave it to me once when I cut my leg open; he said it would bring me good luck. I must have left it in these pants. I throw a dark blue t-shirt on, my eyes skirting over his back the whole time. Trey picks his towel up off of a chair and disappears into the bathroom as I'm digging through my bag. I realize I've left all my sweaters in our dorm room, so I open his wardrobe to steal one of his.

I pull a few shirts and jackets out of the way and freeze. There's a set of Evelyn's dresses still in his wardrobe. I stare at the silky fabric, remembering his spikey ex-Balancer and her hatred of me, and it makes my stomach harden. Why has he kept them? I swallow down the burn in my throat and close the wardrobe door deciding I don't need a sweater after all.

A gust of wind whips around us as we climb the final few feet up the hill to the academy, and I shiver. For a brief moment, I wish I hadn't been stubborn and had grabbed a sweater. But then I remember what was in his wardrobe and decide I'd rather be cold.

"Everything alright?" Trey says as we reach the front door of Stratera. "You've been quiet all morning."

"I'm fine," I say through gritted teeth, pushing open the large oak doors.

Professor Astra walks across the foyer toward us. Today she's wearing black skin tight jeans and a halter neck top, her bronzed shoulders on show. Behind her, the First Fallon is waving her wand over the Door of Fates and staring at it with an intense expression on her face.

I turn to Trey, but his hand is on my back encouraging me into the foyer.

"It's fine," he breathes, "Professor Astra is here, and students are already starting to arrive. She's not going to do anything."

"Good morning, Fallon East, Fallon Luchelli," Professor Astra nods to each of us. "I'll need you to hand out tour timetables to the students. They should know what time theirs is, but there's a pile of tour timetables in that box just in case." She points to a stray box on the other side of the foyer. "Could you give those out. Oh," she says reaching into her pocket, "and these are your official head boy and girl pins. I promise the rest of the year isn't as menial as this."

She affixes a cog shaped broach to Trey's top. Then moves to me. The bronzed cog is simple, with the words 'With knowledge we shall judge' inscribed on it.

"What's the First Fallon doing?" I ask as she pins the broach to my t-shirt.

"Investigating. The Door of Fates has remained dormant for centuries, perhaps millennia. But last night a student walked through the foyer and reported that it was vibrating. It appears the maroon threads in the frame's marble are pulsing somewhat."

Trey looks at me, and I swallow hard, hoping our ceremony didn't cause the activity.

"I'll see you in the induction," she says, and disappears.

Students push open the door to the foyer and stumble in, carrying coffee cups and bags of toast and baked goods. I pick up the timetables and hand Trey a wad. Both of us spend the next half an hour doing our best to direct students and avoid the First Fallon. But the flow of excited Keepers pushes me closer and closer to her until someone bumps into me, sending me tumbling into the First Fallon.

"I... umm. I'm sorry, Your Majesty," I say, searching for Trey.

But the First Fallon has already grabbed my wrist to stop me falling over. She wrenches my arm around and lifts her fingers. Her eyes fall to the scar on my wrist and they narrow, her milk-white skin hardening as if she wants to question me. But she doesn't. Instead, her fingers close around my arm, and a burning pain shoots through my wrist under her fingertips. I bite my tongue to suppress the scream.

"We're at somewhat of an impasse, don't you think?" she growls under her breath, then smiles to a student walking past.

"I'm not sure I know what you mean, Your Majesty."

"Don't bullshit me, Eden," she breathes, "we both know what that prophecy says." The heat in my arm sears to an eyewatering temperature, and I wonder if she's done this to Trey.

"Don't think I've let that little episode in the truth trial go."

"I promise you; Victor is back. I wasn't lying."

"Don't you understand? It doesn't matter. Even if he is back, it's nothing more than trickery and magic. Without..." she stops, straightens up, and continues, "look, I assure you, Rozalyn cannot break her banishment." She loosens her grip on my hand. "It doesn't have to be this way; we're not on different sides. We both want what's best for Trutinor. We both want Balance. If I wanted you dead, you'd be in Obex already. There can be another way, prophecy or not..."

Her eyes flash to the Door of Fates, her expression wavering for a second. She's worried about something, and I want to know what she stopped herself saying. Trey appears, his jaw hard as he places his hand on top of the First Fallon's. She stiffens and immediately withdraws her hand from mine.

"Trey, my dear boy." Her voice is cold as his expression.

"Your Majesty," he says as a flicker of fiery blue flashes across his eyes. "We ought to be getting to our induction."

"Indeed, I was just leaving anyway. Eden," she says, giving me a curt nod, "remember what I said." Then she spins on her heel, walks a few paces, and vanishes in a puff of navy smoke. When the smoke dissipates, and I'm certain she's gone, I let out a huge breath and rub my arm.

"Are you okay?" Trey says, looking me up and down.

"I'm fine." I give him a weak smile, "Thank you for getting rid of her."

He pulls me into his arms, but I'm stiff, still upset about the dresses I found this morning, and I wriggle out of his grip after a few seconds.

"I'm just going to get some fresh air. I'll be back in a second." His face falls, giving those me sad baby blue eyes, and I instantly feel a pang of guilt. I reach up and kiss him. "I'm fine, honestly."

I push open the foyer door to the street outside and collide into a girl.

"Bo," I say, looking up to see who I've bumped into.

"Eden, hey. You okay? You look... umm... Harrassed?" she scans me up and down.

"One of those mornings."

"Do you want to talk about it?" she asks, touching my arm. She's wearing a long-sleeved shirt with a high collar and black jeans, the right leg of which is cut off at the knee displaying her shiny silver prosthetic. She adjusts her stance, the brassy cogs clicking and whirring in her foot as she does.

I consider telling her about my run-in with the First Fallon, but that's not what's furling my insides. "Did Kato ever, you know... Like kiss anyone before, or anything?"

She frowns, "Not to my knowledge. Is this about Evelyn? You know he couldn't help that."

"I know. It's not about her but what I found this morning."

"What you found?" she waggles her fingers, "sounds kinky."

"I'm not joking, Bo."

"Okay, sorry, I'll be serious. What did you find?"

"He still has some of Evelyn's dresses in his wardrobe."

Her mouth twitches as if she wasn't expecting my answer. But then her face relaxes, "Honestly? Don't read into it too much; maybe he just forgot to clear them out."

"Maybe. I mean, it's not like we've spent much time together, we haven't even..."

Bo's eyes widen, "You haven't had sex yet?"

"Shhh," I snap, glancing around us. "And no. I've only spent a couple of nights with him because of all the bloody State business and the fallout from the summer. And now I feel a bit weird about it."

"Because of Evelyn?" She links her arm around mine, pulling me back toward Stratera foyer.

"Yeah, I haven't slept with anyone and he and Evelyn... I guess I always thought whoever I was Bound to..." I shake my head, "maybe I'm being ridiculous."

"I get it. You've been through a lot too over the last few weeks. We all have. But seriously, if he's anything like Kato, you're missing out on a hot bod."

I laugh, knowing full well that the hot body gene definitely runs in the Luchelli family.

"We should go to the induction lecture," I say.

"I know, it's...," Bo says, and is cut off by the front door of a dormitory building on the opposite side of the road swinging open and slamming shut. A girl who looks vaguely familiar stalks across the pavement, crosses the road, and marches toward us.

"Ah yes," Bo says, "meet my newest family member."

I squint at the girl as she takes giant, angry strides.

I turn to Bo, unable to hide the surprise, "That looks like Renzo Winkworth? Sort of..."

Bo pulls out her red lipstick and swipes it over her mouth nodding to the girl as she notices us. Either the girl doesn't notice, or she chooses not to return the nod.

"And just so we're clear..." I start, "that's who Cassian's Bound to?"

Cassian is Bo's recently discovered brother. He was born before her parents were Bound, which made him dangerously Imbalanced. Maddison, Bo's mother, hid Cassian on Earth and lucky for him, he was temporarily Bound to me, which Rebalanced him enough for the First Fallon not to slaughter him on the spot. In the space of a week, Bo lost one brother and gained another.

She turns to me, "Apparently so. We found her two weeks ago. Or, more accurately, she found us. The pull from the Binding got too much, and she had to come back to Trutinor. Believe me when I tell you, she was not impressed."

I notice Renzo is wearing a scowl that's as unimpressed as Bo's description, and it makes me laugh. "Where was she? Boarding school?" I ask, "Arden's always been kind of secretive about her."

"Yes to boarding school. But not where you think."

"Go on...?"

"She was at school on Earth."

"Shut up? The entire time?" I ask, staring after her.

"The entire time."

Renzo Winkworth, Fallon of the West and Arden's remaining daughter, approaches us, dressed in black leathers, chunky shoes, and a dark t-shirt with the sleeves cut off. The t-shirt hangs off her tall skinny frame like an oversized, nightie, but it's held in place by a gaudy rainbow-colored sweater tied at her waist. Her hair, like her sweater, is a mangle of colors and drawn back into a scruffy ponytail.

Both her nose and lip have a silver ring through them, the latter of which she's sucking in and out of her mouth. When she passes us, I swear I smell the faint whiff of smoke – human smoke: cigarettes.

She doesn't acknowledge us.

"What was she doing at a boarding school on Earth? She's only just been Bound. How did she even get away with that? It's not like she's any old Keeper. She's a Fallon."

"Special dispensation. I hear there's an elite Keepers School on Earth."

"Oh," I say, suppressing the gnaw of jealousy. Bo and I were never allowed to go to Earth before being Bound because of the risk to our lives. The fact my father used to smuggle me out to Earth to practice is beside the point.

"Yeah, I know, I don't get how she was allowed either. But do you want to know the weirdest part?" Bo turns to me.

But as she's about to tell me, Cassian bursts through the same entrance Renzo left. He spots us, and her, and rolls his eyes, mouthing 'women.'

"Rennie, babe. Wait," he bellows in her direction.

She looks over her shoulder, gives him the finger, and continues marching off in the direction she was going.

"Dammit, Ren," Cassian says, running his hand through his hair. "RENZO WINKWORTH, I said wait." Cassian waves his arm. But it's too late, Ren is already far off in the distance, her rainbow-colored hair bouncing around her shoulders as she disappears.

"Awkward," I whisper to Bo.

Cassian's cheeks flash pink, then he stands tall, shrugs, and says, "What?"

"Having trouble?" I ask.

"Oh, piss off, Eden."

I laugh, so does Bo. He gives us the same finger Ren gave him before jogging off after her.

"Cassian doesn't strike me as the type of guy to get rejected often," I say, leading us to the foyer doors. "You have to tell me what all that was about."

"You're not going to believe this." She waves to Kato as she spots him.

"Go on..." I say.

"Cassian dated Ren when he was living in Camden."

"You're right; I don't believe that."

"Seriously. She's pissed at him because he hid who he really was from her."

"Did she tell him who she was?"

"Nope. But apparently, that's not the point."

"Wow. High maintenance or what," I say, spotting Trey in the corner handing out a load of papers.

"Which is exactly why they're made for each other. She's going to knock him down a peg or two, and I'm going to love watching every minute of it."

TEN

'Potential Ceremony – the ceremony in which the name of the most likely candidate fated to be Bound to a Keeper or Fallon, as decreed by the First Fallon, is announced formally.'

From the Dictionary of Balance

'Misbind - the name for a Binding pair that differs from the Potentials called.'

Excerpt - Myths and Legends of Trutinor

In the few minutes I was outside, the foyer has filled with excited students, most of whom are congregating outside the main lecture hall ready for induction.

I scan the sea of faces, searching for Trey and any classmates from Keepers School. I spot a couple of classmates who smile and wave, but I wasn't close to them, and they seem engaged in conversation with someone else anyway. The main door creaks open, and Rita Runskall and Trat Riplock walk in. Rita is an Elemental Keeper I've known for years. Her mom and dad worked for my parents in the East, and we've always been placed in the same class. It reminds me of what Felicia said about the broken Bindings. Rita's Bound to Trat now, but her Potential Balancer was a Siren called Tiron Galsworthy. During our ceremony, he was Bound to a girl called Eloise. Rita was heartbroken, but she soon recovered when Trat swaggered on stage, all tall, toned, and handsome. It probably helped that he's from one of The Six families. His father, Obert, is the head of the second most powerful family in the North, which is how Trat was such good friends with Victor.

Rita notices me and smiles, her thick black hair falling over her shoulders. She looks a little pale; our desert skin is usually bronzed, but I guess she's spent the summer in the freezing mountains. She's wearing a floor length dress that clings to her body and has sleeves to the elbows. Trat spots her smiling at me, and his face falls, his eyes darkening with a hardness that makes my insides squirm. I murdered his best friend; he was never going to thank me for that.

Rita places her hand on his forearm, her lips moving as though she's talking, but her eyes don't reach his. They stay rooted to the floor. I frown, trying to work out why I'm so uncomfortable watching them. Then Rita lets go and steps toward me. Trat grabs her wrist, and she jolts to a stop.

He leans into her ear whispering, and as he does, I swear she flinches.

My fist balls, and in the palm of my hand a spark of static pulses, threatening to erupt into lightning. Bo's hand reaches for my arm. "You can't," she says, holding me back. "They're Bound now; it's for her to deal with."

"What if he's..."

"You can't intervene. Not in here anyway. The Riplocks have an unhealthy relationship with their public appearance. If he thinks you suspect something is off and he's as much of an asshole as I think he is, it will only make it worse for her."

Rita's eyes meet mine, all round and full of tension. She shakes her head at me. I nod, accepting her request even though it pains me not to help her. Instead, I pull out my CogTracker and type out a message. Whatever's going on, she's not happy, and I want her to know I'm there if she needs help.

Bo points at the back of the foyer to the set of large oak doors nestled in the wall that Trey and I directed the students to.

We creep into the huge lecture hall and sit in one of the furthest rows back. Down at the front is a stage with a lectern lit by a spotlight ready for the head of the academy to welcome us.

We sit in the comfy royal green and maroon seats and wait. I pull out my CogTracker and flick through the reams of CogMails from Nyx: decisions on funding allocations, new skyscraper bridges, civil war discussions and last, a video message. I pop a headphone in and play it.

Her pale face and thick black spiky hair appear on my screen grinning at me. But the smile disappears as soon as she starts talking. Instead, the birthmark on her cheek darts around her expression the more animated she gets.

"Eden, sweetheart. I love you dearly; you know that. But you have duties here. I know the academy will have you run ragged and there's only one of you, but seriously, I've got mounting piles of paperwork that need dealing with. You've got public appearances to book, and that's without the East State Council meetings. Have you thought any more about that long weekend?"

She sighs, her expression softening. I pull the CogTracker closer; her birthmark seems even darker than last time. It must be the video. Then she starts talking again.

"Listen. I know you've struggled to be in the East since your parents... What I mean, is that I understand. But, honey, you have responsibilities. You can't avoid them forever. I miss you. I love you. Tell Titus when he can come and get you. Please come home. Even if it's just for the weekend."

She blows a kiss at the screen, her eyes welling as the screen goes blank. I pull the headphone out and slump in my seat. She's right. I have avoided going home. But only because it doesn't feel like home anymore. Not without my parents. Even though I know my home tower will be a hive of Keepers and Elementals bustling in an out, busying each other and me, I still can't stand the thought of walking in there because no matter how full it is, to me, it will always be empty.

"You still getting those dreams?" Bo says, jolting me out of my thoughts. She takes out her CogTracker and messages Kato our location.

"Every night. It's probably nothing," I say, "left over trauma from the summer." But my stomach twists in disagreement.

"What was last night's dream?"

"Do we have to do this now?"

"Eden. I'm serious," she barks a little too sharp. "You shouldn't ignore them."

I look at her, scanning her face. That's the second time she's been off with me. "You'll be pleased to know I didn't have one last night."

She frowns as she looks at me, her porcelain complexion crumpling, "Actually, no. That's even more of a concern. You've had them consistently. So what changed?"

I was in a blood-drugged state and totally high on power?

"I was probably just exhausted," I say, "but fear not, Trey is making me see a dream Keeper."

Trey and Kato drop into the seats next to us. "Yes, I am," he says, wrapping his arm around my shoulders and placing a kiss on my lips. "Everything okay now?" he whispers.

I close my mouth and nod. Bo is right, the dresses probably are nothing, and I shouldn't read too much into it.

A professor walks on stage, positioning himself behind the lectern, ending our conversation. He's average height but appears taller because of his slender stature and plain beige suit; unusual attire for an Elemental. We're outside so often, we're more suited to fatigues and flexible clothing. His eyes are orange, like his hair, but his mustache is the same deep brown as his skin. As his face changes expression, it wriggles out of time, as if it's not quite attached to his upper lip. My guess is a fire Elemental.

He taps the microphone on the lectern, but nothing happens. He presses a button and a screech echoes around the lecture hall causing half the audience to clap their hands to their ears. When the echo dies, he speaks.

"Welcome, Keepers, Fallons, and friends from other realms, it is truly an honor to welcome you to Stratera Academy, where we strive for the knowledge to help us judge the fate of others. For those of you that don't know, my name is Professor Cuthberg; I'm the Director of Academic Studies and Performance here at the academy. I'll keep it brief for now; I know that today is overwhelming and the second years are ready and waiting in the foyer to give you tours of the campus. A few quick notices. The library and the training towers are open twenty-four hours a day, but private study rooms shut at 10PM sharp. There will be a formal Christmas ball, and the tickets will go on sale next week. The canteen opens for breakfast at 6AM, lunch at twelve and dinner at 6PM. Classes start officially tomorrow. And last, I'd like to formally welcome our head boy and girl. They are your student representatives to the academy's senior board and will have the ability to deal with any pastoral issues you might have. Where are Fallons Luchelli and East?" he says, squinting into the rows of seating.

I glance at Trey; he looks as impressed as I feel. The position of head girl and head boy is automatically given to the highest scoring students at Keepers School. I came top of my class, but Victor didn't pass. Something that caused more than a little controversy, especially when Trey was given the role of head boy. My insides squirm, but if I don't stand up I know someone will point us out, so, reluctantly, I stand and pull Trey up. "Here, Professor."

"Lovely, lovely," he says, nodding his head with such vigor I swear the mustache will fall off his face. He wafts his hand at us, which I take as a gesture to introduce ourselves, so I nudge Trey.

"Good morning, fellow classmates," he says, sounding super formal. My mouth twitches as I suppress a grin.

"I'm Fallon Luchelli, Siren Fallon of the South. I'm majoring in Siren studies and Council politics, with a minor in Elemental studies. And this," he says, inching out of the way to nudge me forward, "is my Balancer and head girl, Fallon East."

I shuffle forward, noticing a sea of eager faces looking at me. "Hi, I'm Eden East, majoring in Elemental studies and defense of the Balance with a minor in Siren studies and because I'm a glutton for punishment, another minor in Council politics. We're your head boy and girl, so umm...I guess if anyone has any academic or pastoral issues you can find us in the penthouse dorm across the street, or we will pin our CogTracker details to the notice board in the foyer."

"Lovely, lovely," Cuthberg says, "does anyone have a question or comment for our head boy and girl now?"

A dozen hands scattered across the lecture hall shoot up. I know before the professor even asks them, that the questions are about Victor. I glare at the professor, wishing I had psychic abilities.

"You." He points to a boy in a middle row who's wearing a maroon waistcoat and matching glasses.

The boy coughs and glances to his friends who are all flashing surreptitious glances between themselves. My jaw tightens in anticipation. Trey slips his hand into mine, and a warm silky throb fires from his palm into my forearm, and my jaw relaxes. The boy sits up a little, the question I'm dreading forming on his lips.

"So is Victor really back from the dead or was that network takeover a sick joke?"

And there it is. I smile as sweetly as I can and say, "Does anyone have a question not related to Victor?"

The rest of the hands drop.

"Then I think we're done for now, Professor?"

"Indeed. Lovely," the professor says with the same virulent nodding as before. "Thank you, everyone, enjoy your tours and welcome, once again, to Stratera Academy."

ELEVEN

'If one were to gather magics with sufficient potency, the stripping of one's essence is theoretically possible,' postulated Professor Linus in 1507.'

From the History of Forbidden and Lost Magic

A day into Stratera, and I already have my least favorite day. Tuesday lectures drag until late afternoon, mostly because it's the only day I'm not in any classes with Trey, Bo, or Kato. I enter the academy foyer after a double class of history of the elements in which Professor Cuthberg talked at excruciating lengths about the creation of the earth and water elements and the detailed workings of their chemical alchemy.

I head to the right-hand practice tower; I've been looking forward to my next class all day: advanced defense. It's also run by two family friends. I exit the foyer and take the corridor that leads up to the practice towers.

"Eden, hold up. We got to go," Kato says, rushing down the hall to meet me.

"Go? Where? It's my first advanced defense class. I've sat through a painful day of lessons; I'm not missing the best class of the week. The only place I'm going is up that tower and into the fighting ring."

His eyes flick over my shoulder to the practice tower door. The wrought iron gate rises ten feet up. Snaking through the black metal are the five State symbols: North, South, East, West, and Ancient Forest. Behind the gate are my twin tutors: Archie and Arna Frothburn, fire and water Elemental Keepers that used to sit on my parents' East State Council, and they don't look impressed. They're both tall and thin, their bodies equally toned from practical work. Archie's skin is darker than Arna's; his cheeks blaze red like the fire he controls. Arna is a water Elemental; her skin is paler, with a strange blue hue like she's gotten too cold in the snow. They're young but highly skilled, which is why they rose through the ranks of my parents' State Council. Mom and Dad were fond of the twins and when they died, the twins took over a lot of their duties with Nyx. I've been getting it in the ear from them about returning home too.

Archie rubs his forehead; his hand is striated with burn-scars from the constant use of fire magic.

"Are you coming?" Arna says.

"Can't it wait?" I say to Kato, glancing between him and the twins.

"Not really," he says, pulling a face. He mouths, "Libra," at me.

No then. I close my eyes, frustrated with myself for forgetting. I hesitate; all three of them are wearing unimpressed expressions. Either way, I can't win.

"I'm sorry," I say, looking back at the twins, "I promise I

will make up for it. Extra classes, double coursework, what-ever you need."

Archie doesn't say a word; he glares at me then stalks up the tower stairs.

"Eden, head girls need to set the standard. You can't miss classes even if you're ahead of the workload," Arna says.

"I'll catch up on practice, I prom..." I start, but she too, walks off up the stairs and out of sight.

"Bit harsh," Kato says, "are they always like that?"

"Yes... well, no," I say, rubbing my face, already tired at the thought of how long the day is going to be. "They were close to my parents. I guess they think they're looking out for me. I totally forgot about the Libra meet. I'll just have to come back for practice after. You in?"

"No chance. I'm going to be studying Bo very closely this evening," he says, winking at me.

"There is a line, you know. Ever heard of social boundaries?"

"Is that a nightclub?" he says, smirking.

"I'm not even going to justify that with a response."

With a final longing look at the iron gates, we exit the tower corridor, enter the main foyer, and make our way to the entrance as Trey appears. His hair is pulled back into a loose knot, showing off his freshly trimmed stubble. It makes butterflies flutter around my stomach. When his hair is pulled back like that his blue eyes seem even bluer. He's wearing skinny maroon jeans and a plain white top, with short sleeves. He said he wasn't going to wear a vest for a while until he'd found a way to tell Kato what happened to him. I'm only disappointed I don't get to stare at his muscles all day. Although the top he's chosen is skin tight, so it's not all bad.

"This is just an initial meet and greet, is that right?"

Kato nods.

"Okay, how are we getting to Luna City?" I ask.

"Ah, well, the uglier Luchelli here," Kato says, looking at Trey, "brought our train."

"Watch who you're calling ugly, runt," Trey says, slapping Kato upside the head.

"Children, please," I say, smiling and wrapping my arms around Trey's waist. He picks me up and twirls me around as I kiss him.

"I missed you," he says, "advanced Siren studies was beyond dull. Are you ready to go?"

"I am, but I've got to come back and catch up with study. The twins are less than pleased with me for missing their first class."

"Your defense tutors?"

"Yeah," I say, leaning into his chest and sniffing his aftershave: frankincense, but today, instead of summer, he smells of spice.

"So," he says, pulling my chin up so he can kiss me again. "What you're saying," more kisses, "is that you're going to come back for late night studying in the hot sweaty fighting ring?" He leans into my neck and nips my skin in several spots, making me giggle, and Kato looks mortified.

"Guys. Boundaries. We're in public," he says, imitating my voice.

"Sounds like something I ought to study with you," Trey says, ignoring his brother, "you know, just for safety."

I look up at him, the grin spreading to my eyes. "For safety purposes, I agree, that would be most appropriate." I smile and kiss him again. I'll never get bored of kissing him.

"Come on," I say, "before we're late. Where's Bo?"

"She finished class early," he says, "she's already on the train."

I wonder why she didn't come and meet us but figure it's nothing to worry about. The train ride is fast, a little under an hour because Magnus, Trey's Steampunk Transporter, uses a private line instead of the busy South to West commuter rail line. The private line skims the coast the entire way to Luna City rather than winding inland and stopping at all the border towns on route.

Using this line also means we get a gorgeous view of the costal sunset over dinner. Trey dishes out the noodles and veg that Magnus must have picked up somewhere before we got on the train.

As the sun dips lower in the sky, it throws intense pinks and reds over the horizon. This is my favorite time of day in the West. The ocean glistens as if its surface is a blanket of sparking embers. In the distance, a fin, followed by a tentacle, rises out of the water and disappears again. Then there's an explosion of frothing and spitting water. Something that looks like it used to be a fin flies out of the water, detached from its previous owner, and splashes back down sinking into the murky red depths. I swallow down the mouthful of food I just ate, hearing Father's words echo through my mind, "It's called the Blood Ocean for a reason, Eden. Don't ever get complacent; the most beautiful things are usually the deadliest."

We arrive in the West just as the sun sinks below the horizon and the rich pinks turn to navy and gray as night falls.

Bo, who's been quiet the entire trip, takes my arms as we get off the train at Luna City central station and holds me back. I give her the 'is everything okay?' look, but she shakes a nod at me; I'm not sure if it means yes or no.

"You two go ahead," I say to Trey and Kato. "I've got gossip to tell Bo. Very boring girl stuff."

They shrug and walk off ahead of us, down the platform, and out the exit toward the city center.

"Okay," I say, taking Bo's arm, "fess up, what's wrong? Is it you and Kato still?"

"No," she says, rolling her eyes. "Things are getting better. I mean, he's not totally off the hook yet. But, well..."

"He's Kato?" I say.

"Exactly. Even when you want to, how long can you actually be mad at Trey for? It's bloody impossible because of the Binding."

I know what she means; the pull of the magic Binding our souls together makes being cross with him hard. The need, the longing, the completeness: it's systemic.

"So what is wrong?"

She gives me a hard look. "Okay, but no judging," she says, chewing her bright red lipstick pout.

"When do I ever judge?"

"Yeah," she says, "but you're not going to like it."

"Okay," I say, her tight expression giving me the first flicker of unease in my gut. We walk down a sandstone pavement and turn left. The streets become dense with bungalows. Luna City reminds me of the houses from the human fairytales Father used to read me as a child. Either side of the street, cottages with thatched roofs and window boxes overflow with budding flowers. The road itself is cobbled and made of the same sandstone as the pavement and the bungalows.

Luna station is a mile or so inland, and while the ocean is just out of sight, there's no mistaking it's nearby. The air is cut with enough salt to chaff the cheeks. Peppering the pavement are enchanted street lights that, as the last of the daylight disappears, wink to life. They're green, the Sorcerers' State color, and cast an eerie glow over the pavement that makes you want to check over your shoulder.

"I want to meet my real father," Bo says, as lines appear in her forehead.

"Well, that's a great idea. Why were you worried I'd judge?"

She glances at Trey and Kato several feet ahead of us and lowers her voice to a whisper, "Because I think Aurora is the only one who can tell me where he is."

"Oh," I say, my eyebrow hitching up a notch. Now she has my attention. I can't say I'm surprised she wants to meet him; I'd want to too given everything that's happened.

During the summer, Bo discovered that the man who brought her up, Israel Dark, wasn't her biological father. It's the reason her blood is poisonous to anyone who touches it. Maddison, her mother, made a blood oath with Aurora, the banished Mermaid Queen, in exchange for some magic that would protect her Unbalanced baby, the baby that turned out to be Cassian.

Bo is the result of that oath. In exchange for the ancient Mermaid magic Aurora gave her, Maddison had to bear a female child. The catch was that it couldn't be Israel's daughter. Aurora wanted a female Mermaid heir, which meant Maddison had to have a child with Aurora's son. We still don't know why Aurora wanted Bo and given she turned out to be a Shifter, we might never know. But we also haven't found out where Bo's real father is.

"What about Israel?" I say as we turn right and down a narrow path at the back of two rows of bungalows.

"I know, I know," she says, "I feel awful because I still can't bring myself to tell him I know."

"Well, don't you think you should?"

"Honestly? I don't think he needs the added stress. Mom's been more than a little fragile since Victor..."

We both fall silent. I'm sure she's lost in the same turmoil I am. The guilt for killing someone in her family, mixed the knowledge that you had no choice, and the worry that maybe, this time, your best friend hasn't forgiven you.

"I'm sor..." I say, softly.

"Don't," she says, "it's hard enough bearing the weight of what we've done. Let's not make each other feel any guiltier."

"Okay," I say, squeezing her arm, "...So, Aurora? Really though? I mean, do you have a death wish?"

"Have you got a better idea?" She cocks her head at me.

"Well, no." I'm quiet for a bit, trying to think of a better suggestion. When I can't, I say, "Have you got any idea where she is? It's a pretty big ocean out there, and she's been banished for like a million years. I've never even heard of a report of a Mermaid sighting; it could take years to find her. Let alone your father."

"I know. But I want to try anyway," she says, looking at me.

"Is asking your mom out the question?"

"It isn't. At least it's not if *you* have a death wish."

I laugh, "Then I guess old CogNews records are a good place to start looking for sightings and maybe a trip to Aurora's cove for a spot of fishing? Unless you or Kato know some ancient Siren that has a good memory?"

Her eyes pop wide as I say Kato's name, her jaw flexing, as I realize just how loud I said his name.

"What's that about me?" Kato says, turning around. I wince an apology at Bo.

"Nothing," Bo says, smiling sweetly at him.

"Beatrice Dark, how long have you been my betrothed? You think those lashes are going to work on me?"

"They did last night."

"That's it. Stop it. Neither of you say another word," I say, pretending to cover my ears.

Kato laughs and wraps his arm around Bo's shoulder, "Seriously though, I heard my name."

Bo glances at me, but this time, I'm on his side, "I think you should tell him."

She glares at me, then sighs, resigning herself to confessing.

"Fine. But just so we're clear, you're not stopping me from looking."

"Looking for what?"

"Aurora."

Kato and Trey stop dead in the middle of the pavement. "Have you lost your mind, Bo?" Kato says, his face turning a deep shade of red.

"See, Eden? This is why I didn't want to tell him." She shakes him off and stalks ahead. Kato runs after her as she bellows, "You've got two options, Kato: get out of my way, or help me prepare."

Trey glances from them to me and opens his mouth, but I cut him off, "Before you start, I know you're going to say you don't want me going out there either because it's far too dangerous. But seriously, what would you rather? Bo crossing a deadly ocean totally alone?"

His mouth closes, and he folds his arms, staring at me, "Well, when you put it like that, you make it sound so appealing."

"Maybe not the best description, I admit. But I can't let her do this alone."

He's silent; I can tell from his expression this won't be the last time we discuss it.

I understand his hesitance; there's a long history of war between the Sirens and Aurora's Mermaids.

Aurora was banished to the ocean when centuries ago, she waged war against the Siren Queen, Karva. Mermaids and Sirens are closely related, and Aurora thought she deserved to rule over both. Karva thought different. A brutal and bloody war raged. Karva won, so the First Fallon banished Aurora, and no one's seen a Mermaid since. But Karva's win came at a grave cost to the Balance. Thousands of lives were lost, including her own, and the ruptures in the Balance took decades to heal, mostly because Aurora, in a fit of rage, continued to slay any Siren that dared to cross the ocean. One of Trey and Kato's ancestors put a ban on any Siren entering the ocean, and that was that. No more dead Sirens, and the Balance eventually healed. I've always wondered why there isn't more written about it in our history books.

Bo slows until she's back at my side, and I lean in to whisper, "What did you expect? This is Aurora we're talking about. It's only right you tell him though. If anything happened to us while we were hunting her, it's not like they can come and help us."

"Us?" Bo mouths at me.

I glance at Trey's back, but he's not paying attention. Anything could happen, and if neither Trey nor Kato can go, then I guess it has to be me.

We stop outside a dark green door to one of the tiniest cottages on Herb Street. Kato's shaking with fury. The door to the Libra Legion safe house opens. "We'll talk about this later, Beatrice," he growls.

Bo and I look at each other. Her neck is pink, and she's shaking as much as Kato is.

Trey glances at me, but I gesture for him to go in. Once he's out of sight, I turn to Bo."Okay," I say.

"Okay? As in, okay you approve?"

"Okay, as in, I'll help you find your father even if it takes a decade. Which frankly, I think it will."

Her shoulders sag, and she pulls me into a hug, "Friends always..."

"And forever Balanced," I say, finishing her sentence buried in her shoulder. We enter the green door after the boys, and it creaks shut behind us. A flash of orange hair and pointy ears tells me Hermia shut it.

"Hermia," I say brightly, as she double bolts the door and twists several cogs attached to a metal bolt. She digs her hand into her navy First Fallon uniform jacket and throws a sparkling grey substance at the door.

"Eden," she says, still looking at the door. She tuts and throws another fistful of the powder at the door. When nothing happens, she swears under her breath and kicks the green wood, which groans in response. The cogs finally turn and the seal slides over the frame.

"Piece of Elf shit," she grumbles, giving the door a last kick for good measure. She turns to us. "Now, where was I...?"

We're in an empty room save for a single table in the middle; it's just like the safe house in the Keepers School grounds that Arden took us to over the summer. I assume this safe house is the same; what you see above ground is just a façade. The real safe house is underground.

"After me," she says, leading us to the center of the room where the table is. Next to it on the floor, is a hatch. She picks up a glass from the small table, swallows down the drop of liquid left in it then glowers at the glass.

"Hurry up," she says, "I need another drink."

Once the hatch is sealed, the house is soundproof, magic proof, and just about everything proof. We climb down the ladder, Bo first, followed by Kato, then me, and last, Trey. Once Hermia seals the hatch, she leads us into this evening's meeting room. It's a spacious but dim room. The walls are made of a tatty dark wood and chipped green paint. Dusty paintings dot the walls, and the floor is filled with old wooden stools and tables. The floorboards groan and creak as you step over them; if they're as old as the room looks, I'm surprised they don't snap underfoot. At one end of the room is a small stage, and at the other is a bar with optics hanging on the wall and beer pumps along the front.

"We're in an underground pub?"

"My favorite kind of place," Hermia says, pulling me to the side. "Have you told him yet?" she says under her breath. Wild orange curls bounce around her face like arrows, which combined with the fiery look she's giving me, make me wriggle under her glare.

"Eden. I mean it. You tell him or I will. I practically raised that boy. And I get that you're family now too, and even though I agree with you that he needs to confront this, we shouldn't be keeping it secret. You have to tell him. The longer you leave it, the worse it will be."

"I know. I'm sorry. I will tell him, I promise."

"You better."

"I swear on the Balance..."

She rolls her eyes at me, "Just don't take forever."

"Can you tell me what the issue is finding her?" I say, changing the subject.

Hermia ducks either side of me, checking who's around

us, then scruffs my shirt and pulls me down to her level, "I don't think she has an essence."

"What? What do you mean? How is that possible?"

"I have no idea, but essences are how I track people. The magical fingerprint is so unique, that once I find it, I can use it to track a person. But I'm certain the reason I can't find her, is that she doesn't have one. It's like... It's like she stripped herself of her essence and made herself human. You're going to have to ask Cassian where she is. I don't think I can help you."

Disappointment and frustration flood my chest. I really don't want to involve anyone in this when I haven't told Trey.

"Drink?" Trey says, interrupting us.

"I'll get them," Hermia says, abandoning us as fast as she can for the bar. She clambers up a stool and slams her glass on the bar.

"Same again," she says to the barman, then glares at me and nods her head violently at Trey. *Subtle.*

"What have you done to Hermia? And why does she look like she's going to crack her neck?" Trey says.

"Long story." *And not one I'm going to tell you today,* I add silently.

I spot Nyx's jet black spiky hair in the corner of the room as she leans onto her arms and rests on the table, staring at her pint. Titus rubs her back, and my chest tightens. She looks exhausted.

"I'll be with Nyx and Titus," I say, and leave Trey to help Hermia with drinks.

Arden smiles and gestures for me to come over, but before I can talk to him, Nyx's face beams at me, "Eden."

I lean down and embrace her. She squeezes me far too tight, and I have to pull myself out of her arms.

Titus leans over and kisses my head, patting me on the back.

"Hope the first few days have been good," Titus says. "Now the new train is refurbished, I'm going to be jobless without you toing and froing from the East."

"I know, I'm sorry. I will come home soon. I promise. But with all these meetings and academy work, I've been so busy."

Nyx turns away, her lip quivering, and it makes my chest ache. I don't want to hurt her or leave her to pick up all my Fallon duties. But being at home still hurts without my parents there.

"Okay," I say. "I promise to come back for the long holiday weekend."

She sits up, her vertical green cat-eyes bright and wet, "Really?"

"Really. If Titus has an opening in his schedule to come and get me, that is."

He smiles, "I'll have to check."

Nyx gives him a jab, "Oh stop that. Of course he'll come and get you. I'll plan the entire weekend. It will be fantastic. I'll make sure you're not too overwhelmed with business, and we'll have that welcome home ball I've been threatening you with."

Before I can protest, Trey brings the drinks over, without Hermia, I note, and Kato and Bo take seats on the table next to us. Bo sits closest to me. Israel nods to me from a few tables away. Maddison, sat next to him, gives me a weak smile. While she's being civil, she hasn't forgiven me for what happened with Victor, and I don't think she ever will.

The rest of the faces, apart from Arden's, I don't recognize. Cassian and Ren enter the pub. Cassian joins Israel and Maddison, but Ren's swept into Arden's open arms, and a strange dance of stiff bodied shuffling ensues. As if they don't quite know how to hug each other. She disentangles herself to give him a pat on the back. *That's weird.*

Someone closes the door, signaling for the room to fall silent. Cassian waves, Ren barely manages a curt nod before turning back to the conversation she was having with him. I squint at her; there's a dark smudge around her eye, covered in far too much concealer. I nudge Bo's leg and flick my eyes to Ren. But she shrugs like nothing's wrong.

"Has she got a black eye?" I whisper under my breath.

Bo looks over her shoulder and then stares at me with wide eyes, "Yeah, you're right. Weird."

Before I can contemplate it further, Arden takes a mug and perches on the front of the stage "Welcome, Libras and new recruits," he says, and takes a sip of whatever is in his tankard. He winces, blows out some air, which makes his handlebar mustache quiver, and takes another smaller sip. He's wearing his usual green sorcery robes, although he has a new wand belt cinching him in. "It's an informal one tonight, folks. A general catch up, discussion of next steps, and a social to welcome our potential new recruits and a chance for them to ask questions. On the tables are information packs. I'd ask that you read through them here, and leave them in the pub. Before we start, does anyone have any other business?"

I pick up the top sheet and scan it. It has information explaining the Libra's goal – to end the First Fallon's reign, as well as their values, which include: minimizing casualties, avoiding unnecessary risk, and ensuring they have an evidence base before acting. I hesitate, wondering what the rebel group's values are. I scan the sheet again, unsure if I agree with these principles or how the Libras want to fight this war. Isn't part of war about taking risks? Aren't there always casualties?

I stand up. "I do," I say, answering Arden's question, and the room turns to me.

"Eden, please," Arden says, gesturing for me to take his place. He slides into one of the more comfortable fabric chairs, the arms frayed with puffs of stuffing hanging out.

I hop on the stage and clear my throat, "I have information on the rebels who attacked the Council a couple of weeks ago. It appears they might not be our enemies."

There are a few puzzled looks exchanged across the room.

"But they attacked the Council," Israel says.

"I know. But I think that's because they don't know about the Libra Legion and what you're trying to do. I have a source that says they're comprised of a group of people whose Bindings are faulty. Some of them weren't Bound to their intended Potential; others have Bindings that just don't work."

"Where did you get this information?" a Shifter with a mop of dark hair sat at the back asks.

I glance at Trey who shakes his head.

"Let's call it an anonymous source. But one that is extremely trustworthy. And while the attack was happening, I noticed a few of the rebels had damaged Binding scars."

Arden nods and stands. "Thank you, Eden. This is excellent intelligence. Julian..." he says, indicating the Shifter who asked about my source. "I want you to work on this. I've had an update from the Guild of Investigations. Trey and Eden captured one of the marble cases from the rebels' smoke bombs. The Guild has analyzed the residue from inside the casing, and it appears that they're using a rare plant, the Mizzenbud. It's only found in two places in Trutinor, the northerly part of the Ancient Forest and the valleys of the Eris mountains. Can you liaise with the Guild and narrow down the search areas?"

Julian nods and writes some notes on his CogTracker as Arden speaks.

"Oh," Arden says, "and put it out through our informant network too. Someone must have heard something or seen something, if not in the valleys then in the forest."

Julian nods and taps out more lines of notes when something occurs to me.

"Arden?" I say, "do you think we should be investigating the Binding process?"

Ren shifts in her seat, and there's a smattering of conversation around the room. A Sorcerer in long green robes sat behind Israel pipes up, "Fallon East has a point. If the thing that unites the rebel group is the fact their Bindings are faulty, then there must be something wrong with the Binding process itself. Which isn't exactly news to us given the events of the summer."

"Yes, and we all know who'll be tampering with them," I add. The muttering is louder this time; a few pints are slammed against the table in solidarity, and a couple of older Elementals in the back of the pub cheer.

"Simmer down, Libras," Arden says, waving his hand at the room. "I agree, we should be investigating the Binding process. But we must tread very carefully. If, as Eden is suggesting, the First Fallon is tampering with the Binding process itself, then we may have an opportunity to prevent her from doing it in future."

"I can use the academy library for research," I say. *In all the spare time I don't have,* I think, immediately regretting offering.

Arden nods, "Israel and I will use the Keepers School library to do the same thing, and Julian will contact the informant network to see if there's a contact connected to the rebel group. The rest of you, business as usual."

Arden comes over to our table. "What do you think so far?" he says to me, "are you ready to take the Libra oath?"

"I... Umm. Potentially, yes."

"Potentially?" Arden laughs as if I was joking. I wasn't.

"I mean, obviously," I lie. "The next Oath Ceremony isn't for a while though, is it?"

"No," he says, shaking his head, "we're going to have weekly meetings, which you're welcome to attend, but because we're trying for a big recruitment push, we're holding out for an official Oath Ceremony."

I nod, grateful for the time to think about it. I decide I have to know who the rebels are and what they want, and I don't know if I can take the oath until I have. Arden turns back to the room, seemingly satisfied.

"Oh, and at the next meeting, I'd like a recruitment update," he says, raising his glass, "cheers, Libras. To Balance and truth."

"Balance and truth," the room answers with a round of clinking glasses.

TWELVE

'It is argued that the soul is the source of our strength. But I beg to differ; the heart is much harder to control than mere mind and will power. But that makes it all the more fun to play with.'

Karva Arigenza, in discussion during the creation of The Book of Balance

"I'll see you guys tomorrow," I say, waving to Bo and Kato outside the main entrance to Stratera.

"You're actually going to study?" Bo says, looking at her watch. "It's almost eleven."

"I know, but I promised the twins. Besides, the training room will be empty, so I'll be able to practice in peace."

"Yeah, 'peace,'" Kato says, nudging Trey.

"Goodnight, Kato," I say, and slip my hand into Trey's to lead us through the huge oak entrance doors. We walk across the foyer's black and white checkered flooring and into the corridor leading to the practice towers. Fire lanterns hanging on the wall light the way as we pass the wrought iron gates and climb all the way up to the fifth floor.

Our first-year practice room is a large round training area that reminds me of the London cage fighting gym we first found Cassian in.

The same lanterns hang in here as the hall, although there are also spotlights in the ceiling. Next to the spotlights are a set of free-standing black separators resting on the wall, which must turn the room into a simulator. Dangling from the furthest side of the room are five drapes, each embroidered in gold with our State symbols.

The air has the faint smell of animal, ash, and sweat; signs that whichever class was in here last, worked hard. The walls have a row of hooks for our combat bags and spare kit, and above them are paintings of all the great Trutinor wars: The Mermaid-Siren War, the first North-East battle, and the West War. All of them are graphic, filled with blood, scenes of torture, and dismembered body parts. They serve as a reminder and a warning: war only causes Imbalance.

Next to the drapes is a bookshelf and next to that, a wooden bar with a folder on it. I pick up the folder; there's a note scrawled on it from Arna telling me what I need to do and what books I need to read. I turn to the drills section in the folder. Some of it's simple stuff: use of essence power in defense, combat drills, and then some more complicated Fallon specific drills. For me, I also need to practice simultaneous use of multiple elements and running various drills with a squadron of front-line Keepers.

"What's the damage?" Trey says, turning the lanterns up, so there's more light in here.

"Two sims, some drills, and homework."

"Okay, I'll call the drills," he picks up the folder and nudges me into the center of the room but grabs my arm, stopping me from moving, and pulls me back in, "kiss me first."

I smile into his lips; I love it when he does that. Wrapping my arms around him, I kiss him hard, my insides tingling as I do.

"Enough," I say, grinning and untangling myself, "I have to practice before I lose the will to do it at all."

"I think you should lose the will," he says, his blue eyes burning hot and intense like he's about to compel me to stop.

"Trey Luchelli, behave yourself." I put my hand on my hip and open my mouth again, but he holds his hand out to cut me off. "Fine, let's be boring." He pushes a life-sized plastic training-dummy into the middle of the room. "Ready?"

I nod, pushing up my sleeves.

"First drill: arm swipes and hand grips. I'll help."

He comes in front of me and grabs for my arm, "Now swipe your hand over mine twisting my arm over."

I do as he says and it works; the power shifts from his grip on me, to my grip on him.

"Again," he says.

So again, he grabs, and I twist out.

"This is too easy, we learned this in Keepers School. What's next?"

"Alright, show off," he says, grinning at me. "Second drill: fireball. Fireball. Water cuffs to the ankles, and finish with a two-element combo: fire wrapped in electricity, straight to the chest."

I take a deep breath, close my eyes, and draw on the elements. They're sluggish today. I coax and pull water and fire from deep inside my chest. Fire comes first. No surprise there. After air, it's the one I find easiest to control. Much to my father's disappointment, I always struggled with his water essence.

The silky cool sensation of water eventually slides into my veins, ready to submit to me. My eyes fly open. I launch the fireballs fast, spin around, and drop to the floor as I shoot the water cuffs at the dummy's legs. I roll forward, leap up, and unleash a stream of fire from one hand and entwine it with the bolt of electricity pouring from my other one. The electricity loops around the dummy's chest, but the fire ricochets off it like the two elements are magnets repelling each other.

"Again," Trey says.

So I do. Throwing fire, water cuffs, and dropping to the floor. But again, the fire and electricity ropes repel away from each other.

"Dammit," I say, launching a ball of fire at the floor. It rolls a couple of feet then fizzles out, so I throw another one at the same spot.

"What did the floor do to deserve that?"

I glare at him, raise my palm, and create a flame, bouncing it up and down mock threatening him, "Do you want one too?"

He grins, his eyes twinkling as he does, "Only if you give it to me in the bedroom."

My gut clenches, remembering Evelyn's dresses in his bedroom. "Do you ever think about anything else?" I say a little sharper than I intended. But the thought of his hands on her body, her hands on his back, makes my skin crawl.

"What was that?" he says, putting the drill sheet down.

"Nothing. Can we get on with this? I'm better than that shoddy performance. I'll get it right this time."

"Eden," Trey says, his voice softening, "it wasn't just your expression, I *felt* it too. So it's not nothing. What's going on?"

"I don't want to talk about it." I take a step back, then turn, and walk over to the bar, switching on the sound system, cutting him off. A killer base beat rumbles through the room, growling and vibrating so hard I swear the drapes are moving to the rhythm. He raises an eyebrow but stays quiet, as his gaze follows me back to my start position where I reform my fighting stance.

I really don't want to talk about it because even if those dresses are in his wardrobe by mistake, they still represent the years he spent with Evelyn. I can't take those away. Just like I can't take his scars away. I know that even if he says he didn't love her, he had to spend years pretending he did. They did all the things we should have done. The First Fallon took that time and those 'firsts' away from us, and nothing can change that. And maybe, if I'm honest, that's why we haven't had sex yet. I know it's pathetic; he can't help what's happened, but I can't help how I feel either.

I launch the fireballs, one after the other. Larger, hotter, and angrier. I fling them so violently at the dummy I knock it over. Dropping, rolling, and sliding the water cuffs over the ground, I manage to get them to loop around the dummy's ankles faster than the last time. I jump and straddle the dummy. Evelyn's face appears like a ghost over the dummy's. A roar erupts from my belly as I punch the fire rope around the dummy's chest and finally fuse the lightning rope into it.

"Enough," Trey says, touching my shoulder. A thick gooey sensation, like a cooling foam, pours from his hand into my shoulder and suffocates my emotions, extinguishing the fire and dampening my powers.

He hoists me off the still-smoldering dummy and leads me to the bar so he can turn the music down to a soft rhythmic hum. Staring into my eyes, he puts his arm around my waist and pulls me close, "What's going on?"

"Please don't. I really don't want to talk about it. It's not even worth it."

"Well, the dummy sure as shit thinks it is."

I give the smoking carcass a sideways glance, "I'll have to replace that."

Trey snorts, "I'm sure they have a million spares. Are you going to tell me what's wrong with you or do I have to compel it out of you?"

I look away. He pulls me a few feet around the circular wall where there's a pile of discarded fighting pads. We sit down and lean against them, and as we do, the words spill out before I can stop them, "Why do you still have Evelyn's dresses in your wardrobe?"

His lips quiver as if he's suppressing a smile, "Is that what the dummy abuse was about? A few of Evelyn's dresses?"

"And that right there is exactly why I didn't want to talk about it," I say, slamming back against the pads.

"She's dead. What on earth have you got to be jealous about?"

"Because she's had you. *All of you,* and you can't take that back."

Trey pulls his hand through his hair and sighs, "Yes, she's had me. Yes, I had sex with her."

Deep down I already knew he had. But hearing the words hurts more than I want it to. I swallow hard, trying not to let the bile in my throat turn into vomit. My eyes sting worse than my throat, and I have to draw on the water element to force the tears away. I don't care if Trey can sense I'm using my power to stop myself from crying. I won't let Evelyn be the cause of any of my tears.

"You know when I was Bound to Evelyn, I thought I'd lost you? You're the only thing that matters to me. The only thing that's ever mattered to me, and I thought you were lost to me. Forever. So I chose to carry on because I didn't think we, 'this,' would be possible. But I swear to you, Eden, she never had my heart. And she knew that too. It's why she hated you so much. She had me physically, but she couldn't have the one thing she wanted..."

"Your heart?"

He nods, "You know as well as I do, my Binding to her was a farce. No matter how strong the First Fallon Bound Evelyn and me or how hard she tried to keep me and you apart, nothing Evelyn or the First Fallon did could ever change what was, and always will be, in my heart."

"Then why do you still have her dresses?"

"Because her parents asked me to send her things back to them, and I've been shipping it in batches. I had to unravel three years of living together and pull the entire mansion apart looking for her belongings."

He lifts my chin up to his, "There's only one person my heart has ever belonged to."

I attempt a smile, "What if I'm not as good as her?"

"Eden, my life without you was nothing. Just a vague half-life. Evelyn was only ever a duty forced upon me by a corrupt Council and a cruel Fallon. But you... You were and always will be my salvation. Every second I stole with you, every touch, every night by the Pink Lake. It was all worth it just so that I could have one more moment with you. And if you're not ready, then I'll wait, even if that's forever because I'm happy just knowing I have you in my life. You're the missing piece of my soul, Eden. You and you alone."

I inch back toward him, slipping my hand under his neck and around the back of his head, pulling his lips onto mine. The jealousy evaporates.

"Okay," I say between hot kisses, my lips moving over his, "Okay." I straddle him and pull him as close as I can. His arms wind their way around my waist, under my top, brushing over my skin like hot static. I want him. All of him. I no longer care if he's been with Evelyn; he is mine and always was. I pull his shirt off, running my hands over his shoulders and down his abs. His hands slide up to my bra, unhooking it from behind. He grabs my hips and flips me underneath him, lying on top of me, smothering my neck and mouth with kisses. His touch makes me catch my breath.

The spotlights flick on, startling both of us. I scrabble to readjust myself, re-clipping my bra. Trey grabs his top and twists his back away from the door.

"Kato, seriously. Did you ever think to knock?" I snap.

"Why would I?" he says, "I thought you were studying." He feigns innocence, but the way his jaw is jutting out, it looks more like he's wearing his 'I told you so' face.

"What do you want?" I ask.

"We have a problem..."

THIRTEEN

> *'Soul Death – The absolute and final destruction of a soul, thereby preventing it from resurrection and severing the eternal tie with its Balancer, forever.*
>
> *N.B. Performing a soul death is treason under the jurisdiction of The First Fallon Law.'*
>
> From the History of Forbidden and Lost Magic

Kato leads us out of the training tower, down the stairs, and through the foyer.

"Where are we going?" Trey says, upping his pace to keep up with Kato.

"Library. Arden's waiting for us there."

"Arden?" I say, frowning, "but we only just left him in the West a couple of hours ago."

"Like I said, we have a problem," Kato says, and breaks into a jog.

Much like the Keepers School library, Stratera's library is buried deep in the belly of the central academy building. We descend down a set of spiral marble stairs, the heat sucked out of the air by the cold stone. At the bottom of the stairs is a short corridor that ends at a set of arched wooden doors with a metal ring for a handle and a plaque in the center of the door that has the academy motto on it:

WITH KNOWLEDGE SHALL WE JUDGE

Kato pushes open the door, and the three of us walk in and down the central aisle between two long racks of all the editions and versions of the Book of Balance through the years. When we reach the center of the library, it breaks open into a seating area, with long thin mahogany tables decorated in maroon leather down their centers, book rests, and dim-lit brass lamps. The air smells of musty books, leather, and insomnia. Even at midnight, the library is busy.

In the furthest corner of the breakout area behind the study tables, in an area of armchairs and coffee tables, are Bo, Arden, and Hermia, whose eyes look glazed; I'm not sure if it's because of the amount of alcohol in her blood or tiredness.

We sit, Kato next to Bo and Trey and me in a two-seater sofa. I rest my bag on the floor and dump my CogTracker on the coffee table next to Trey's.

"What's going on?" I say, trying to keep the worry out of my voice.

"There's been a development," Arden says, leaning forward and lowering his voice.

"What kind of development?" Trey asks.

"One that if it comes to fruition, will have consequences," Arden, says his jaw tightening. Kato, Bo, Trey, and I exchange worried looks.

Hermia shuffles forward, and Arden nods to her. "Before the First Fallon banished her sister to Obex, it didn't exist," she says.

"I didn't know that," I say to both of them. "When we were in Obex, the Last Fallon said that her sister had banished her and that the Imbalance we're all sending to Obex is slowly killing her, and everything in it, but she never mentioned that Obex was created specifically *for* her."

Hermia rubs her hands over her face as if trying to rid herself of her stupor, "Well, it was."

When she doesn't elaborate, I turn to Arden. "When both the First and Last Fallon lived here, in Trutinor, Balance and Imbalance co-existed in a perfect equilibrium. Obex is... Or, I should say, was a part of Trutinor."

"Like its Balancer?" Trey asks.

"Exactly," Arden replies. "But in her quest for a Balanced utopia, the First Fallon tore Trutinor apart to separate Balance and Imbalance."

"So what's the development?" Bo asks, chipping in.

"The other night, the Door of Fates starting vibrating, and the threads in the frame started pulsing," Arden says.

"I know I saw the First Fallon examining the door before our induction," I say, my fingers brushing against my arm as I remember the pain from the First Fallon's grip.

"I thought the history behind the door was all just a myth," Bo says, frowning.

"Wrong," Hermia says, pulling out her CogTracker and tapping some buttons. When nothing happens, she glares at it but continues talking anyway, "And until this evening I've been struggling to work out what Victor was up to. I was trying to correlate the dark spots. But they're so sporadic. Castles, ancient ruins, open fields, coastal positions," she wallops her CogTracker when it refuses to display her findings.

"Piece of Elf shit," she growls.

Kato picks it up and strokes it. "You have to woo it," he says, "like a lady." Within seconds, he's got the tracker projecting a map of her findings. Then lines appear connecting the locations, followed by a table of data.

"How'd you do that?" Hermia says. "I haven't ever managed to get the mapping program to do that."

"I told you, seduce it."

She raises an orange eyebrow at him, "If you can put the ego aside, we should talk. We could work well together."

"Can we get back to the point?" Bo says, taking the Tracker from Kato and putting it on the coffee table in front of all of us.

"As I was saying," Hermia says, narrowing her eyes at Bo, "until this evening I thought his movements were meaningless."

"But they're not?" Trey asks, leaning in to look at the map.

"No, they are," Arden says.

"I don't get it," I say.

"Hang on, how are Victor's random movements connected to the door?" Bo asks.

Kato's eyes widen. "Oh my God, Beatrice Dark, you're brilliant," Kato says, grabbing her cheeks and kissing her. "That's why his movements have been so sporadic. He must be looking for a key or something to open it."

"That's exactly what he's doing," Hermia says, her eyes

glittering at Kato in a way that can only mean she's scheming.

"A key for the door?" I say, frowning. "But there's no lock."

"Correct," Arden says, "he's looking for the lock too."

"Okay," I say, an uncomfortable gnaw forming in my gut, "say he finds this magical lock and key, what's on the other side of the door? Where does it lead to?"

"It's not where it leads that's the problem," Hermia says. "It's what it lets out that's the issue."

My blood turns icy as I recall Victor's face on the CogTV in our room, the threat of Rozalyn's return.

I swallow hard, then look at the group, "The Last Fallon...? Victor's found a way to bring her back."

FOURTEEN

The four soul categories:

Lost Soul – categorized as demon – A soul that died from Alteritus, or failed to be Bound before death.

Obex Soul – Obex inhabitant – A soul waiting for its Balancer in order to pass onto the next life.

Absent Soul – A soul that has passed into the next life without its Balancer.

Deceased Soul – A soul that has been destroyed.
    The Dictionary of Balance

"We think so," Arden says.

"What I've gathered from working with Cecilia, sorry, the First Fallon," Hermia starts, "is that the door was used to seal the barrier. Think of the barrier between our worlds as a scar. I guess the door was the plaster that stopped Trutinor bleeding."

A silence falls over us, and my mind drifts to my dreams. The fractured images of a broken Trutinor - I've seen it bleed enough, I don't want to see it in real life.

"Before I set out for Stratera, I had a quick strategy meeting with the Libras that hadn't already left the safe house. We're convinced, given what Victor announced on CogTV, that the Last Fallon is trying to rip open the barrier between our worlds. She wants to reunite Trutinor and Obex so she can start the prophesied war."

Trey and I simultaneously lean back in our chairs. The prophecy says that a fated pair who Inherit power, will unite with the Last Fallon and destroy the First Fallon.

"War aside," I say, when I've regained composure, "is reuniting Trutinor with Obex such a bad thing? If our worlds are meant to be joined, then what's the problem with reuniting them?"

Arden shakes his head, "*Were*. They were meant to be joined. But like any anomaly, once it occurs, it changes everything. Look at what's happened to Victor. Just before I left Luna City, I spoke to a couple of senior Guild Sorcerers in the Libra Legion. They think the barrier really is a sort of scar in the fabric of the universe. And if you cut open scar tissue, it doesn't tend to heal well; the scars get bigger, and more damage is done."

"Oh," I say.

Bo puts her head in her hands and mumbles from somewhere behind them, "So we need to find the lock and key and stop Victor opening the door?"

"Essentially," Hermia says.

"Sounds like there's a but," Kato says, picking up Hermia's CogTracker and scrunching his face up as he taps at the keyboard.

"There is," Hermia says, then adds, "why isn't there a bar in here?"

"Because it's a library," I say, shaking my head at her. "Stay on point. What's the but?"

She glowers at me but answers anyway, "We don't know what the lock and key look like, let alone where they are."

"Can't we just ask the First Fallon what she did with them?" Kato asks.

Arden and Hermia both give each other a sideways glance as a heavy silence falls over us. One by one, we all turn to Trey.

"Oh," he says, breaking the silence, his face crumpling, "because of all the memory wiping I've done on her, she can't remember what she did with them?"

"And that's the 'essentially,'" Hermia says.

After Trey Inherited, the First Fallon experimented on him testing the limits of his Imbalance. She refused to let him see me, but he managed to sneak out on several occasions anyway. When he returned, she was furious. The first time he wiped her memory it was an accident, but then he learned to control the ability, and he used it to see me more often. Wiping her short-term memory so frequently didn't help her sanity or, apparently, her long-term memory.

"Okay, so what's plan B?" I say.

"Research," Bo says. "We scour the library for anything we can find on a magical lock and key. Records, rumors, historic texts, anything."

"Good idea," Kato says, "I'll go back to the East with you, Hermia. I think I've got an idea on how we can triangulate the Imbalance spots, and you'll have all the tracking hardware in your shop. I reckon I can reprogram our trackers as locators. And I'm hoping you'll have some kit I can use to pin down the source of Victor's network hack."

Hermia whistles, her eyes popping out of her skull, "Yeah, me and you are definitely having that chat, Kato. We could make mega bucks together."

"I'll go back to the Guild to see if they have anything that can help," Arden says.

"Okay," I say, "that leaves me, Bo, and Trey to hit the books."

"I'll have a hunt through the records section and the old CogNews to see if there was anything discovered or reported," Trey says.

"I'll look in the history section," Bo suggests.

"That leaves me with Imbalanced magic," I say.

Arden, Kato, and Hermia say goodbye and leave the library, and Bo, Trey, and I all split up.

The library is cut in two by the central walkway. The older, ancient texts are on the left, and nestled behind them in the back are the Imbalanced and dark magic books. On the right are the newer more modern books, research texts, and the records section. Bo and Trey head right, and I turn left.

I wander deeper through the rows of leather and dust. Each rack stretches high above me; I'd need a ladder to reach the highest shelves. On the ends of some of the shelves hang bags of cotton gloves for the oldest and most delicate texts. There's a thick musty scent in the air, and I can't decide if I love it, or if the tickle it's creating in my throat is annoying.

I skim my fingers down the spines of a row of brown leather books; it disturbs a layer of dust that fills the air and makes me sneeze. I spot a copy of Trutinor State Defense – the history of civil war, tactics, and Fallon reign, the text Arna said I'd need to read so I pull it out.

As I slip the book under my arm, my head snaps up; gooseflesh runs down my back. My element senses kick in. The air is moving, wrinkled with the movement of a body, yet there's no one in my aisle. I glance behind me: nothing. The air slows, and settles, but still there's no one around. I try to shrug the uneasy feeling away and continue heading toward the dark magic section.

As I meander further into the library, the light fades, the fire lanterns dimming as if a draft is blowing through the library. I reach the next break in the shelving and stop. Again. I look left and right up the aisle, but there's no move-ment and no one nearby.

The air grows cold, cold enough that the lantern hanging nearest me dies. My heart thuds in my chest as I skirt the area looking for the source of wind. *It's just a draft, Eden. Stop being pathetic.* But even as I think it, I know there's no draft because I can't feel any wind in the air, and my powers are uncomfortably silent. *Get a grip.* I steel myself, stand tall, and step into the break between the shelves. The dark and Imbalanced magic books section is right in front of me.

I'll start here, I think, as a hand slips over my mouth making me stiffen. I figure it must be Trey playing a stupid joke on me and force myself to relax so I can kick his ass for frightening me. But the hand shifts position and my spine tingles. It's not a hand, it's a paw, and it's half covered in fur.

I spin around. Knocking the paw away, I stumble into

the dark magic section and face the boy I've already killed once, "Victor."

My hands immediately ignite with electricity. I take a defensive stance, hands raised, ready to finish the job I started.

"Eden," he says, that peculiar maroon vein pulsing down his face. "I meant it when I said I'm not here to hurt you."

I shift from foot to foot, wondering if I should scream or wrap a bolt of electricity around his throat. But for some reason, I don't do either of those things. I stay still.

Realizing I'm not going to scream, his shoulders relax. I scan him up and down; this time, he's wearing leather trousers with some kind of extensive belt with loops and pockets filled with magical items hanging off it. His top is maroon and covered by a leather jacket. He looks surprisingly good for a dead guy. As he leans against the book shelf, I can see just how fitted his outfit is. His trousers and jacket are snug to his tall, no longer slender, body. He seems to have put on some muscle since he died. *Is that even possible?*

I roll a small flame around my palm and then flick it over to the lantern that snuffed out. When the flame flares back to life, Victor's face is tight. I frown. As much as I hate him, I've known him long enough to know when something's wrong.

"I know why you're here. What you're looking for. And I'm not going to let you take it."

He grins, the light from the flames glowing in his eyes. "Took you long enough," he says.

"Do you really think we're going to let you cut a hole in the universe? You'll destroy everything."

"Rozalyn disagrees."

"You're on first name terms now... Wow, Victor, you're moving up in the world."

He ignores my comment, "She believes this path is the right one for Trutinor, Obex, and for Earth."

"And what if it isn't? What if all it's going to do is destroy all our worlds?"

He sighs, "You're going to have to pick a side, Eden. One way or another, you're either on the First Fallon's side, or you're on Rozalyn's. And we both know whose side the prophecy says you're on. So why don't you stop delaying the inevitable and get out of my way so I can get what I came for."

"What did you come for?"

"Unicorn droppings and candy corn. We're in a library, idiot. What do you think I'm here for?"

I grit my teeth to stop myself from burning his eyeballs out. The longer I keep him here, the more chance I have of getting information from him.

"So you're a minion now?" I say, in the most patronizing way I can.

"I prefer messenger," he says, rubbing his face. He scans the shelves, then his fingers tap the vein pulsing on his temple, and he pulls his ear.

If that's his lame attempt at a coded message, I'm not buying it.

"Whatever," I say, rolling my eyes. "I've had enough. I'm taking you into custody. You can't gatecrash my corona-tion and waltz around Trutinor creating Imbalances. You're supposed to be dead. And right now, there is no war. Which means there's no side to pick, and honestly, my coursework is more pressing."

"You know you're not taking me into custody," he says, his eyes narrowing into slits.

"Fine. Then let's stop this slow dance and tell me what you want from me because you didn't appear in the library right behind me by accident."

His face softens, but his eyes stay pinched as if he's pleading with me. He rolls out his non-pawed palm. Scribbled in wonky handwriting are the words 'DON'T PANIC and TRUST ME.'

Huh...? He grabs my hand and touches it to his temple. The vein is cold and wet under my palm.

Throbbing through it, with every beat of his heart, I sense the darkness, the void that always signals Imbalance. It nudges against my essence, calling to the vault buried in my mind like it's a long- lost sibling. Her face, the Last Fallon's, flashes through my mind. Then the library dissolves into darkness.

FIFTEEN

'We all fear something, even the powerful who hide it like a shameful secret. But the powerful are foolish, for they only fear things more powerful than them. The truth is, there is only one thing we should fear: the heart. When whole, it harbors enough power to give life where it was taken, destroy life that shouldn't be, create new worlds and sentience, or tears the walls of all our universes down. Fear the heart and fear the Keeper that controls it.'

Excerpt – The Lost Scriptures

"What the hell have you done to me, Victor?"

"I haven't done anything. Shut up and listen, I can't hold her off for long. I need to tell you what's going on."

I'm surrounded by a darkness so thick I can almost touch it. I try and move, but my body doesn't respond. My hand rises to touch my cheek but that, too, doesn't work. There is no cheek, no hand, no body, nothing. Yet I can feel my heart hammering against my ribs. A cold prickle slithers down my back.

"I told you to trust me. Please don't panic because if you do, you'll jump out, and we won't be able to have this conversation."

"Jump out? Of what? Where am I?"

"Are you going to shut your fucking mouth so I can explain?"

That, at least, makes me laugh. He might be dead, but he's still a total prick. My heart slows enough for me to control my breathing and to shoot, what I think, is a disembodied glare through the darkness.

"I don't even need to see you to know the expression you're pulling." He sniffs. "I..." his tone breaks; his voice echoes, as if he's not in front of me but around me.

"Am I in your head?"

"Yes," there's a cough and a shuffle somewhere in the blinding darkness.

"The vein," he continues, "is linked to the Heart of Obex. It's what the Last Fallon is using to keep me alive here and to control my every move. She's manipulating everything I say and everywhere I go. I'm just a puppet."

The Heart of Obex? That must be the other half of the heart the Sirens guard. It's in Obex? "So that's why you couldn't tell me what you wanted out loud?"

"Finally, she catches on."

"Do you want me to play nice?" I snap. "How am I inside your head?"

"Dead-guy trick. Picked it up in Obex. Tantamount to a

minor haunting, mixed with a little essence manipulation. You'll feel super queasy after and probably pass out for a couple of hours."

"Thanks for the warning. Okay, get to the point, it stinks of dog in here. What do you want from me?"

"I need your help."

I laugh, but it's more of an indignant snort. "Help? You tried to kill me and Trey for that matter."

His turn to snort, "Are you kidding me? You actually *did* kill me."

"Fair point. Doesn't mean I'm helping you. Do you really expect me to trust you after everything that's happened?"

"No. But given you knifed me. In. My. Actual. Beating. Heart. I expect you to at least let me show you what's going on."

"Fine."

The darkness glimmers, lights and colors swirl into focused images, reminding me of mine and Victor's final Earth simulator exam at Keepers School.

A tall slender woman stands on a set of spiraling stairs crying. Her skin is as smooth as silk and deep brown. Her lips are perfectly pointed and atop her head is a mop of pure white curls. She's stunning.

"Who is she?" I ask.

"She's the first," Victor says.

"The first?"

"The first of many things but specifically, the first anomaly. She's like me, an Unpredicted."

"I said who, not what." I squint at the image, wishing I could make Victor's brain zoom in. There's something about the curve of her face that's familiar.

"She is one of the First Children. You're looking at

Karva Arigenza."

"When you say first, you mean like..."

I search my brain for my history lessons, trying to remember the names and order of the First Children: Darique came first, he was born to Rozalyn and was the first Elemental. Then, Rueben, he was Cecilia's first child and the first Shifter. Then Cecilia had Karva, the first Siren, followed by Aurora who was Rozalyn's and last was Clarissa, Cecilia's third and final child; she was the first Sorcerer.

"Yes," he says, with an air of smug in his voice, "I mean the first ever Siren."

I give a low whistle. "But, I don't understand," I reach to scratch my head and remember that inside here, I have no head, or hand for that matter. "Why is she an anomaly?"

"Because like the First and Last Fallon, the First Children are meant to be immortal. Only Aurora killed Karva," Victor says, his voice drifting around my back as if he's walking behind me.

"But the others died too. Aurora's the only one left alive. How come they're not anomalies too?"

"Because an anomaly only occurs once. Karva's death changed the Balance. After, the deaths of the other children became part of the Balance's plan. Once any kind of anomaly occurs, the Balance readjusts itself onto a new path."

My head swims with information as I try and put the pieces together.

"Why are you showing me her?"

"Because you need to bring her back."

"What do you mean, bring her back? How is that even possible?"

"Don't worry about how for now..." There's a scuffle

and a squeezing sensation, like Victor's stiffened.

"What's going on?" I say.

"Rozalyn's coming. I have to be quick. She wants me to open the door for her to walk through. The only way to shut it is to have a certain type of soul walk through it instead. So, I'm giving you a choice. Rozalyn or Karva?"

"Doesn't sound like much of a choice."

"Would you rather I let Rozalyn through?"

"Obviously not. But why Karva? What's in it for you?"

"She's...Shit."

There's a shuffling, more muffled swearing, and I'm yanked backward and into the dim light of the library.

Victor blinks at me, his eyes wide with a hardened stare. This time, his coded warning is loud and clear.

"Eden, dear..." Victor says, his voice strained, higher pitched. It's not him.

"Your Majesty?"

Victor's mouth peels backward, displaying yellowed incisors. His face convulses, Rozalyn's appearing over it like images flashing through TV static. Her face fades in and out of focus. But her blood red eyes remain solid, and they bore so hard into mine that I'm frozen to the spot.

"Are you ready to join me and fulfill your prophecy?" she asks.

"I...," I shift on the spot, hot under her gaze. Something is stopping me agreeing. There are too many unknowns, too many questions.

"It's fine, dear; you don't need to decide now. In fact," Victor leans down, bringing her face closer to mine. The coldness in her eyes oozes into my body, making me shiver. "You don't have to help me at all. But if you don't, try not to get in my way. Prophecy or not, I'm going to destroy my sister."

Victor snaps back into a standing position, "Hurry up, Victor dear," he says in the Last Fallon's strained tones. He gives me a pained look, reaches for a book on the shelf, and then his black wings slink out of his back and over his skin shrinking his body down until he vanishes from sight, taking the book with him.

I stagger back to where I left Trey, my stomach rolling with the nausea Victor promised. I wipe my sweaty brow and cling to each table as I stumble toward Trey. Bile clogs the back of my throat. My knuckles whiten where I'm gripping the tabletops. What the kind of magic did Victor use? There's a beeping, and I'm vaguely aware it's a CogTracker. I stagger across the rug, reaching the seats I left Trey in, and freeze.

It was my CogTracker, and he's standing over it, his face pale, eyes full of tears.

"I'm sorry," I say. I don't have to look at my tracker to know what he's staring at. "I'm sorry," I mumble again. I lean on the table, the floor swaying underneath me.

"You couldn't leave it alone?" Trey says, anger burning through his voice. "Not only did you not drop it, you're actually searching for her?"

I open my mouth to respond, but he cuts me off.

"And worst of all, you're using Hermia to do it. *Hermia*? Dammit, Eden."

"Trey, please," I say, but my stomach rolls again, and I scout the area for a bin. "Let me explain," I say as I stumble toward it.

"Don't bother," he says, and storms out of the library, leaving me clinging to the bin.

"Trey...Wait," I shout. But he's gone, and as soon as the words leave my mouth, I heave over the bin and empty my stomach.

SIXTEEN

'Dream Fever – An infection of the dream. A hallucinatory nightmare that's impossible to wake from. Dream fever causes the fracturing and separation of consciousness, subconsciousness, and dream state, trapping the mind in a permanent nightmare until the body starves and death occurs.'

From the Annals of Sorcery

I get up and grab my CogTracker, which Trey left open on the coffee table, Hermia's CogMail still on display like an accusation.

"Eden? Is everything okay?" Bo asks, appearing from the central aisles. Her eyes furrow, "You're green."

"Dodgy food," I mumble, grabbing my belongings. "Going home. Catch up tomorrow."

She flashes me a dirty look for abandoning her, but I leave before she has a chance to stop me. I have to call Trey and apologize, but the thought of explaining makes my stomach churn like I'm on one of those absurd human rollercoasters. I stumble out of the library, across the foyer, and out the front doors.

For a few seconds, the cool touch of night air makes the nausea settle, but then I take a step forward, and it comes rushing back. I dash to the closest dumpster and throw up. When I recover, I open my CogTracker and scroll to find Trey's number.

It rings a few times and then goes to voicemail. I redial immediately. But this time it goes to voicemail after just one ring. I let out a frustrated shout, which turns into a gagging session as bile crawls up my throat. He's not going to pick up, so I switch to CogMessages.

Trey, I AM so sorry. Please know I would never do anything to hurt you intentionally. You thought you were doing the right thing when you took my memories, and as much as you disagree, I believe I'm doing the right thing now. I was going to tell you, but the right moment never came up. Please don't be mad. I love you... In all the lifetimes.

Three dots appear as I take a steady walk back down the hill toward Stratera station. There's no way he'd go back to our dorm. Not if he's this angry with me, and I doubt he's gone back to the bar either because that's the first place I'd look. My guess is he's heading for his mansion. The dots stop, but no message appears. So I type out a second message.

I know you're there. Talk to me. Don't shut me out because I made a mistake. We have a lot of

years left together, and it's going to be an awfully long time if we spend it in silence. Neither of us are perfect; we're both going to mess up over and over again. But I'll still love you anyway, and I hope you'll love me...

The dots appear and disappear again. The muscles in my neck flex although I'm not sure if it's frustration or the urge to vomit. I decide to change tactic. No matter how annoyed he is with me, I know our Binding will bring him back eventually, but I want him to *want* to come back.

You can't ignore me forever...

...I'm far too cute.

Finally, he replies.

Ha.

There's a pause. But then a second message arrives.

You are. But I'm still angry with you. I've gone to the mansion, please don't come after me, I need some space. I promise I'll come find you tomorrow.

There's another pause, and then a third message appears.

I still love you. T x

I reach the station and come to a stop. My legs feel like bricks, and a wave of exhaustion hits me. Victor warned I might be tired once he threw me out of his head. I'd walked this way thinking I was going to find Trey. I glance back at his messages, toying with going to the mansion anyway. But then I remember the cannon ball of emotions he shared with me in the Council foyer; I decide to respect his request and give him the space to process.

I scroll to the offending message from Hermia.

From: Hermilda.Endlesquire@TrackerServices.com
Subject: RE: Lost & Found??
To: Eden.East@FallonCogMail.com

I didn't like to mention it in the library, and I know you'll be furious, but this whole thing is getting ridiculous. I caught up with Cassian after the Libra meeting.

Dammit, Hermia. I didn't want to involve anyone else.

He confirmed my suspicions; Lani did strip herself of her essence, and that's why I can't locate her...
He also said he would be willing to take you to see her.
Think about it before you say no, and for Trutinor's sake, tell Trey. He needs to know.
H

I slam the CogTracker shut and glance at the station clock; it's nearly 1:30AM. I drag myself onto the next train heading into Siren City. Trey might not be at the bar, but that's exactly where I'm going. I'm tired, fed up, and in need of a drink.

The public steam trains are basic at best. The carriages are cold. No matter what State you're in, an icy chill seems to grip the brittle walls. Our private trains have expensive heating and cooling systems and insulated walls; these trains do not. But this time, I'm grateful for the cool air because as the tiredness grips my body, it will get harder to stay awake. I don't want to sleep. Not when my dreams are full of blood and ruin. And definitely not when I've just been inside Victor's head. I sit on a hard-wooden seat, which creaks under my weight. The cushion backs are frayed and puff out a cloud of dust when I poke them. My nose wrinkles as I inhale stale air. It's an unpleasant mix of old sweat and fast food. I flip open my CogTracker. There's a message from Nyx; I press play, and her bright face and green cat-eyes appear in the screen.

"Eden, darling," she says, and wipes her hand over her face like a cat cleaning itself.

I frown, there's no doubting this time - her birthmark is definitely darker. Instead of pale orange, it's a deep brown. I hope she's not sick.

"I'm so happy you agreed to come home. I'm having your room revamped. I thought it would help, a new start so to speak. If you like, I can overhaul the entire tower? I know you said you weren't ready to come back, so I'm going to box your parents' belongings and move them into storage until you're ready to go through them. I'm hoping that will make it easier for you to come home..."

Her eyes bug wide, her black hair sticking on end.

"I mean, if that's not what you want, I won't touch anything. You might want to do it yourself. I just want you to be happy and comfortable coming home."

She looks away from the screen. Blinks a few times, and then shakes herself.

"When you come back in a couple of weeks, you're going to need to make a decision on your East State Council members. I know we went through suggestions on the train, but you didn't make any definitive choices. You need your own Council, honey, especially while you're at Stratera. They can take the brunt of the local work, and you can sign things off in batches here, or Titus can courier things to you weekly during the term. There's one more thing..."

She pauses for breath, then continues,

"...There's trouble brewing on the border again. Rumblings of Shifter attacks. We need you to review the peace keeper strategies for the borders with Trey. Did he talk to Bo? I'll send the strategies by encrypted CogMail..."

She pauses; her lips flutter as if she wants to say something but isn't sure how. She shifts behind the camera.

"I'm very proud of you, Eden. I just needed you to know. I know I've been tough on you and expecting a lot. But I want you to know how proud I am. Sometimes we don't say these things enough. But I am so very proud of you, and I love you with all my heart, darling."

I'm not entirely sure what to make of her message. I reply, telling her how thoughtful I think it is that she's redecorating the tower and giving me a chance to recover before I have to sort through my parents' stuff. I sign it off asking if she's okay because she doesn't seem herself. But I don't expect a reply any time soon; it's nearly 2AM.

By the time the train reaches Siren City, the exhaustion is making every step like trudging through drying cement. The city is asleep, the streets quiet save for the occasional late night drinker stumbling home.

When I reach Luchelli Lane, my t-shirt is wet, and I'm dripping with sweat. This deep in the valley, there's no wind to cool you down. My heart sinks when I scan the street: it's dark. I check my CogTracker; it's 2:30AM. I hoped they'd still be open but they must have shut for the night. The red glow that spills onto the street, and the regulars who fill the cobbles with their laughing and chatting are gone. The lane is desolate, except for the remnants of overpowering perfume, discarded drinks, and tacky patches on the ground. I kick a stray bottle in frustration and slouch on a pile of chairs chained to the shop next door to Trey's bar. I'm so tired, and all I wanted was a drink to wash away the guilt.

I lean my head against the wall. I must fall asleep because the next thing I see is a pure white flash, and then I'm standing atop Stratera hill looking down at Siren City. I turn around; the academy is no longer the building I remember but made of bone and crystal. The two towers that usually stand either side of the main block are shaped like enormous tusks lancing the clouds. The building between them is made of a strange crystal that shimmers, not like the sparkle of the sun on the ocean's surface, but like the glint of something sinister in the First Fallon's eye.

Keepers emerge from the buildings. All of them silent, their skin the color of dried ash and bone. Their faces devoid of any expression, their eyes locked on the floor. They move in couples and uniform steps.

What is this place?

As a couple passes in front of me, the girl's head snaps up. "Help us," she says. Before I can answer, there's a piercing scream. But none of the Keepers around me turn to investigate, they just continue trudging on to wherever they were going.

I find the source of the scream: it's Lani. Her bronzed skin is pale, her face smothered in tears as she looks up at the tusk-shaped towers.

At first, I can't understand why she's crying; then I squint up at the towers. There's a limp body broken over the top of the tusk, skewered through the chest, arms hanging slack, blood seeping down the tusk's ivory exterior. It's Trey. A guttural scream rips through my chest.

"Eden?" a disembodied voice echoes around the street, drawing me out of my panic.

"Eden," it calls again, "wake up. Wake up now."

The dream collapses into darkness, and I'm pulled, no, yanked into consciousness. My eyes open, and I gasp for breath.

There's a woman holding my arm. She's breathtaking. Her face is covered in freckles, which make her vibrant green eyes stand out even in the dim street light. The only blemish on her freckled face is a thin scar on her forehead that I think is her essence scar – three circles that connect in the center. As she steps closer, a few loose strands fall from the messy knot her chocolate brown hair is tied in, and her bohemian trousers tinkle like bells as she moves. But the strangest thing about her is the series of markings on her arm. Shapes and symbols cut into the skin. Some of them are faded, but others are raw like they're fresh cuts.

She smiles at me and nods to the shapes. "They're my dreamers," she says as if I know what that means. "It's nice to meet you officially, Eden." She holds out her hand, which I shake, trying to rid my brain of its sleep addled state.

"Sheridan?" I say, tentatively. She looks totally different. The woman I saw in the bar last summer was a shell, frail and willowy. Felicia has done an amazing job healing her.

Sheridan smiles, "You were having a nightmare. Figured I'd help you out."

"I appreciate it, thank you," I say.

Felicia steps out of the bar, locks the door, and grins as she spots Sheridan. She bounces over to her, clearly not spotting me leaning against the wall in the shadows. She throws her arms around Sheridan and locks her lips onto hers.

I give an awkward cough, and Felicia leaps a meter away from Sheridan, her eyes as wide as orbs as she sees me in the darkness sat against the shop wall.

"You scared the Balance out of me," she says, her body relaxing when she realizes it's only me.

I can't help but laugh as she gives me a playful thump on the arm. "What are you doing here at this time of night?"

"I needed a drink."

"Yeah, you look like you do too," Felicia says.

"Is it the nightmares?" Sheridan asks.

"In part. But also a minor disagreement with Trey."

The pair of them give me a knowing look as if they've had their own fair share of disagreements.

"Early Binding relationships are hard," Felicia says.

"Tell me about the dreams," Sheridan says, "when I came out, you were screaming. Without doing a proper dream share, I couldn't see your entire dream, but I caught flashes and images. A bone tower and a lot of blood."

"They're getting worse," I say, "I don't know if it's some kind of stress, or trauma from the battle with Victor, or some subconscious fear I have. But I'm afraid to sleep."

Sheridan nods, "Come with us. Trey has organized an evening together in a few days. But you're here now, and we're about to walk home, so unless you've got somewhere else to be, you might as well come with us."

Trey doesn't want to see me until later in the morning, the bar's shut, and I have no idea whether the trains will still be running this late at night. Unless I plan on sleeping rough, I'm not sure I have another option.

"I'd really appreciate it, thank you," I say, and pull myself off the wall.

It takes us about ten minutes to get to their house, winding our way through the rows of white marble mansions, porches with giant stone columns and naked statues that frequent the streets as often as road signs.

We slip off the main roads and enter a street with a row of more modest houses, although when I say modest, they're still several story high town houses made of the same luxurious marble as the mansions.

We reach their place, and Sheridan slips out a key opening the front door into a corridor. There's a set of stairs at the end of the corridor and a lift next to them. Besides us are two doors.

"It's apartments?" I say, surprised.

Felicia laughs, "It might look beautiful outside, but not every Siren can afford a mansion."

Their apartment is the first one on the left. Underneath their door is a welcome mat that makes me smile; it says 'Sleep Tight, Sleep Balanced.'

We enter a spacious sitting room; the floor is made of a plush cream carpet. The sofas are cream too, and the rest of the furniture is oak and wood. It smells like burnt lavender, chamomile, and incense. On the coffee table is a pestle and mortar, a box containing lots of green things, some incense, and some candles probably left over from a ritual.

Opposite the front door is a long corridor with the lights off.

"Take a seat," Sheridan says, "will you get some drinks, Fliss?"

"Sure," she bounces down the corridor, switches on the light, and disappears into the room furthest away. I think she's the perkiest person I've ever met; even the thought of trying to be half as energetic as her makes me yawn. Sheridan takes off her shoes and sits cross-legged on the carpet opposite where I take a seat. I sink so far into their cream cushions, I'm not sure how I'll climb out again. Felicia returns, putting three steaming mugs on the table. I reach for one, but Sheridan puts her hand over it. She picks out some herbs from her box, drops them in my mug, and swills them with a short stubby wand that's the same pinky-red color as the marks on her arm. She shoves the mug toward me as Felicia drops into the single armchair and swings her legs over the side.

"Thank you for agreeing to help me."

"It's an honor to help one of our Fallons. Although technically, I haven't agreed to help you yet..."

I'm not sure what to make of that comment, but she motions for me to drink up.

"What is it?" I ask.

"I love this part," Felicia says, grinning.

Sheridan picks up the slate grey mortar and empties it into something under the table. Then she picks her way through a pile of assorted herbs in her box on the end of the table. She frowns at twigs, sniffs others, and dabs the occasional green leaf on her tongue. She chooses a small selection and drops them into the clean mortar. Then she picks up a long needle and looks up at me.

"To help you, I need to see your dreams. The drink opens your dreamscape up to me. Have you ever shared your dreams before?"

"No," I say, shaking my head. "Is that a problem?"

Sheridan glances at Felicia and pulls the herb box back adding several more dried brown and green herbs to the bowl. When she's finished crushing the pile, she puts her tools down and the pestle clinks against the mortar. Then she picks up a needle again and hands it to me.

"Not a problem, exactly."

"Sounds like there's a but?"

"There is," Felicia says, curling her legs under her.

"Sharing your dream space isn't like using any other Keeper magic," Sheridan says.

"It isn't?" I ask, looking between them.

"No," Felicia says, her grin widening as her Siren-blue eyes light up.

"There are a few things you need to know before you agree to share your dream space with me," Sheridan says, picking up the pestle and mortar to grind the mixture again.

"Okay?" I say.

"The first is that this is a permanent sharing."

"Permanent? You mean you see the dreams of everyone you've shared dream space with every night?"

She tilts her head at me, "If I wasn't skilled, yes."

"But you are skilled?" I ask.

"The most in all of Trutinor," Felicia interrupts, her face beaming as she looks at Sheridan.

"So how do you stop them?" I ask.

She lifts her marked arm, "Fail-safe."

"It's awesome, she designed the fail-safe mechanism herself," Felicia says, the grin stretching even further across her face. "She was awarded a prize in advanced sorcery for it and had a bunch of academic papers published. It's a huge deal." Felicia uncrosses her legs and leans forward.

"It's not just that I can see your dreams," Sheridan says,

dismissing Felicia's compliments. "Because you're a Fallon, your power is stronger than any of the Keepers I've worked with before."

"Which means what?"

"It means," Sheridan says, glancing at the powdered mixture and placing the pestle and mortar on the table, "that there's a chance you'll see mine too."

"Ah... I see why you haven't agreed to help me yet," I say.

She gives me a sad smile. "My dreams have always been my own. While I've entered many others, mine have been private."

"We don't have to," I say, feeling guilty for the second time this evening.

"It's fine," she says, "if we don't use our gifts for good, we might as well not have them."

"Okay then," I say, eyeing the liquid and taking a gulp. It tingles, like static, but instead of tasting the liquid, I smell it: flowery charcoal. I stare at the cup in amazement.

"Okay," Sheridan says, sitting up a little higher.

"So the fail-safe?"

She pushes a lock of her chocolate waves behind her ear.

"The fail-safe will help. It should more or less stop you seeing my dreams and if necessary, stop me from seeing yours. Our fail-safe will be a unique shape, something meaningful to you and will form a mark on our skin." She points at the markings on her arm that I noticed outside Trey's bar.

"A replica will appear as soon as you start dreaming. When you want to stop the dream share, touch the fail-safe, and it will eject me. Think of it as a trap door."

"Or a vault," I say, thinking about the similarities to the vault I already have in my head.

"A vault?" she asks.

"Nothing. Sorry. How do I create the fail-safe?" I ask, yawning and taking the final slurp of liquid from my mug.

"You don't. That's the beauty of the spell," she says, her green eyes twinkling.

"It comes from your blood."

I frown, wondering what happens if it doesn't form. As if she knows what I'm thinking, she smiles, "You'll be fine."

"What will it look like?"

Sheridan smiles, "Like your safe place. Or at least a representation of whatever makes you feel safe anyway."

"Okay," I say, still not comfortable with the fact I have to go into the dream share without the fail-safe already in place.

"The first time will be intense."

"Intense how?"

"Most likely you will flip between dreams. You may even head hop between my dream and yours. It will be disorienting; it takes practice to allow someone into your mind. Minds don't like to be shared."

I shift in my seat. My mind is not a place that should be shared; there's too much darkness and Imbalance inside me. What if having Sheridan inside my head makes the vault burst open?

"When you say 'mind'..."

She smiles, "Don't worry, I'm not a mind reader. I can't influence your thoughts, or see into your subconscious, just your dream space."

"There'll be nausea afterward, won't there?" I groan, thinking of Victor and the library, which already feels like weeks ago.

"Possibly," Sheridan says, "but the herbs should help combat it."

"Okay," I say, relief washing over me. "Then if you're still willing to help me, I think I'm ready." I yawn again as if my body wants to prove how tired it is.

"Bring the needle," Sheridan says, and takes my hand to guide me along their corridor until we stop at the first room on the left.

"Last chance to back out," she says, grinning.

There's no way I'm backing out now. "I need to know what the dreams mean," I say.

"Then welcome to the dream room," she says, and pushes the door open. The room is painted black, except for a speckling of bright white dots over the walls and ceiling that appear to glow like stars freckling the night sky. Unlike the thick incense from the living room, there's a fresh clean smell in here, like the sharp cut of the wind, and it makes me feel like I'm outside, lying on my back, looking up at the stars.

"It's beautiful."

"Thank you," she says.

There's no bed, which seems odd given that we need to sleep. But as I step deeper into the room, I realize the entire floor is spongey like a mattress and covered in blankets and pillows.

"We have to sleep next to each other. I need to be close to you the first time to ensure the connection sticks."

I shrug, "Fine by me.

We sit, and Sheridan pushes the mortar toward me, "I need a drop of your blood."

I push the silver needle she gave me into my index finger and wince as it pricks open my skin. I squeeze a few drops into the mortar and hand the needle back to Sheridan, who does the same. She stirs the mixture, reaches for a small purple vial that must have been tucked down the side of the mattress, and pours a couple of drops of clear liquid in. Then she reaches for her wand. Green wisps of magic flow from the end of her wand as she whispers words I don't understand. The threads of green whisk the mixture in the mortar until it whips up and out of the bowl in the form of a mini tornado. The bowl rattles against the table spinning faster and faster until it bursts into flames and disintegrates into ashes.

"Interesting," she says, and picks the bowl up, "ready?"

"I am. What was interesting?"

She smiles, "I don't always get flames."

"This is going to be one hell of a ride," Felicia says, sticking her head around the door, "I'm almost tempted to hop in just for the fun of it."

Sheridan glares at her, "Behave, Felicia."

"Good luck," Felicia says, and closes the door.

What's the powder for?" I ask, looking at the bowl in her hands.

"That, we use now."

She dips her fingers in the white powder and smudges a circle on my forehead. Then she does the same on hers. It's hot at first; then the circle gets cold. Icy cold.

"Why a circle?" I ask.

"Because of the infinite connection between the mind. The three circles on my forehead represent consciousness, unconsciousness, and the dreamscape. Are you ready?"

"I am."

"Then dip your finger in the powder and dab it on your tongue."

I reach down smearing some of the ashy powder on my finger and touch it to my tongue. It tingles, light and full of electricity. A giggle erupts from my belly. As soon as Sheridan slides a pillow out for me to lie on, my eyes roll back in my head, my body drops to the pillow, and I slip into unconsciousness.

SEVENTEEN

'Dream Share – The population and
subsequent witnessing of a single dream
by two or more Keepers.'
The Dictionary of Balance

I'm at the top of my home tower roof in Element City. My
feet teeter on the edge of the parapet as a wave of horror
chills my body. The sun is tinged maroon and black. Blood-
red streaks dirty the clouds making the air thick and choking. The heat from the desert has gone, and cold winds
whip around the building. In the distance, instead of golden
waves of sand, the desert dunes are singed black. On the
building next to us, I spot a lone figure, which I think is
Sheridan.

My beautiful cube city is broken. The buildings closest
to me have been sliced in half. Their innards: metal girders,
cement, and steel rebar, are displayed like carcasses. Towers
crumble, bricks splinter off and drop to the streets below as

if the entire city is decaying. Bridges between the buildings are rotten and collapsing. Great chunks have been bitten out of the sides of the skyscrapers. What city-sized monster has eaten my home? Tears run down my cheeks. The ground beneath my feet wobbles as my home tower rots and collapses like the rest of them. I fall, not to the ground but into the darkness of sleep.

When I wake in my next dream, I'm standing in a dim corridor. The walls and floor are made of smooth white marble – we're in the South. Inlaid in the floor is the Siren symbol. I kneel down to examine it. Our symbols are made of gold, but this is made of a creamy substance that ebbs and flows and sparkles like there are fragments of diamond in it. I'm in the corridor under Trey's mansion; we're near the heart.

I stand, noticing Sheridan standing someway down the corridor. She keeps her distance, observing rather than interrupting my dream. A sharp pain radiates in the fleshy part near my elbow. I stare at the inside of my arm, a hexagonal coin shape appearing on my skin. The fail-safe. I touch my trouser pocket where the real coin sits and smile. Father. The fail-safe is shaped like the coin Father found in London; it was on the same trip he brought Mustard, our dog, back with him.

Trey materializes, holding my hand. He tugs my arm and starts running, dragging me down the corridor. The wrought iron gates are already open.

A bolt of pain slams into my head, and I stumble forward letting go of his hand. The dream melts as I fall. When I land, it's on rock. I can't breathe. My head's swimming, my skin itching like it doesn't belong to me. Nothing looks right, and everything's tinged with a strange green hue. I roll around the rocky ground beneath me, scratching at my blistering skin until I remember: I'm dreaming. I sit bolt upright. This isn't my dream. It's Sheridan's.

She's walking, bare foot, across the rocks and down into the valley. Her trousers thwack against her legs as they jingle in the wind. The breeze whips her chocolate colored hair around her head. I get up and run toward her. As I step over the peak of the hill, I pull short and blink. When I can't work out what I'm looking at, I squint. At first, I think it's a sea, with ripples and undulations on the surface. But I realize the hue of the dream is distorting the colors. I'm staring at fabric. Hundreds and hundreds of feet of fabric all stitched together in a mosaic of creams and browns. Tucked in the crooks and edges of the valley is a village of tents.

Sheridan stops and turns toward me, frowning. She raises her hands and puts them flat out facing me.

"You shouldn't be here," she says, and pulls her arms back and shunts them forward.

My elbow burns where the coin's mark imprinted my skin, and I'm flung backward into darkness. The hilltop wind roars in my ears as I fly through the darkness, then as I slam into a hard, hot surface, the wind ceases.

Rubbing my eyes, I pull myself up and realize I'm standing on my home tower roof again. This time, the sun is high enough in the sky that my arms sting from the heat. In the distance, desert surrounds the city of skyscrapers. Lonely train tracks traverse the sandy dunes, and if I strain, I can make out the faint outlines of the other East State cities: Ignis, Caelum, Oxonia, and Terra. A shadow moves in my periphery. *Trey.* I reach for his hand but recoil as I touch fur.

"Victor."

On my right, Sheridan's figure ripples in and out of focus as if she's struggling to stay in my dream. I blink, and

Trey is standing on the parapet, his heels edging backward. I leap forward, trying to grab his hand, but it's not me leaping. It's Victor, and instead of grabbing Trey's hand, he grabs his throat and holds him over the edge.

"Wars are never really won," Victor says, my mouth curving around his words. I fight, straining inside Victor's body to pull Trey back over the edge to safety. But Victor has control of my arms.

The dream cracks, and like the splintering of a mirror, sharp pieces of buildings and sky shatter and fall around us. Until there's nothing but darkness. Pain rips through my skull, that familiar itching, crawling over my skin as I slide into Sheridan's head.

Her mind is tighter this time, the images faint, like a watercolor painting. She's trying to control what I see, and I don't understand why.

I'm in a small room, in a bed covered with patchwork blankets. I sit up, trying to make out the details, but the harder I stare, the weaker the dream gets. I clamber out of bed and hold onto a set of drawers to steady myself. The dream shifts in and out of focus, the ground moving like a see-saw. My stomach curls and more of the color drains from the dream. The vault rumbles, my frustration fueling its anger. I try to push the vault back, force it into submission, but I'm asleep, and so is my conscious brain. A hairline crack appears in the surface of the vault, just enough for a slither of Imbalance to leak out, and there's nothing I can do to stop it.

The color pours into the dream. Sheridan materializes in the door; her mouth falls as she stares at me, and she grips the door frame so hard I think her fingers might break. Threads of black dance around the room like spiders' legs, skittering over the walls and ceiling, and they all originate from me. I try and grab them, but my fingers swipe through them as if they're nothing more than smoke and shadow. More images pop into focus: colors like an explosion of summer.

A distinctive white mask appears on top of a set of drawers. My eyes widen, I know exactly where I've seen this mask before. I reach for it, but as my fingers brush the surface, a thread splinters from the wall, twisting and undulating as it flies toward Sheridan. Her eyes skit from me, to the thread, to the mask. She shakes her head, almost apologetic, at me. Then she raises her hands and twists them into various shapes until I'm yanked backward, and the dream whites out.

Dammit, Sheridan, what are you hiding?

I'm back in the corridor under Trey's mansion. My back is against the wall, my legs wrapped around him. His hands hold my thighs, and his mouth wanders over my skin. He plants soft silky kisses everywhere his lips roam. The Imbalance is gone. I'm confident Sheridan's okay because I can still feel the pressure from her sharing my mind. The dream fractures and reforms in a different room.

Trey's teetering on the edge of another precipice. Only this time, it's the edge of the Heart of Trutinor's fountain. Beneath him, the thick creamy blood shimmers, sloshing and splashing on the floor with a ferocity that feels like a threat, and it makes my heart pound. In the center of the fountain, is the giant white beating heart. On the other side of the fountain, Sheridan's body fuzzes in and out of focus. I move forward, my arms stretching out in front of me to loop around Trey's arm to pull him off the ledge. But he doesn't move. He grips my hand and pulls me up and onto the ledge with him. Our chests press against each other, locked in the perfect balance. One step forward, and

Trey will fall, one step back, and I'll pull him down to safety.

The heart behind him thuds – slow steady rhythmic beats, that pulse so hard my dream vibrates, and my head fogs with the hypnotic drumming. Trey inches back, frowning at me.

I look down; I'm in Victor's body. Sheridan steps round, coming closer so she can watch. Victor's furry hand jerks out, his claws protruding from his paw pads. His arm punches into Trey's chest.

I scream and yank Victor's hand out. But Victor's body is gone, and I am left holding Trey's heart in my hand. It beats once, twice, thick warm red blood spilling over my wrist and dropping onto the fountain's rim. I go to grab Trey, but my fingers don't reach him. A disembodied scream rushes around the room before being swallowed by the padded walls. I try to pull Trey off the ledge, but my body is moving in slow motion.

A smile hovers on Trey's face, then he coughs, spraying blood over my cheeks. A river of red bubbles over his lips until his expression slackens, his face lifeless. Dead. My fingertips skim his chest but too late, he's already falling backward into the fountain. As he disappears, the white fluid splashes up, drenching me in hot metallic-tasting blood. Panic grips my entire body in great spasming shudders. I drop the heart, stepping backward and falling off the fountain ledge, through the floor into darkness, until my eyes open, and Sheridan's hand clamps over my mouth.

EIGHTEEN

'Fate is decided. But a decision can be corrupted.'
Rebel Proverb

I grip her hand, but she pulls me onto my side to face her. She shakes her head at me, her brow carved deep with wrinkles and a finger pressed to her lips. When I nod, her grip loosens. I'll stay silent, if for no other reason than I want the explanation for why she's dreaming of the mask the rebels wore during the attack.

She sits up, takes her pinky wand out, and moves to the back wall. Despite a night of sleep, her hair still looks styled. I pull my hand through my less styled, more tangled hair and straighten out the t-shirt and combat pants I fell asleep in.

Sheridan waves her wand over a patch of wall, and a window ripples into view shining bright morning light into the room. She taps the corners of the frame with her wand,

and a foam liquid rushes out creating a seal around the window. Then she opens the door and shouts for Felicia, who slopes in, yawning and rubbing her face. What is it with these two looking immaculate first thing in the morning? Felicia's dark crop of pixie hair is as perfect as if she'd just had it cut. She lies down on the mattress, and Sheridan seals the door the same way she did with the window.

Sheridan turns to me and says, "Okay, it's safe to talk now. You never know who's listening."

I have so many questions rushing through my head; I'm not sure where to start. "Those weren't your dreams, were they?" I say, scanning her face.

Her mouth twitches, as if she wants to hide the truth from me, but then her shoulders sag, "No. They weren't dreams."

"Memories?"

She nods. Felicia glances from Sheridan to me, and frowns, "How did Eden see your memories?"

"I don't know," she says, looking at the mattress and picking at a stray thread. But she does know. Of course she knows; I saw the fear in her eyes as the threads of Imbalance went for her.

"Because there's residual Imbalance inside me," I say. "I should have told you before you agreed to dream share. I'm sorry. I didn't think it would be an issue because it's in my subconscious. It was risky and stupid, and I'm sorry."

"Residual what?" Felicia says, sitting up, awake now. "You're still Imbalanced? I thought that disappeared once you were Bound to Trey?"

"It did and it didn't. We have more control now. But it will never disappear completely. I think it's what connects us to the prophecy."

"Are you hurt?" Felicia says, grabbing Sheridan's face

and pulling her this way and that. "Any signs of infection? I only have one vial of dream fever antidote in the apartment. I'll have to..."

Sheridan silences Felicia by touching her hand. "I'm fine," Sheridan says. "She didn't infect me. I don't think she can. It's not me that's inside her head anyway, just a representation of me."

"Yes, but it's your essence," Felicia says, throwing her hands up. Her face is dark, like thundering clouds. In all the times I've met Felicia, I've never seen her anything other than bubbly. It makes me nervous.

"Honey," Sheridan says, "I'm fine. I'm not hurt, and I don't think I will be."

Felicia gives Sheridan a stiff but satisfied nod before lying back down, arms folded, though the scowl furrowing her forehead starts to flatten out.

"Why do you have memories of rebel masks?" I ask, pulling some pillows together to lean on. "There was a rebel attack at the Council... All the attackers were wearing the same mask."

She hesitates, "If I tell you..."

"You can trust me. We're connected now. My dreams are yours. You've seen something you shouldn't have too."

"The heart?"

I nod.

"Heart?" Felicia asks, but thankfully Sheridan doesn't reply. We share a look, of faith and respect and secrets, and I know that Sheridan is going to become a good friend.

"Guess we're going to have to learn to trust each other." She takes a breath, "I was born in the rebel base. My parents are both rebels, as were their parents."

I frown, "How long have there been rebels?"

Sheridan laughs, "Since the First Fallon tore Trutinor in two."

The Libra Legion has only been working against the First Fallon for a couple of decades; I almost feel sorry for their plight.

"Do you really have agoraphobia?" I say, eyeing her.

She smiles, narrows her eyes at me, and says, "No comment." She sits up a little and continues, "I can only tell you so much. While my family is free-born, we're not high ranking enough within the rebels to know the details of their plans."

"Then what can you tell me?" I say.

"That they'll never give up."

"What do they want?"

"What they've always wanted."

"Justice, Balance, and freedom?" I say, echoing the words of the rebels from the Council attack.

"Exactly," Sheridan says, "there's a larger plan that I don't know anything about. What I do know is that they've spent a long time working toward a way to end the Binding system."

"The Binding system?"

She nods, "The First Fallon has poisoned the system. She's using her position to manipulate the Bindings, and that's why there's an increasing number of them failing. We call them Misbinds."

I should be surprised. But after what happened to Rita and me, I just feel relieved to be able to put a name to it. Then I realize Rita never replied to me, and I make a mental note to message her again.

"Then why not stop the First Fallon poisoning the system and creating the Misbinds? Why do you have to end it for good?"

"Because if not her, then someone else. Systems can be abused. They always will be. If the embodiment of Balance itself is corruptible then so is everything else. Besides, do you really think our fate should be decided for us? That we should have no choice over who we love and who we're Bound to for the rest of our soul's eternal life? It's unjust," she says, her voice getting louder. Felicia places her hand on Sheridan's arm as if to tell her to calm down. Sheridan takes a short breath and lowers her tone. "The only way to stop the injustice is to end the system completely."

My fingers skim over the ridges of my Binding scar, tracing the dips and curves of both our essence's markings. Could I live in a world with no Bindings? What would my life look like without my Binding to Trey?

"Isn't destroying the system as bad as corrupting it?" I say, finally.

"Perhaps," she adds, "but there are only two sides to every war, and we all have to choose."

"Maybe," I say, staring out the window at the rising sun, "you're not the only one who thinks that." Victor's said it, so has the Last Fallon as has Hermia. But what if they're all wrong? "Or maybe we shouldn't have to choose sides at all," I say, more to myself than her.

I fall into a frustrated silence. There's so much I don't understand. There's a war brewing in Trutinor. I know whose side the prophecy says I'm meant to be on, and I know who my parents would want me fighting alongside. But what if I belong on another side entirely?

"Do you want to talk about your dreams?" Sheridan says, after a while.

"Right, yes. My dreams," I say, focusing on her again. "I'd nearly forgotten. Trey dies every time. All the dreams are different, except the two versions of Trutinor - the crumbling one you saw and the washed out white one with all the bone buildings. But everything else changes including how Trey dies. Do you think they're prophetic? Is Trey going to die?"

She twiddles with her wand, avoiding eye contact as she spins it between her fingers as though trying to drill a hole in the mattress.

"Well, the bad news is, I can't be certain. Not enough dream time with you yet. But I have some initial thoughts, and the good news is that I know where to research for more answers. We can get to the bottom of this." Her eyes stay fixed on her wand.

"Sheridan?"

She looks up, "Mmm?"

"What are you not telling me?"

"Nothing," she says, giving Felicia a sideways glance.

"Sheridan...?" I say, harder this time.

She puts the wand down, "Fine. But I don't want you to jump to conclusions."

"Okay," I say, my stomach tightening. "But they are dreams of Trey dying. Kind of hard not to jump to conclusions."

"You're not a scryer," Felicia says, "you can't be seeing the future."

"Then why is Sheridan wearing that expression?" I ask, laughing nervously.

"You can't technically predict the future," Sheridan says. "Only scryers have that ability... In theory."

"Theory?" I say, my heart racing. "But you think that somehow I am...? Predicting the future, I mean."

"I'm not sure. Maybe variations of," she twists her wand on the palm of her hand, her eyes all distant and glazed.

"That's not possible? Everyone's fate is predetermined,"

Felicia says, sitting up.

"Precisely, there's a prophecy...," I say, wishing she'd hurry up and get to the point.

"Which is exactly why I need to investigate. I'm not certain of anything," Sheridan says.

"But there's a chance I'm seeing future versions of Trey's death?" My chest is so tight I can barely breathe. She looks at me now, giving me an apologetic smile, "Sorry, I should have led with the part where I don't think the prophetic part of your dream is Trey's death. The part that concerns me most is the consistency of the two versions of Trutinor. I'm not convinced they're prophetic, but they're also not nothing either."

"So there's still a chance they're just nightmares?"

She hesitates but nods.

"But you don't think they are just nightmares?"

She shakes her head once.

"And Trey's repeating deaths?"

Sheridan's lips pinch as if she doesn't want to tell me what my heart already fears.

"Sheridan?" Felicia says, frowning, "she came here for us to help her understand what the dreams were about. You can't not tell her the bit she needs to know."

"It depends," she says, reluctantly.

"On?"

"On whether the versions of Trutinor you're seeing are prophetic or not. If they're not, then the likelihood is that Trey's deaths are just your subconscious fear of losing him."

That's not subconscious; the thought terrifies me. I've lost my parents - I can't lose him too, it would break me.

"And if they are prophetic?" Felicia asks.

Sheridan swallows hard, "Then Trey's deaths might be too."

NINETEEN

Lani Luchelli, Personal Journal.

12th October, 2017

Paris

Cassian has only returned once. He promised he would be back to visit, but I've seen Renny more than I've seen him. She's still furious of course, but honestly, I'm not sure if it's because Cassian lied, or the fact she's Bound at all. She says she visits me when she returns to see her friends from Earth school, but I'm not sure I buy it. But I don't mind much, I'm grateful for the news she brings, of Cassian, the boys, and of... Him. She says Eden is looking for me, and she only found out because Hermia asked Cassian why she couldn't track me. So now they know: I'm human, essence-less. Powerless. Strangely, it's a relief; knowing they know feels like I'm stripping layers of filthy secrets away that were suffocating my skin. Finally, I can breathe. Ren says Eden is trying to convince Trey to look for me, but she won't succeed. That boy is as stubborn as Kale was. And even if she does, I'm not sure I can face him, either of them. Not after what I did. But I've also decided I won't run. Not anymore. There's something about Paris; I like it. It could be home: the vintage architecture; the lilted accents; the permanent smell of warm pastry and sweet wine. Ren is certain Eden is coming... Well, I guess this is where she'll find me.

I blink, her words churning inside my head. The walls in her dream room seem to shrink. My chest clamps, my breathing spiraling out of control.

"I don't think so," Felicia says, gripping my arm and pumping a wave of Siren compulsion through my body. She holds my arm until I calm down.

"Thank you," I say, "for the..."

"It's nothing," she says, letting go of my arm and shrugging. "Lucky for you, anxiety happens to be my speciality." She winks at me, but I only manage a weak smile because my insides are still slick with panic. I make my excuses, telling them I need to find Trey and sort out our disagreement. But really I just need to see him, to feel his chest rising under my hand; to know with my own eyes, and hear with my own ears, that he's alive.

We exchange CogTracker details. Given Sheridan and I will likely invade each other's dreams for the rest of time, it seems courteous.

I leave their apartment, but I've so rarely spent time in

the South that it takes me a minute to push the rising panic down long enough to work out which way Trey's house is.

The air is cool and bright. The morning sun isn't quite high enough to take off its evening jacket and shower heat on me. I flip open my CogTracker and scroll to the notifications. My blood runs cold. There are eleven missed calls from Titus, five from Trey, and a dozen more CogMails.

Something's wrong.

I locate the main road that will take me back into the center of Siren City and sprint the entire way up it. My lungs burn by the time I reach the center of the city, and I'm forced to slow down. Once I've caught my breath, I pick up the pace again. Despite the throb in my thighs, as I enter Siren City high street and spot the back of Trey's mansion at the other end, I burst into another sprint. I ignore the smiles and nods of various Sirens and Keepers I know as I run past the row of huge white mansions, marble pillars and marble statues filling the streets. On the other side of the road, the lower floors of the mansions have all been carved out to make way for shops and restaurants filled with glass windows and the smells of breakfast and coffee.

When I reach Trey's mansion, I hesitate. The rational part of my brain says he's left me five missed CogCalls so he must be alive and wanting to talk to me. But he also left me in the library because I'd gone behind his back. Despite my fears, and the fact I don't want to hurt him, I also can't let this go. At some point, he is going to have to confront his mother. But now is not the time for that argument, so I decide I will drop it, at least for a while. I push open one of the rear doors, into a modest kitchen. There are a couple of chefs frying eggs and popping toast. My stomach growls in response. I've only had a few hours' sleep, and I can't remember the last time I ate. But there's no time to stop, so I steal a piece of toast from the pile and keep walking. I climb a set of marble steps and push open the door to the cellar kitchen. The main foyer is the other side of the mansion, but Trey's bedroom wing is this side, so I take the white marble staircase to his floor.

As soon as I step out of the stairwell my skin prickles. My Elemental powers fire to life, roaming the air for anomalies. There's a tang, cold and sweaty, like dread, and the movement in the molecules is juddery, like someone's pacing. My legs spring to life, hurtling me down the corridor and straight into Trey's living room. I throw open the door, my eyes skipping around the room until they settle on him, and I physically drop to the floor, crushing the toast in my hand as relief washes over me.

"She's here. She just walked in; I'll get her out the door, and we'll be on our way in five minutes," Trey says.

My head snaps up, remembering that there were a dozen missed calls from Titus too. "What's happened?" I say, pulling myself together. He's on the far side of the room pacing, one CogTracker between his shoulder and his ear and another one in his hand.

He cuts the call off, "Where the hell have you been? Have you not checked your CogTracker?"

My blood instantly heats. "Hang on a second, Trey. You left me in the library. Remember?" I say, my voice hard. "And thanks for asking, I've had one hell of a night, you could have been dead for all I knew." As soon as the words are out, I realize how ridiculous they sound. Of course he wasn't dead, I'd have known because of our Binding.

"What?" he says, his forehead creasing.

"Doesn't matter. What's happened?" That's when an icy shiver slithers down my spine. The look in his eyes; pain knotting his brow; the stiffness of his posture.

"Sit down," he says. But I don't because now I'm terrified.

"Just tell me what's going on," I say, and glance down at my hand. I unfurl my palm; three crescent-shaped marks have dug into my palm where I'm clenching my hands so tight.

"Nyx is missing."

I close my eyes, a dark veil slipping over my mind as my world shatters into a million fragmented loved ones, all lost, or dead, or gone.

"What happened?" I say, my voice a whisper.

He moves across the room and pulls me into his muscular arms. Even though he's standing with his arms around me, I can't help but do my ritual: I put my hand on his heart and listen to its thump, thump, thump.

"It's going to be okay, we're going to find her," he breathes.

And maybe we will, but my chest is screaming like it's already too late.

"I don't know all the details," Trey continues, and where my cheek is pressed into his chest, his voice rumbles against me. "But Titus said she was preparing for your return home. He went to take her dinner, but she was missing. Her CogTracker is hanging off the dial, papers are strewn across the ballroom, decorations torn, and lights ripped off the ceiling."

"There was a fight?" I ask, closing my eyes again, imagining horrible scenes playing out, blow by blow.

"Titus thinks so."

"Any blood?"

"Some."

I stiffen. "We have to find her," I whisper into his chest. My eyes sting, but I refuse to let tears of defeat out. I tell myself we can save her, over and over again. We can save her because we have to.

"I know. Magnus has already prepped the train. We'll go east first, straight to your tower to meet Titus. Then we'll make a plan to search for her."

He untangles himself and grabs my hand. We race through the foyer, out the mansion, and down the hill toward the station. I want to shout at Trey for not having a station built under his mansion like I have. But I bite my tongue because I know it's fear making me cross, not anything he's done.

We reach the station, both of us panting and sweating. It's a relief to see the train's sleek maroon exterior and the long black chimney puffing and chugging out smoke, ready to move. Magnus holds the door open, and we clamber on. Within seconds the train jolts forward, the metal undercarriage grinding along the tracks as the train moves out of the station.

Even using the private lines and at top speed, it will be an hour or two before we reach the East. Siren City is in the south-west of the State, and it's a trek home.

Trey clunks plates and glasses behind the bar in the corner of the carriage. I sit in the largest maroon booth under a window and pull my legs up under my chin watching the city blur into a streaky pallet of color.

He brings a plate of food and two mugs of coffee over and sits, just far enough away, that I realize the caring embrace he gave me in the living room hasn't erased our fight in the library. The gap between us feels like an ocean of unsaid words and resentment. I hate it. I long for him to put his arms around me and for all of this to be forgotten.

I look up at him. He pushes the coffee across the table and a piece of toast, and I can't help but smile.

"What's funny?" he says.

I take a sip of coffee, "I think I've left a piece of crushed toast in your living room."

"Oh," he says, smiling but doesn't look at me. Instead he looks through the window and eats his own toast in silence. I shift in my seat; we have to talk about his mother. I can't keep hiding things, and he can't stay angry at me.

"I'm sorry," I say, putting the coffee down.

"Are you though?" he says, refusing to look at me. "You say you are, but you knew how I felt, and you still didn't drop it."

His words hurt. I'm not used to coldness in his silky tones.

"Trey... If I had the chance to see my mother one more time..."

He turns to me, his eyes bright, burning hot blue. "This isn't the same thing. Your parents were loving and devoted and sacrificed their lives to save yours. My mother ran off. Abandoned me... It's not even close to the same thing."

I reach for his hand, but he flinches as if he's going to pull away. He doesn't, so I pick it up. "I know that's how you feel, but I don't believe that's what happened. Yes, maybe I'm projecting because of what's happened with my parents. But they're gone, and I don't have the chance to ask them why. All I'm asking is that we find out what really happened to yours. Mothers don't abandon their children for no reason. Hermia said she stripped herself of her essence. I can't imagine how horrific that was for her. You need to find her and ask why. For Kato. For you. Maybe even for me too."

He turns back to the window, his jaw flexing and clenching.

"And when you find her and I'm right?" he says, giving the blurry scenery a hard stare.

"If..." I say, squeezing his hand, "if you're right. Then I'll drop it. I'll never speak her name again. But if you're wrong...?"

He turns to me, his eyes stony, "*If*... Then yeah, sure I'll hear her out, why the hell not?"

I close my eyes and let out a deep breath. When I open my eyes, Trey's face is close to mine. He scoops his arms around me, pulling me in close. "I hate arguing," he says, inching closer, "you're everything to me, Eden. I don't want anything to come between us."

"Neither do I," I say, and slide my lips over his, my hands slipping under his shirt and over his warm back. His hand tiptoes up my arm and under the back of my head, his fingers curling into my hair as he pulls me onto his lap.

"You're so beautiful," he says, pausing for breath.

We stay wrapped in each other for the rest of the journey, sharing kisses, memories, and dreams for the future. Our fingertips trace each other's outlines, feeling every curve and dip of our bodies. And for a few short moments, I forget the world, forget the fact Nyx is gone and Victor is back, and I live in the moment. Just Trey and me. Tangled in our own little world of love and lust and happiness.

When the light dims as we enter my home tower's underground station, my heart beats faster; by the time the train docks, my mouth is completely dry.

With the exception of the Dusting dinner, which ended in Israel's arrest and me running away to Siren City, I've barely been to the East at all and never to my home tower. We leave the train and cross the underground platform. Trey walks up to a short set of steps and holds open the door to my foyer. But I'm frozen to the spot. When I don't walk through, he stops and looks down at me at the bottom of the steps.

"Oh," he says, noticing I've turned into a statue. He returns to me, wrapping me in an embrace.

"I don't think I can," I mumble into his chest.

"Kind of ironic this."

"Ironic?" I say, untangling myself from him to frown.

He smiles, "What was it you were just saying about me burying my head and not confronting stuff with my mom? I know it's a different situation, but you're doing the exact same thing."

I blink at him, processing his words, and then a laugh bubbles up from my belly. He's right. I'm being a total hypocrite. "We really are meant to be Bound."

"Yes, we are," he says, and kisses me, soft, loving, and as his lips touch mine, warmth trickles from his mouth into mine and fills my body with the glow of reassurance. Just enough compulsion to make me step forward. "I'm right here, okay? If you need a moment or you want to leave. I'm here. But this isn't about them today. It's about Nyx."

"Okay," I nod.

"Are you ready?" Trey says, sliding his hand into mine.

"No."

"Good. Let's go," he says, and tugs me up the stairs.

I take a deep breath, push open the tower doors, and step into my home for the first time in weeks.

I stand in the middle of the foyer, scanning the room. Keepers bustle in and out of rooms, corridors, and lifts. Faces I've known my entire life. All of them hesitate when they see me and stop to give me smiles filled with sad eyes. I don't want their pity. I'm meant to be their leader. Leaders shouldn't be pitied. And for the first time, I understand why Nyx has been pushing for me to return home. I've not been here, not been present, and not been in control, and now they think I'm weak. This isn't what I wanted, and it's not what my parents would want either.

"Come on," I say to Trey. This time I tug him into the lifts and push the button before anyone else can enter with us.

"What's wrong?" he says.

"I just... I should have been here. It's fine. I'm going to change that now."

We exit the lift on the floor below the penthouse into a long corridor. This is where the highest-ranking Keepers in the East either live or have business quarters in order to be close to my parents for work. My eyes glance up at the ceiling; the penthouse is home. As my eyes scan the ceiling, I picture all our rooms in order, but I have to pull my eyes away because the aching in my chest gets too much.

The corridor is bright; this high up in the tower, there are no other sky scrapers blocking out the light. The desert sun streams rays of light in through the two end walls, which are made of glass. It makes our lilac carpet and the East State symbol printed at equal distances along the runner sparkle like shiny brooches.

I knock on Titus and Nyx's apartment door; there's a scuffling inside, and then it opens. Titus looks awful. I fling my arms around him, and he sucks in a stilted breath.

"I'm so sorry I wasn't here," I say.

"Don't say that," he says, putting me at arm's length. "This isn't your fault. You've had academy work, and I know you're still struggling with Lionel and Eleanor."

"But maybe if I was here...?"

"No, sweetie, you couldn't have stopped this," he says. He goes to shake Trey's hand, but Trey bats it away and pulls him in for a hug. Titus coughs as though he's trying to stifle a sob. After a minute he straightens himself up and shows us into the living room before wandering into the kitchen. Cups rattle, and the click of the kettle follows.

"Tea?" he calls.

Trey looks at me; I nod. "Sure," Trey shouts back.

The room is spacious; there's a rectangular cutout hatch in their kitchen. I can see him pottering around through it from where I am. The room is separated into an open plan diner-living room. On the other side of the room, their dinner from last night is still set. There's a lingering aroma of fish and steamed vegetables, but the two plates are full, the meals untouched and cold. Just another shadow to add to my home tower, I think, before shaking the thought away.

I pick up a photo of Nyx and two other women on a side table. It's crinkled and stained like it was left in the loft before someone decided to frame it. In the photo are two other women with the same wild black hair as Nyx. All three of them have the same birthmark she does on her cheek. Must be a family trait.

Titus puts three cups of tea down and slumps into one of a pair of tatty arm chairs. In front of the chairs is a coffee table and opposite a larger sofa, which Trey and I sit on.

"What happened?" I say, picking up my tea to drink it.

"She was working in the ballroom on the first floor. Organizing a themed ball for when you returned. She'd been busy all day, and I'd barely seen her. Once I'd finished some routine maintenance on the trains, I decided to make her dinner and take it down so I could give her a hand finishing the basic decorations. She was planning an elaborate element theme..." He pauses, his voice cracking. "She was going to use air, just for you. The room was going to be full of electricity lights and those glow bugs. She even booked a specialist Elemental chef to make the food tingle with static."

My eyes sting at his words, but I refuse to cry when I know he must be hurting so much more than me.

"What happened when you took her dinner?"

"Well, I didn't get the chance. I set it out and went downstairs to fetch her, but as soon as I left the apartment, Archibald collared me and asked me to help him downstairs with a sofa."

Archibald is one of my parents' senior Elementals. He lives on this floor, but he decided to retire when my parents passed away.

"When we reached the foyer, we heard thudding and crashing on the first floor. We ran upstairs, but by the time we got there, it was too late," he says, his hand scrunching into a fist. "She was already gone. The ballroom is exactly as it was when I opened it. Her CogTracker cracked and left in the middle of the room, the furniture all scattered... She was just gone. I phoned the Guild immediately and they sent the group of investigators. They're down there now."

I glance at his forearm, his Binding scar poking out from under his sleeve. I want to ask the question fluttering on my lips, but I bite it back because I'm not sure I want to hear the answer.

"She is alive," he says, looking from his Binding scar to me.

"Of course she is," I say, silent relief washing over me. I sink a little further into the seat. "Nyx is a survivor. I expected nothing less."

Titus tries to smile, but it's weak, and he looks more like he's about to cry. I reach out to touch his hand, "I didn't mean to bring up..."

"No, it's fine," he says, patting my hand. "You're right. She is a survivor; I should take comfort in that."

I nod, and we fall into silence. Nyx was orphaned as a child. Her parents died when she was only eight. She didn't have any other family. She survived for a couple of weeks by herself until the food went moldy, and the heating cut out. The Northern Eris mountains are always cold. Even in the valleys closest to the border, if the heating cuts out, you know about it. She shifted and ran away, figuring she could survive easier in her cat form. She made it to the Ancient Forest and spent the next few weeks scavenging and eating mice. That's when my mother found her, thinking she was actually a starving, flea-bitten kitten rather than an orphaned Shifter. Nyx was too weak to shift back to her Keeper self, so Mom had no idea. Anyway, she took Nyx home and nursed her back to health. Which is when Mom got a shock. A few days later when Nyx had the strength to shift again – Mom found a sleeping girl in the cat basket. Of course, my grandparents wouldn't let Nyx go to an orphanage. So they gave her a scholarship to Keepers School, and that was that. Nyx was family.

I blink back the tears, forcing the growing lump in my throat to subside.

"Will you show us the ballroom?" I say, breaking the silence.

Titus looks up, blinking his own tears away and gestures for us to move.

We take the lift down to the first-floor ballroom in silence.

"Wait...," Titus says, clutching my wrist as we reach the ballroom door. "It's not nice in there." The color drains from his face.

I give his arm a reassuring squeeze, "We will find her, I promise. But to do that, we need to speak to the Guild Sorcerers to see if they've found anything."

Titus nods, but his brow and upper lip are shiny with sweat. I glance to Trey and flip my eyes to Titus. Trey's eyes blaze to life, a fiery blue coating his pupils. He places his hand on Titus' shoulder, "We're not going anywhere Titus," he says.

Titus' eyes gloss over, the stiffness in his shoulders dissipates, and the hunch he was cradling vanishes. As I stare at Titus, who is clueless to what just happened, I wonder if Trey was right. If Keepers can't tell when they're being compelled, maybe Sirens are the most dangerous and powerful Keepers.

"We're not going to abandon you, Titus. Nyx means everything to me; you're both family."

Titus nods, his eyes wet as he pushes the ballroom door open. It creaks as it swings, as if it too, is reluctant to show us the devastation waiting inside.

I blink as we enter, my heart hammering in my chest. The hall is a mess. There are Guild Sorcerers milling around, a cluster at the back embroiled in a deep mumbled conversation. Another Sorcerer is standing by a table that runs along the side of the room. On top of the table is a medley of smashed glass, broken stands, and jumbled cutlery. Pieces of paper are scattered everywhere, torn, crumpled, and sprayed in dark red. I swallow hard, realizing it's not paint. Strings of lights that once adorned the ceiling hang low like a willow tree's branches. Most of the bulbs are smashed, and glass is sprinkled across the floor like confetti. A broken ladder is abandoned at the far end of the room. But the thing that makes the hairs on my arms stand up is the patch of blood in the center of the room. A hand print smears it out in a long, violent streak like someone was dragged. Images rip through my mind: flashes of Nyx screaming, her attacker pulling her, legs convulsing as she tries to escape. I swallow down the swell of nausea.

"Are you okay?" Trey says, placing his hand on my back. Where his palm touches my skin, a warm pulse flows through my skin and attaches to my essence like a calming massage.

"I'm fine. Really," I say, and I am. Right now, the only thing that matters is finding whoever hurt Nyx and wiping them off the face of Trutinor. I kneel by the patches of blood, examining the marks on the floor around them. There's a trail of tiny red paw prints that track a few feet away toward the door, then stop suddenly. She must have shifted and tried to make a run for it. The paw prints are uneven like every third step was stumbled.

"She's injured her leg," I say, more to myself than Titus and Trey. For Titus' benefit, I add, "But there's not enough blood for this to have been fatal."

My fingers skim the floor, crumbs, tacky liquid, and glass pressing into my fingertips as they move over the flooring. There are a series of gouge marks in the tiles. It looks like a knife was responsible, or maybe a set of sharp claws. I close my eyes, seeing the play-by-play again. A paw swipes at Nyx; she ducks, the paw misses and takes a chunk out of the tiles instead.

My eyes trace the lines and dips until I notice a clump of fur. It's not black and short like Nyx's cat fur. But long and speckled grey-brown like a wolf. I sit bolt upright, the color draining from my face.

"What is it?" Titus asks.

"Who's in charge?" I say, "I need Forensic Sorcery."

Titus scans the room then shouts, "Winston."

A short round Sorcerer wearing equally round spectacles leaves the group of investigators at the back of the room and wanders across to us. He has a mustache that despite filling his upper lip, also appears to be round.

"Can I help?" he asks.

"Have you taken samples?"

"Of course," he says, raising a bushy eyebrow at me.

"Show me," I say standing, "because I need to know if that fur belongs to who I think it does."

He leads me, Trey, and Titus, over to the group who part to let us in. In the center of the huddle on the floor are several CogTrackers analyzing different samples. From each Tracker, a holographic projection beams up into the space between the Sorcerers. Their wands are extended out, prodding and poking at the images digging deeper through the analysis. A taller female Sorcerer with a mop of mousy colored hair uses her wand to direct the projection containing the fur toward us. She pokes a translucent button on the projection, but it's still analyzing.

"Keep it there," I say, reaching to stop her flipping past it. "I want to see what the fur analysis says once it's done."

She cocks her head at me and glances at Winston. He nods approval, so she shrugs and drops her wand. I skim the lines of text appearing as the analysis runs. The graphs dissect the fur variations and the strands of animal hair and DNA until my eyes settle upon a single word that confirms what the gnawing in my gut is telling me.

Fur analysis complete: Victor Dark - deceased

A shocked gasp echoes around the group.

"I knew it."

TWENTY

'The separation of life and death is a thin veil covering the soul. The soul rarely sees the difference, noting only the presence or absence of its Balancer. But absence it must feel. For that yearning is what guides the soul to finding its Balancer in the next life. This is why the folds and fabrics of Obex must prevent the live from finding the dead, not out of malice or Imbalance but for the protection and longevity of their Binding.'

Excerpt - The Book of Imbalance

"Titus, we have to go," I say, turning on my heel, grabbing Trey, and heading out of the ballroom.

"Wait for me," he shouts, catching us up. "Do you have a

plan?" He's shaking and pale. I would be too if it was Trey that was missing. I hug Titus and whisper that it's going to be okay. He sucks in a breath and gathers himself together.

"We will go to Hermia's shop first because Kato headed there last night. They've been working on a tracking program to find Victor. We need to know whether they've located him and make a plan to hunt the bastard down. This time, I'm going to finish what I started."

"Eden, wait," Titus says, grabbing my shoulders. "I should go, I should be the one to kill him."

"Titus," I say, gripping his arm, "We don't know what he's capable of, let alone what he is."

I love Titus dearly, but as a Steampunk Transporter, he isn't trained for combat. If anything happened to him, I'd be heartbroken.

"I'll tell you what he is, a walking dead guy that's about to get a lot deader," Titus says, and the first spark of fury lights in his eyes. "Victor's taken enough from us. He's not having Nyx as well."

"I know. But, Titus, please, I need you to take the train to the Guild of Investigations and find Arden..."

"Why? I'd be an asset."

"You would, but we will need supplies, and you're the only one that can drive the train."

Titus hesitates, staring deep into my eyes as he weighs up his options. "Okay," he says, "but when you find him, you stick it to that son of a bitch for me."

"I can guarantee it," I smile. "Tell Arden to gather a team ready to track Victor. Even if Hermia and Kato haven't zeroed on his exact location yet, they should have an idea of what State he's in. They can send us specific coordinates while we're on the move," I pause, trying to control the stream of consciousness. "We don't know what back up

Victor has. So can you ask Bo to bring The Six? The more back up we have, the better."

Titus stands a little straighter. The spark in his eyes is now a roaring furnace. He's ready for the fight, and so am I.

"When I get them, I'll send the coordinates to your CogTracker," I say.

"Okay," he says, pulling me in and kissing my head. "I'll take the private lines so I can get back from the West in time. I'll meet you at the nearest station to Hermia's shop."

"Perfect. There's a station two streets up; I think it's called Light Street station."

"Okay," he says, "I'll be as quick as I can." Then Trey and I leave.

Hermia set up a shop several years ago after her husband died. Trey said she called it insurance should the First Fallon ever sack her, but he didn't believe her. He thinks Hermia uses the shop as a front so she can try and track her husband down in Obex because she doesn't believe he crossed over into the next life. Trey and I had the unfortunate opportunity to be in Obex for a few hours during the summer. While we were there, she explained that Obex constantly moves and shifts. The streets are never in the same place for long, so even if you wanted to find a loved one, it's almost impossible. It's as though Obex itself tries to stop you finding them. Like the Balance plays one final cosmic joke, only allowing you to reunite with your soul mate in your next life. And yet, despite knowing full well the chances of finding him are infinitesimally small, she won't give up.

We take the skybridge route as it's faster and more

direct. In the center of Element City, the bridges between the buildings are solid metal, with glass roofs, like the towers themselves have arms sticking out. But the further out of the center you get, the less sturdy the bridges are. The view of the pavement hundreds of feet below on the glass bridges used to make my stomach coil. But today, I sprint across them with Trey trailing behind; I'm too desperate to find Victor to care how high up we are. As we reach the city perimeter, the bridges turn from glass to wood, so I slow down because they creak with every footstep making them more perilous than sturdy. We step across the slats of a bridge between two dingy residential sky scrapers when I halt mid-stride. Scanning the ground below, I realize we're already deep inside the Eastern district, and we need to get to the ground to locate her shop.

Stepping out of the skyscraper, the heat hits us like a rush of dry sauna air. The bridges were high enough that what little desert breeze there was, could at least blow the sand off your face and dry the sheen of sweat.

It's late afternoon, and ground level is sweltering. The buildings are packed even denser in this region than in the center of the city, and at this time of day, the desert has had plenty of time to oven roast the buildings. Heat has stolen its way into every corner and alley, and it's stifling.

We walk in single file through the dark and oppressively narrow streets. Sand carried on the air sticks to my skin and what falls away, rolls in dusty clumps over the pavements. I crane my neck up. Daylight struggles to reach the streets, but every so often a single shard spears between the buildings like an arrow to illuminate a patch of the road ahead.

Awnings jut out of street-level windows, with trinkets, incense, and magical devices hanging from them. Under the smell of magic is the aroma of cooked spice, and it makes my stomach growl. There's a high population of air Keepers in this part of the city, and it gives the sandy air a hum like bees are buzzing in my ears.

By the time we reach Hurst Street, we're both an exhausted mess, and I'm in desperate need of food and water. Hermia's shop is in the center of the street. The block is a long residential tower, with the ground floor devoted to shops and trading services, most of which look suspiciously like they're selling Imbalanced magic.

Her front door is cut in two, like a stable. The lower door is for the Elves who must frequent her shop and the outer door for everyone else. There's raucous laughter coming from inside the shop and the clattering of objects. I turn to Trey who raises an eyebrow and holds the door open.

Hermia's shop is as dim as the street outside. When my eyes adjust, I see just how full her shop is. There are gadgets and devices everywhere, only a small number of which I can identify. There are bottles and boxes with different signs and symbols on them and a shelf full of herbs and ingredients. Below it is a cabinet, that's locked and full of what I think are tracking devices. I spot a tuft of curly orange hair under the cash desk. But there's no head and no body attached to the tuft. Kato, however, is standing, one leg raised, on top of the cash counter, his glass full of a blue liquid, his blond hair in disarray and a distinctive rosy tint to his cheeks. When he notices us, his leg drops, and he slides the glass behind his back.

Hermia's head pops out from under the till as she launches something round into the center of the shop floor toward a glass bowl. It clips the bowl and shatters the side, spraying glass everywhere. Three tall glowing candles balanced on a stand at the back illuminate the shop in an eerie evergreen color. It makes the cluttered store and the explosion of glass look more like the place was just burgled than a professional storefront.

"Weeeeeey," she cheers, slamming her other hand, holding a glass full of the same blue liquid, down. It sloshes over the counter, and then she spots us.

"Oh, fu..." she starts

"Hermia?" I interrupt. "Did you, by any chance, get Kato drunk?"

"Nope," he says, sliding off the counter and grinning at me. He walks - or staggers is more accurate - up to me and gives my cheek a gentle tap, "Not drunk. Tipsy, perhaps. But swear to Trutinor, this is my first. It's just happened to be a strong first." He plonks a sloppy kiss on my cheek.

Trey slaps him upside the head, "Watch where you're putting those lips, Luchelli."

"Oi," Kato says, swiping for Trey and missing, "we're celebrating."

"Celebrating?" I ask, "did you find Victor?"

"Oh," Kato says, his face falling. "No, not yet although I'm narrowing the search parameters as we speak. I did, however, quit Stratera."

"You did what?" Trey bellows. He grabs Kato's glass and dumps it on the counter.

"Yeah. We're going into business. Hermia and me," Kato says. "Hence the celebratory toast. We're the ultimate dream team. The dog's boll..."

"That's enough," Trey says, and Kato falls silent. "We'll talk about Stratera later. Right now, we have a problem, and you need a clear head to deal with it." Trey turns to Hermia. "Eden and I just walked from her tower; I don't suppose we could have some food and water?"

She points in the direction of a door in the corner of the shop.

"So... Eden... Long time no see," Hermia says as we enter her living room, her eyes darting from Trey to me.

"He knows," I whisper, "Kato doesn't."

Hermia nods, satisfied, but I'm sure I hear her mumble 'about bloody time' under her breath. I choose to ignore it because I still have to convince Trey to tell Kato. Kato drops onto Hermia's sofa and leans back on the pillows as if he might fall asleep. Trey sits opposite him. Hermia's already in the kitchen making a racket.

Three green sofas fill her modest sized living room. All of them made of old leather and covered in throws the same orange as her wiry hair. The walls are littered with what looks like broken or defunct prototypes. I've never been in Hermia's house. I knew about her shop, but I didn't realize her house was attached to it. Behind one of the sofas, is a photo. The only one in the room. It's another Elf, with short orange hair –orange hair like Hermia's. But where she has bright green eyes, his are ocean blue. He's smiling, but the photo is aged and faded.

"Is that her husband?" I whisper to Trey, glancing at the kitchen door.

"Yes," he whispers, "his name was Bellamy."

I take a seat next to him as Hermia returns bringing drinks and food for everyone. She lays out an enormous range of odd-shaped fruits and bread on the coffee table between the two sofas and shoves two glasses of water at Trey and me, "Here you go then, killjoys." She digs Kato in the ribs, "Oi, wake up, lightweight."

He sits bolt upright, his face fading to an unhealthy shade of green.

"I had like three sips of that stuff. It's factually impossible that I'm drunk."

"Oh, for Balance's sake," Hermia says, "drink this before you puke on my blankets." She hands him a frothy mixture and then swallows the other glass of it down in one.

Both their faces twitch as they gulp the liquid. Kato grabs his head and moans for a good ten seconds before looking up at us, his eyes fresh and perky.

"What in the name of holy Obex was that?" he says.

"Rapid hangover inducer and cure. Now," she says, turning to Trey and me, "what's going on?"

"Victor's taken Nyx," I say.

"Kato, get the CogTrackers," Hermia says, piling the fruit and bread back onto the tray. I grab various bits of food, throwing a chunk of bread and three pieces of fruit at Trey before she lifts the pile off the table and places it on a chest of drawers in the corner. Kato returns, grinning as he brandishes what looks like his old tracker, only now it's been supercharged. It's twice as big as it was, with six cogs and various dials and aerials attached.

"Has the program finished running?" Hermia says as he places it in the middle of the coffee table.

"Almost." He taps a few buttons on the keyboard screen, and a projection appears above the table. Lines of data stream across the projection, interspersed with newspaper snippings, Balance readings, and photos of Victor.

"This," Kato says, brandishing his tracker, "is the reason we're going into business. It takes Hermia's skills in locating essences and injects them with my programming skills. It's like tracking on steroids. This puppy is going to make us millions."

"Kato," I say, raising an eyebrow. "You already have millions."

"Not the point, Eden. Not. The. Point."

"So it's reading all the data, combing records, and combining them with the dead spots Hermia located?"

"Exactly. Then it uses statistical probability and a program I designed to read essences and predict locations based on all the data." Kato taps various screens making the lines of data speed up.

"How accurate will it be?" I ask.

"It won't be perfect. Not to start with at least. But we should be able to pinpoint it down to a mile or so."

"That's still a big radius if we're on foot."

"Would you rather scour the entirety of Trutinor?" Kato asks, and I fall silent.

"Right, quit bitchin' and check this out." He prods a sequence of three keys. The data lines stop and swap to a map of the North State.

"Well, well, well," Kato says, folding his arms, "somebody decided to go home."

Victor's home mansion towers out of the mountainside. Tall dark turrets jut into the clouds like swords. The rest of the projection is just miles and miles of mountains, all barren and rocky and covered with snow.

Kato frowns and presses a few more buttons, and the image races forward deeper into the Eris mountains.

"Minor error," he says, coughing, "he's about five miles south-west of his home castle. But it's a complete wasteland. There's nothing there apart from valleys and minor hills. I can't see why he would be there, and it's going to take you days to search that area."

"Then you'd better get some coffee, and start working on improving that program," Trey says, standing up to steal more food from the tray Hermia put aside.

"We're going to head north. Send us more detailed coordinates when you have them, and send Titus those details now. He can figure out what station in the North we need to go to. I've asked Titus to liaise with Arden, Bo, and The Six," I say.

"Okay, I will," Kato says, his face furrowing, "look after Bo, won't you?"

"Of course, although I think she's more equipped to take care of us."

Kato smiles, pulling his shoulders back as his face fills with pride.

"Wait a second," Hermia says, fidgeting in her seat as if she's trying to figure something out. Her eyes scan the projections.

"What's wrong?" I ask.

"It's just that... We haven't stopped to ask why he's taken Nyx, and I think I just figured out why."

Kato, Trey, and I all stop what we are doing. But it's Trey that speaks first, "Go on..."

"Remember the library? We said Victor was looking for the lock and key to the Door of Fates?"

"Yes..." I say, my stomach coiling at the thought of how Nyx could be involved. I was so concerned with finding her and killing Victor for good this time, I hadn't stopped to think about why he took her in the first place.

"Hang on," I say, remembering Victor's appearance in the library. "I haven't had a chance to tell you, but Victor actually appeared in the library."

"Pardon?" Trey says, a flash of anger creasing his face.

"Don't start, Trey; you were cross with me."

His jaw stiffens, then he says, "Fine. What happened?"

"Well, he told me the vein thing on his temple is how the Last Fallon is controlling him. But the weird part was that he said he needed my help and that I had to bring

Karva Arigenza back from Obex. Why would he ask for help and then take Nyx when he knows how important she is to me?"

"Forget that, come here," Hermia says, waving us over and sitting up straighter. She taps out something on the supersized CogTracker, and several files shoot across the screen.

"Well talk about Victor later," Trey growls in my ear.

Nyx's face appears, bright and smiling, with her vertical green cat-eyes. Next to it is a series of photos of faces that are familiar and a string of file information. When Hermia brings the photos next to each other, I realize why I recognize them. It's her mother and grandmother; I saw their faces in the photo at Titus' place.

"Did she ever talk to you about her birthmark?" Hermia says, zooming in and cropping each of the women's photos.

"No, but I did notice the fact that it was hereditary," I say.

"What's this about?" Kato interrupts, shoveling a hunk of bread into his mouth and pushing the empty cup of froth away.

"I don't think it's just a birthmark. One of the benefits of my continued service to the First Fallon is overhearing conversations and seeing documents that would otherwise be hidden. I heard her talking of a lock once after Trey had compelled her, and she was all confused. She was lost in a memory and ranting about her sister and how she would never be able to open the boundary between our worlds because she'd designed the lock to change continually."

"Continually change?" I say, scrunching my face up. "Change to what?"

"Well, that's the thing. She said it was such an ingenious idea because it wasn't a 'what' but a 'who.' She wove the lock into the genetics of a family. The First Fallon said that her sister would never be able to find the lock because as each new child was born, the lock keeper would change. I never knew which family, and I didn't ask because I knew she wouldn't tell me anyway. But look at the birthmarks on each of their cheeks; they're all identical in size and shape," she says, pointing at the zoomed-in images. "What if Nyx is the lock?"

There's an exchange of looks between us as each of us peers closer at the images. Hermia is right; the birthmarks are identical. Nyx is the lock, and Victor has her.

TWENTY-ONE

If it's rebels you seek,
*   find us where the woods and*
mountains meet.
*   A sign you must leave,*
*   for us to retrieve.*
*   Freedom. Balance. Justice.*
*   Is all you need to trust us.*
*   And our arms and doors will part,*
*   if you can show us what is in*
your heart.
  Rebel whispers

Before we leave Hermia's shop, she affixes locating devices to both of our CogTrackers. Kato hacks the software so he can control them remotely and connect them to his new program.

As we leave, Hermia sees us to the door and waves as

she flips the 'open' sign to 'closed' and draws the blind over the door.

Trey and I sprint through the streets, toward Light Street station. By the time we arrive, Titus is already waiting for us.

We clamber on board the first train carriage we get to, which happens to be a supply carriage. I press the intercom to let Titus know we're aboard and the train jolts forward. The carriage is rammed full of equipment: food; sleeping bags; locators; and various anti-magic Faraday devices, which prevent magic from being used. We leave the supply carriage and step through the gangway into my private passenger carriage.

We take a seat on the comfiest sofa. Trey swings his arm around my shoulder and pulls me in, giving me one long slow kiss.

"She's going to be okay, isn't she?" I ask, leaning into his chest. My eyes close as I catch a whiff of his perfume - frankincense and summer on warm skin.

He stays quiet. As he always does when he knows I don't want to hear the answer. I squeeze my eyes shut harder to block out the worry. Sometimes I wonder whether it would be better if he lied to me and told me everything was going to be okay.

We travel through the night, skirting around the outside of Element City, through the western part of the desert, and into the Ancient Forest. By morning, Kato's sent documents and files to our CogTrackers. Half of them from Bo. She's gathered a dozen folders full of photos, ancient scripture, spells, and rituals Victor might use to open the door. Kato also transferred the series of photos Hermia found of Nyx's family as well as all the history they could find of her.

We pull to a stop in White Willow, the forest's

Northern station. When we disembark the train, Bo and The Six are already there. There's only a short wait before Arden's sleek royal green and gold train pulls up on the platform opposite. Arden clambers off the train with a dozen senior Guild Sorcerers. I raise an eyebrow. They might be powerful Sorcerers, but two of them are walking with canes, a third is more wrinkled than a shriveled prune, and I think the Sorcerer standing next to him might be asleep.

They move to our huddle and Arden raises his green-robed hands to quieten the group. He's in tighter fitting sorcery robes today; a harness style belt hangs from his waist under his belly, which holds his wand, some silvery balls, three pouches of herbs, and a variety of other magical devices only some of which I recognize, and I wonder what the Guild has created this time.

Further up the platform, Titus steps down from the engine cabin. He hangs back, chewing a nail. Even though he's not supposed to come, I won't be stopping him, and I doubt Arden will either. I notice Israel and Maddison standing apart from the group, both of them scowling. I'm surprised Arden agreed to let them come. But by the distance they're keeping from the main group, they must have been given strict orders not to overstep the mark.

"Thank you all for volunteering for this mission," Arden says when we're quiet. "The First Fallon has agreed that it is vital we capture and contain Victor Dark." His eyes cross to Israel and Maddison, and he adds, "Alive." Which garners a nod from the pair of them. "The First Fallon herself wants to question him. Therefore, proceed with caution at all times."

Maddison stiffens at this, but Arden continues.

"I will take the Guild Sorcerers as the scouting party. Eden, Trey, Bo, and The Six will follow behind. Titus,

Israel, and Maddison will bring up the rear with Olivius who will enchant the kit and equipment. We need to break ground in the Eris valley before nightfall. Kato has sent coordinates for a camping spot about ten miles north from here. Any questions?"

Maddison raises her arm, but he ignores it, which makes her scowl practically violent.

"Good. Let's move."

Muted light breaks through the forest canopy, tossing the occasional beam of light into the undergrowth. After a short walk, we near the edge of the forest. The trees grow sparse, scattering as if they're running away from the mountains. Arden's group have disappeared; I'm guessing they've broken the forest line already.

The closer we get to the border between the Ancient Forest and the North, the sharper the air is. The floral aroma from the forest's bushes and flowers dissipates, replaced with the promise of snow.

As we pass the final tree in the forest's perimeter, the State border appears; a line of green grass distinguishes the muddy undergrowth of the forest from the beginnings of the Northern mountains. The grass stretches over a series of fields farmed by Shifters. But as the fields swell into mounds, hills, and eventually gray rocky mountains, the luscious greens and yellows drain from the landscape. Once across any border, the terrain changes so fast I've always wondered if the States were having some kind of territorial war none of us knew about.

I pull to a stop just after the border and frown. "Something feels wrong," I say to Trey and Bo, dropping back behind The Six who march on. This is the North. I know we're only just across the border but still. Shouldn't the temperature have dropped?"

"I don't know, it's pretty chilly," Trey says, pulling the fur cape we were issued around his shoulders. "But I suppose you've got a point. It isn't as cold as it should be."

"And we care about this why?" Bo asks, brushing down her uniform and adjusting cogs on her leg while we pause.

"Because the weather is the only thing that doesn't change," I say, glaring at her because she should know better.

We continue, leaving the forest behind us and trudging through the field on the same path Arden took. Trey stops and kneels in a long patch of grass to examine something on the ground. His shoulders stiffen.

"What's wrong?" I ask.

He stands, holding something between the palms of his hands, his eyes wide and skirting between Bo and me.

"It's dead," he says, opening his palms, "the plants are dying."

In the middle of his hand is a shriveled skeleton that looks like it used to be a flower. Its once bulbous head is mud brown, and the petals are dissolving into the air with every tiny hand movement.

"That's not possible," I say, looking back at the distance between the forest and us. It's less than a hundred meters. "Plants don't die in the forest."

"I know. I mean, technically we're not in the forest, and this land is farmed on a cyclical basis, but...This isn't like seasonal plant death. Look," Trey says, stepping aside to show us.

A circular patch of field about a foot wide has blackened, like the remains of a fire; only there's no evidence of fire or ash. Just sooty earth and a handful of dead plants. I look from Trey to Bo, the color draining from all three of us.

"We need Arden or, what's his name? The herbalist Sorcerer from the Guild, the younger one. Jacobs?"

A shift in the atmosphere catches my attention. Cold whips around us, and something in the forest makes the air change; it rustles, like the crumpling of paper. I tense, my fists balling up ready to attack.

"Something's watching us," I breathe.

Bo's body crumples and appears by my heel, in her wolf form, sniffing the ground.

"Go," Trey says, leaning in to kiss me. "Make sure it's just a stray deer and meet me back here. I'll find Arden." He touches his forehead to mine, making me smile, then he kisses my lips and whispers, "Be careful." He sets off at a sprint, running into the ankle height grass and off into the valleys after the lead group.

With Bo at my side, her nose firm against the ground, we track back, retracing our steps into the gloomy forest.

Her wolf body is slender. Like Cassian, her fur is thick and white. She's a little unsteady on her feet; I remember that she said while the prosthetic limb Titus and Lance created for her is enchanted to shift with her body, she takes the form of so many different creatures that finding stability on her legs is a learning process in each new form.

She darts from tree trunk to bush to tree trunk. Then freezes, her tail out straight, her fur hackles raised. She's found our intruder's scent.

"Go," I say, and she bolts. Powering over shrubbery and stray logs, I sprint after her, jumping and ducking to keep up. Her body disappears into a dense patch of trees.

A girl's voice cries out, "Don't hurt me."

"Rita?" Bo asks as I duck under a branch and into their view.

"Rita? What are you doing all the way out here?" I say.

She's a mess. Her clothes are torn, and her luscious black hair is ratty and full of dirt. But what concerns me most is that her eye socket is black, her cheek purple, and her lip split.

"What the hell happened to you?" I ask, reaching out to touch her shoulder. She flinches and steps back.

"It's fine," she says, her limp hair falling in front of her face.

"It's quite blatantly not fine, Rita," Bo says, putting her hand on her hip. "Who did this to you?"

Her eyes shut, making the bags hanging under her eyes even more pronounced.

"You're safe," I say.

"We'll protect you, from whoever did this. But you need to tell us what happened," Bo says.

"You already know," she says, taking a deep breath and sliding down the nearest tree trunk, "you wouldn't have sent me that message before the induction if you didn't."

"Trat," I say, sitting down on a fallen tree stump next to her.

She nods. "I don't love him," she says, pushing her hair behind her ear. Her shoulders slump, a couple of tears plopping onto the stained fabric of her pants. "I'm never going to love him. It should have been Tiron. It was always meant to be Tiron."

Bo looks at me, her mouth pinching as she swallows down the worry.

"It didn't work, did it?" I say, shuffling closer so I can put my arm around her shoulder.

"At first, I thought it would be okay. He *is* handsome, so I figured I'd fall in love with him eventually. But we're not compatible. And I didn't feel any different. We're supposed to feel something. Aren't we? It's supposed to change our essence, make us stronger, more stable?"

She looks up at Bo, a ray of hope curving her eyes. Bo hesitates. I do too. I'm not sure what the right answer is. Bo and I do feel different. But if we admit that, will it crush Rita? Or affirm her decision to run?

Bo looks at me and shrugs, so I take a deep breath and make the decision for both of us. "Yes, it feels different. There's a wholeness inside me now like I'm finally complete. Before there was a tiny hole, something missing, not from my life so much as my soul, my energy. Like a tiny piece of me was born inside him and a piece of him in me."

Rita's nods. She pushes herself upright, tears still glistening on her lids. "Thank you," she says, "thank you for being honest. I knew things weren't right. And so did he." Her fingers move to her lip.

"Did he hit you?"

She doesn't respond, but she doesn't have to. My muscles tighten, heat flushing my neck. I should have stopped it in Stratera foyer.

"He won't get away with this," I spit, and a small flame floats out of my mouth and drops to the forest floor burning a dried leaf that I have to stamp on to put out.

"He already has. It started a week after we were Bound when I admitted I wasn't in love with him. He exploded. The fact he didn't love me either, didn't seem to be the point. He avoided my face until a couple of days ago. That's when I ran." She hitches up her top, showing a rainbow of bruising across her ribs.

My hand ignites in flames; the vault rumbles threatening to open.

"Eden," Bo growls.

I heed her warning and bury the darkness in my unconsciousness. After several breaths, I calm down and push the vault away.

"I'll get his father struck off The Six for this," Bo says.

Rita smiles, "Don't," she says, and for the first time color floods her cheeks, a rosy glint burning in her eyes. "He isn't going to get away with it. I have a plan."

"What are you going to do?" I ask.

"First I need to make it into the valleys."

"The valleys? There's nothing in the valleys other than grass and hills."

"I heard there's a rebel group."

"You can't. They're an underground group," Bo says, panic in her voice. "They attacked the Council."

I avert my gaze, a strange cocktail of emotions swirling around my body. I've not told Bo what I know about the rebels yet, or the things Sheridan's told me. For Bo, the Libra oath is the only way to fight this war. But I still haven't decided, and part of me wants to know more about the rebels.

"I know it's dangerous," Rita says, "but I'm not going back. Not until I'm strong enough to make him pay. It's not like the distance will affect our Binding or our strength." She raises her Binding scar arm, "This is useless. Besides, they'll believe me. The rebels are meant to be broken like me... I want to be with people like me. You have to let me go."

I glance at Bo, neither of us happy about letting her go alone. "You're not broken," I say, and as I say it, everything that happened over the summer comes back: even though it's fixed now, I witnessed the same looks of shame and fear

Rita will experience if she stays at Stratera. When you've been cast out of a group once, I'm not sure you should ever go back. Maybe that's why I'm not sure where I belong.

"I mean it, Rita, you're not broken," I say, and pat her back. "You're perfect the way you are."

My stomach coils; I'm not sure if I'm saying those words for her benefit or mine, but they have the desired effect because she smiles at me.

"How many days' walk is it?" Bo asks.

"Half a day, maybe a full day if I'm slow."

"Then let us give you some supplies," I say, more to Bo than Rita.

Bo cocks her head at me but agrees.

"Thank you," Rita says, tears welling in her eyes.

Bo's figure drops to the floor, and she sprints away. I rub Rita's back, " I mean it, Rita. I've been there, I had a broken Binding too, remember?"

"I know," she says, giving me a teary smile, "I knew you of all people would understand."

Bo's back within a couple of minutes. She's panting and carrying a small green rucksack in her wolf mouth. The air around her figure ripples and contorts as she shifts into her Fallon form.

"It's got water and food supplies, and this," she holds up a fabric roll, "a sleeping bag. To keep you warm if you don't make it by nightfall."

"Thank you," Rita says, "I won't forget it." She hugs us both, squeezing me for a little longer than necessary. Then she hobbles off toward the border in the opposite direction.

"Should we have let her go? She's all on her own," I ask Bo.

"Did you see the look in her eye? She's not going to give up till she finds the rebels and makes Trat pay."

"Yeah," I say, feeling a strange sense of solidarity. "Something tells me she's going to look for Tiron too. If he hasn't already found his way to the rebels."

"What makes you say that?" she asks.

"Because it's what I'd have done for Trey. That's the thing about true love – you always find your way back to each other, no matter what."

TWENTY-TWO

'Scrying – the ability to see future events.'

The Dictionary of Balance

'Visions – Ambiguous. Limited flashes, glimpses, dreams of potential futures. Usually bestowed upon the 'seer' by the Balance. Warnings.'

The Dictionary of Balance

"Who was it?" Trey asks, as we rejoin him and the small group he's brought back.

"Rita," I say, then pull him off to the side, "she and Trat aren't doing so well. Do you remember the group Felicia talked about in Stratera Coffee? She said Sheridan's Balancer ran off to join a group of people whose Bindings were ineffective."

"The rebels?" Trey says far too loud.

"Shh, and yes. That's where she's gone. And honestly, Trey. You should have seen her. She was a mess. Trat was hurting her."

Trey's eyes burn dark blue. "Stop." I say, putting my hand on his back, "Rita's doing what she needs to. I think she needs to process what happened to her, and we should respect that."

"He needs to pay."

"I know, but something tells me Rita's going to make sure he does."

"What's happening to the flowers?" Bo asks behind us, so Trey and I rejoin her, Arden, and Jacobs.

Jacobs pushes the sleeves of his long green sorcery robes up. His hair is mousy blond, long and dead straight, tied in a loose knot halfway down his back. The knot itself is green ivy and weaves through his hair and under the collar of his robes, and I can't help but wonder what it's attached to. I realize now I'm closer to him that he's middle aged, but his skin is supple, and he looks a lot younger than he is. But when he turns to answer me, the worry lines in his brow suddenly age him.

"Fallon Luchelli was right." He raises his wand, and the dead plant, now held in a transparent Stasis Orb, hovers up from the ground.

"It's dead?" I ask. "How?"

"We don't know. But the CogTrackers are reading high levels of Imbalance."

"And the patch of earth," Bo says.

Jacobs nods. "We've covered the patch in a mini isolation dome to stop it from infecting any other patches of the forest."

"Is it Alteritus?" Bo asks.

"No. That's restricted to Keepers. This is not something we've seen before; we dug the patch, and it doesn't end. It's like the source is coming from the ground, from Trutinor itself."

My spine prickles, flashes of my nightmares, a broken decaying Trutinor, replaying.

"Trutinor's dying?" I whisper, more to myself than the others.

"Well, I think that's a bit dramatic," Jacobs says, laughing in a way that sounds more like he's sniffing. "But it certainly looks like it might have a case of eczema or a cold."

"This isn't a joke," I snap.

I don't hear his response; the air stills, and the sound of their voices muffles as the memory of my dreams crystalizes and makes my chest hurt. There's a hand on my arm; I'm being guided away, toward the valleys and the rest of the lead group. When we are some distance away, the fog of panic dissolves. A cool clean sense of clarity radiates from the hand on my arm, up into my shoulder, and into my head.

"What was that about?" Trey asks.

"This is how it happens. Piece by piece until the sky is burned maroon with Imbalance, and Trutinor is dead."

"In your dreams, you mean?"

I nod and look up at him, "This is how it starts..."

He squeezes my arm. "I'm sure there's an explanation," he says. But I don't have one, and neither does he, so we fall into silence. I wonder if Sheridan's had any luck looking for answers today and pull out my CogTracker to drop her a message.

From: Eden.East@FallonCogMail.com
Subject: Any news?
To: Sheridan.Nikolas@KeeperCogMail.com

Hey, Sheridan,
Any news? I've had a worrying development. Just north of the forest, barely 100m across the border, there's a spot of dead earth. A Guild Sorcerer said he thought it was a case of eczema, but given my dreams, I don't buy it.
What do you think it means? Any research news on what you think my dreams mean?
E x

We walk in silence for most of the next two hours. Conversation is limited to asking if each other is okay and stopping for water or breaks. After our third water break, I check my CogTracker. Sheridan's replied.

From: Sheridan.Nikolas@KeeperCogMail.com
Subject: RE: Any news?
To: Eden.East@FallonCogMail.com

Eden, I hate to say it, but this does change things. Until now there's been nothing to indicate your dreams are manifesting.

I stop reading, gooseflesh running down my arms. There *were* signs, inconsistencies; I just didn't put two and two together: the anomalies in the air in Stratera, the temperature off a few degrees here and there. I keep reading.

I still maintain that given you're not a scryer, it's highly unlikely you're using scrying abilities. But. I have found something, and it's not good news. There's a case: twins. They lived almost a thousand years ago. Sadly, for them, no one took them seriously until it was too late. They were only children, ten years old and they weren't scryers. They had vision-like dreams, or I should say half-dreams. Each twin saw half of the vision, and it wasn't until a dream Keeper examined them both and pieced the visions together that they realized what it was. They saw war. But not just any war, the Siren-Mermaid War. By the time the information was taken to the Council, it was too late. Karva was already dead.

I don't want you to panic. I'm not convinced you're experiencing the same thing. But I do think we need to take this further. I know you'll want to take it to the Council, but I'm not sure that's the right answer either. I can't say it on CogMail. But I think you should visit my home. Tell them. They can help. The rebels.

I'll keep digging and come back to you. Hey, chin up, this indicates it's about Trutinor, so at least Trey isn't about to pop his clogs...

Too soon?

Sheridan

I laugh, as inappropriate as it is, but I'm relieved this isn't about Trey. I drop her a quick note back thanking her for the information and mentioning the anomalies I've been sensing.

I tell Trey the news from Sheridan, and he smiles, "Do I get to say I told you so now? You're stuck with me for the rest of your life. I'm far too stubborn to die." Then he leans down, scoops me into his arms, and kisses the worry away.

We continue climbing up the Eris foothills, which rapidly turn into steep rocky mountains. As the air cools to an icy chill, it makes my chest burn and my breathing labored. Walking goes from difficult to grueling. After another thirty minutes, we reach a plateau, and to my relief, Arden has made camp.

A transparent dome, much like the one from Ignis City when there was an outbreak of Alteritus, and it needed quarantining, covers most of the plateau. This time, it doesn't require proof of Balance to enter. As we pass through the transparent perimeter, it brushes against my skin like silk fabric, and a wave of heat hits me.

"I've never been more grateful for heat in my life," I say to Trey as we maneuver around several Sorcerers using wands to erect tents and set fires to cook dinner. We're assigned a tent each. I argue for a two-person tent, but one of the Sorcerers says there aren't any and tells us to go to the cooking area for dinner.

Bo is huddled with The Six. She looks like the general she is, her black leather uniform, fitted and paneled with enchanted armor that shifts with her. She's attached her fighting prosthetic leg this evening as opposed to the leg she wears to Stratera. This one is more streamlined. The cogs are inlaid into the smooth metallic surface, and it doesn't click and whirr like her other one. The Six are all in matching uniforms: smooth leather, silvery armor, and epaulets that display their rank over their fur cloaks.

Bo addresses them each individually, "Obert and Angus, you take the first watch shift tonight, Markov and Delphine, you're up next, and I'll do the early morning one with Vega."

I tense as I catch Delphine staring at me and wonder how the border is. Maybe I should confront her while we're here. Although Nyx said she'd denied any part in the Shifter attacks. I decide that Mother would have wanted to confront her, but Father would have made her wait, stick to the diplomatic negotiations. Bo continues to lay out various options, plans, and tactics for capturing her brother. She reiterates about five times to capture only, no kills. Trey joins her, swinging his arm around her shoulder. "Evening, boss lady," he says.

She rolls her eyes and grins, "What do you want, Luchelli?"

As I disappear toward the fire, Trey says, "Sadly, nothing fun, I figured we should discuss border control in the East."

The fire's large and burns in the center of the cooking area. I can't help but edge closer to it, drawing off the occasional ember to play with, manipulating and poking it to form an arc, then an orb that I bounce in my palm. A body hovers near my shoulder.

"Israel," I say, startled. "Are you okay? I'm sure this isn't easy for you."

Israel is tall and stocky, his white-blond hair worn in the same topknot at Victor, the sides of his hair shaved with cutthroat accuracy. Thick furs line his back, and he's wearing his customary leathers underneath.

"I am okay, Maddison is less so."

"I'm sorry..." I say, knowing full well her pain is my fault.

When he doesn't respond, I feel awkward, so I make conversation, "I'm pleased the treaty is still in force. Father would have been proud. I know there are still some tensions, but it's promising progress."

He doesn't respond to that either, so I fall silent. After a while, he clears his throat, "I... I wanted to ask you something."

He fidgets with the fur on his cloak, uncomfortable with whatever it is he needs to ask.

"Of course, anything."

"We wondered if you'd had any more engagement with Victor? We all saw the CogTV episode, but we've heard nothing from him since he returned. It's breaking Maddison's heart."

"Oh, I see," I say. Bo had said that Victor hadn't been in touch with them, but I hadn't considered the implications. I toy with not telling him that Victor found me; I've only told a handful of people. But guilt gets the better of me.

"I've seen him once," I say. "In Stratera, he was trying to steal a book."

Israel's back straightens, his face hardening, but I'm not sure if it's because he's angry or if the rapid blinking is because he's trying not to cry.

"Israel, I should explain before you get your hopes up... He's not coming back; he is dead. The Last Fallon is employing some powerful ancient magic to keep him here. She's controlling him, and he only came to me because she wants me to do something for her. I am certain that if he had free will, he would come home..." I pause because he won't like my next words. "I know this won't be easy to hear, but I suspect when the Last Fallon gets what she wants, he will have to go back to Obex." I wait for a response, but he can't look at me, and I've run out of things to say. I leave him by the fire, alone with the pain I'm responsible for causing him. As I walk away, I'm sure I see a tear run down his cheek, but he turns his back on me.

TWENTY-THREE

'Wars are not won by those who brandish weapons; wars are won by the silent heroes you never see coming.'

Balance Proverb

The elder Sorcerers use magic to keep the spit roast rotating until the chicken is crisp and ready to eat. They dish out strips accompanied by boiled rice and water that's tinged orange with a purifying liquid. Chatter around the fire is mostly tactical, discussing the files Kato and Hermia have sent alongside the best ways to capture Victor and what potential magic he will use. As night falls, exhaustion sets in; the last two days have felt like a week. Trey and I return to our tents. I'm about to climb in when I notice Maddison and Israel. They stop speaking and turn to me. Each one gives me a small smile, which I return with a nod. This, I think, is at least progress from Maddison. I kiss Trey goodnight and slide into the tent next to his. I check my CogTracker one last time; Kato's sent an estimated projection of Victor's movements. He should pass us tomorrow morning.

Sleep must arrive at some point because I wake to my body rocking from side to side in slow wave-like movements. My eyes fly open, the sudden realization that I'm neither meant to be rocking nor moving. But as soon as I sit up, a cloth is placed over my mouth, and a sweet chemical stench fills my nose. My body falls limp, and a veil of darkness descends over me.

I've no idea how long I'm asleep for, or who took me, but when I wake, I keep my eyes shut. I've been kidnapped. In the seconds before I was drugged unconscious, I managed to work that much out. If I want to stand a chance of escaping I need to gather as much evidence as I can about my attackers before they realize I'm awake.

I send out my essence; it roams the air, feeling, sensing, stretching as far through the wind particles as it can. It scopes out smells: the faint remains of baked bread and fried garlic – I can taste my kidnapper's dinner on the air. Wherever I am, it's densely populated, not quite a city but more than a village. There are hundreds, maybe thousands of vibrations in the breeze, Keepers moving, busying themselves in the area. But in this room, there is only one body. They're behind me. Their body heat is ruffling the air despite the fact they're motionless – a Siren, I suspect, and probably to keep me calm.

I peel open my eyes. It's dark, still night. I can't have been asleep for long. The Siren moves and leaves the room;

I catch the back of their head as I sit up. It's a girl, short and tanned, with long straight hair.

I scan the room; the roof is made of a creamy fabric, and the floor is a patchwork of rugs, like the bedding I'm in. It reminds me of the room I saw in Sheridan's dreams. Part of me wonders whether she's responsible for this. She told me to speak to the rebels, and given that we're not much further north than the Eris valleys, it's plausible that's who's holding me.

The rest of the room is empty, except for the stool the girl was sat on, which is the remains of a tree stump, smoothed and worn into the shape of a bottom over years of use. There's no door, but the fabric of the tent I'm in serves as a flapping doorway. Who kidnaps someone and doesn't lock them up? I throw the covers off and run for the door, only to smack into an invisible wall. I bounce back, crumpling in a pile on the floor.

"What the f..."

"Good evening, Eden," a voice interrupts. I dust myself down and examine the voice's owner. A tall pale man with silvery white hair is stood in the doorway. His eyes are odd, a mix of silver and green, and his lips plump red ones. I have no idea who or what he is.

He enters the tent and gives me a hand to help me up. I eye him, then slap his hand away and stand up by myself. He smiles to himself, then says, "May I?" but doesn't wait for an answer. He pulls a piece of circular sticky fabric off my pajama sleeve. My fists ball, igniting with electricity. Who the hell does this asshole think he is?

"You can't get out with it on, clever little bit of sorcery that."

"Who are you?" I say, looking him up and down. There's something so familiar about him, but I can't quite place what. I decide he's a Shifter; his blond hair and the faint limp in his walk makes me think of the First Fallon and her essence trace.

"I'm the leader here, Castor Jameson."

I narrow my eyes at him; if he's a leader then this must be the rebel camp. I shift backward, my feet slotting into a defensive position, fire exploding to life around my fists. "Okay, Castor. Where exactly is here?" I ask.

"Here is transient," he says.

"Don't be evasive," I say, and raise one of my fists.

He gives me a warm smile before lifting his hands up, "I apologize for the manner in which you were taken. I assure you that your guards are unharmed, merely sleeping on the job. And no harm will come to you while you're here."

His voice is calming, sincere. I change my mind, wondering if he's a Siren instead of a Shifter. Whatever he is, there's no malice in his eyes, just curiosity. I believe him.

"Fine," I say, extinguishing my fist, "next time use the CogTracker, that's what they're for. What do you want from me?"

"Walk with me," he says, gesturing for us to leave the tent. I approach the flapping door with suspicion, poking my hand out first. When I'm not flung backward, I step out.

I have to stop my mouth from dropping as I take in the tented city I'm standing in. Above me is a blanket of creams and browns. Thick tarpaulins that stretch as far as I can see, with rods and polls piercing the ground and skewering the fabrics to hold them up. It looks just like Sheridan's dream. We're standing in a spacious communal area, with stalls and woks cooking food, and in the far corner are a set of three cave mouths. Although lanterns hang from the cave ceiling, from this distance, I can't see where they go. Castor must clock me looking at the cave mouths because he says, "Don't try and work out where you are. Our network is extensive, and as I mentioned, we move every few weeks. For you, it's the middle of the night, but for us, we work in shifts to ensure our base is always protected. But for the most part, what you see now is temporary. Like I said, transient."

"How is this temporary?" I ask, trying to keep my mouth from hanging open. "It looks like a Bedouin city."

Castor smiles, pride beaming in his eyes, "Thank you, it's taken many centuries for us to perfect our system. We use the tents so that we can move and relocate when necessary. But I'm sure by now you've figured out where you are?"

"Rebel headquarters?"

He nods.

"And the caves?" I say as we pass them and move deeper into the communal area. Scanning the Keepers, my eyes are wide like spotlights. There's so many of them and all from different States.

Castor watches me, his silvery-green eyes glittering at me, but he doesn't answer.

"You understand," Castor says, "that I've taken a great risk by bringing you here. We've bought you into our headquarters because we believe our interests are aligned. But you've seen where we are, how our system works. You are a risk to our safety."

My stomach knots. Is he threatening me?

"We've lived in isolation for thousands of years," he continues, "I hope that the risk I've taken is worth it."

"I pose no threat to you," I say, and I mean it. Something solidifies in my mind – the burning questions I've had, the uncertainty of whether to swear an oath to the Libra Legion. Deep down, I wanted this. I wanted to see the rebels for myself, to know what they were doing. Then I remember Rita.

"There's a girl, a friend of mine, she would have arrived in the last twelve hours or so."

"Rita?"

"Yes," I say, my eyes brightening, "so she did make it. Is she okay?"

"She's in the hospital wing. Mild dehydration and exhaustion, and they're treating her wounds. But she should be fine."

I smile to myself; finally, someone with a happy ending.

"What do you want from me?" I ask, genuine curiosity in my tone.

"For now, we seek to understand what you want," he says.

"What I want doesn't seem to matter."

"Because of the prophecy, you mean?" he looks down at me as we exit the communal area and move through a carpeted walkway.

"You know about the prophecy?" I ask, surprised.

"We know about a lot of things. You haven't answered my question."

I fall silent. Choosing instead to stare into each tented room we pass; Keepers smile and nod at us as they cook and laugh and play games, as if this weren't a temporary city full of rebels but like any normal city in Trutinor. I stop short, looking at one family in particular. This time, my mouth does fall slack. The parents bear no Binding scar.

"How?" I ask, "how is that possible?"

Castor doesn't answer me and guides me away from the door to continue through the walkway so I play back his question. *What do I want?*

"Honestly," I say, looking up at him, "I'm not sure I know."

"I have intelligence that says you are part of the Libra Legion."

"I have attended a meeting. But I haven't taken the oath yet."

"Yet?" his eyes narrow, "but are you invested in their cause to end the First Fallon's reign?"

I fall silent. Again. Is that what I want? Or do I want something more? I rub my hands over my face trying to clear my mind. I keep being told there are only two sides to this war. Balance or Imbalance, but part of me thinks that, just maybe, that's the problem. My heart tells me to finish the job my parents started: side with the Libras and Arden. Plot the chest pieces, and strike only when we're guaranteed to take the Queen. But my head says use the Last Fallon, join her so I can harness her power and take the First Fallon's corrupt reign down while we can. Head or heart; Balance or Imbalance. But what if I listen to my gut, which is screaming that there has to be another way, that I should hear Castor out?

"To some extent, yes," I say, which is the truth. "I do want her reign to end. Am I happy with the way the Libras are trying to achieve that? Not so much."

Castor stops and gestures for me to enter a room. The floor is made of the same patterned rugs as the room I woke up in. There's a raised platform in the center, a square shape with low cushions and a coffee table burning incense with two steaming mugs.

"Please," he says, and steps onto the square and sits cross-legged on the furthest side of the table. He picks up the mug and takes a sip. So I sit opposite him and do the same.

It's herbal tea; a fruity aroma hits my nose as soon as I pick up the cup, and when I swallow the liquid, it's warm, hot almost as it slides down my throat.

"Why did you bring me here?" I ask, putting the mug down.

"To give you a choice."

"A choice?" I laugh. "what choice can you give me?"

"The Libras or the rebels."

"That's not a choice. I don't even know who you are."

He smiles, sips his tea, and pushes a blank coin across the table.

"What's that?" I pick it up and take another sip of my tea.

"It's what we represent."

"Which is?"

He leans back, staring at me as I examine the circular coin. It's made of silver, a smooth disc no larger than the coin in my pocket that Father gave me, and it's completely blank. When he doesn't answer, I look up, "What do you represent?"

He takes a long slow breath, then leans forward, his face tense and serious, "Choice. Freedom. The end of oppression. The end of the entire Balance system... The end of fate itself."

I laugh. I can't help myself, I've never heard anything more absurd in my life. The end of fate? He's insane, or maybe I am because even though every word he's said is ridiculous, I haven't left; I'm still sat here holding the coin, staring at him.

His expression is serious; he believes every word of what he's saying, and as much as I want to tell him he's lost his mind, part of me believes there might be something to what he's saying. I have to know, "Is that even possible?"

As soon as the words are out, the coin slips through my fingers and drops onto the table. I look at it, confused as to how it's on the table, and my fingers are still wiggling in the air. All of a sudden my head is groggy. The room spins as if I've drunk too much of that blue stuff Arden and Kato like.

I glance at the tea, shove it across the table. "You drugged me," I growl, stumbling to my feet. I slip down the side of the square platform crashing to the floor for the second time.

Castor stands, and shrugs, nonchalant. I don't like this side of him. "I might have brought you here, but I don't trust you yet," he says, taking my hand to help me up. "We haven't survived for thousands of years by giving out trust that hasn't been earned."

"You kidnapped me, remember? And drugged me. Twice no less. How do you expect me to trust you?" I mumble. As my eyelids get heavy, his face blurs, and he reminds me of someone, but I can't think who. There's a scuffle, and a girl appears in the room. She's tall and skinny, dressed in black, her hair a rainbow of colors, and beneath her eye, is a black bruise.

"I don't. You're just supposed to choose."

A sleep-filled laugh bubbles up as the girl's face blurs in and out of focus. "Why is everyone so familiar here? You look like Renzo," I giggle.

"You said she'd be asleep," the girl spits.

Then I fall limp in Castor's arms, and the dark hug of sleep takes over me.

TWENTY-FOUR

'Instructions on killing the dead – Lost soul demons are notoriously difficult to kill. They are, after all, already dead. However, to dispatch a Lost soul demon back to Obex, simply burn it.'

From the History of Forbidden and Lost Magic

I sit bolt upright in bed and glance at my fist; it's curled shut. I open my fingers and find a silver coin in the middle. So I didn't dream the rebel kidnapping. I throw clothes on and jump out of bed, unzipping my tent and climbing into Trey's next door. I slide into his covers and stroke his cheek.

"Wake up, handsome," I say, and kiss him.

His nose twitches as his eyes peel open. "Now that's a view I could get used to waking up next to," he grins, kissing me back, and for an instant I get lost inside the moment, but then the coin presses into my hand, and I remember why I'm in his tent.

"I was kidnapped," I say, pulling away.

"What?" His eyes skitter across my face.

"I'm fine. Promise. But last night, I was taken by the rebels."

"Did they hurt you? What did they want? Why didn't The Six stop them?" He's sitting up now.

"Trey, I swear I'm fine. Their leader wanted to talk to me. So they dosed The Six with sleeping drugs and took me to their base."

"They did WHAT? Drugging The Six? What if they'd been caught? What if they'd drugged you?"

I open my mouth to tell him they did but shut it again. His eyes are all fiery blue and flashing maroon.

"You need to calm down, or I'm not telling you the rest."

He glares at me, then closes his eyes. He takes four deep breaths, and when they reopen, his baby blues are staring at me.

"They gave me this," I say, flicking the coin at him.

"What is it?"

"A symbol for what they represent."

"Which is?"

"A fresh start, I suppose. But choice. Freedom. The end of oppression. The end of the entire Balance system. The end of fate itself," I say, echoing Castor's words.

"That's not possible."

"That's what I thought. But, Trey, I saw them: adult Keepers with no Binding scars. I don't know how, and I don't know why. But I want to find out... Castor asked me where my loyalties lie."

"Castor?"

"Their leader," I say.

Trey stiffens, "Oh. And where do they lie?"

I glance at him. Really? He chooses now to get all butt hurt, "Not like that, he's old enough to be my dad."

Trey's shoulders relax, and I have to fight myself not to roll my eyes at him. "Honestly?" I say, "at this point, I'm not sure."

My essence pokes me. It's wandering off on its own, like a defiant child trying to get my attention with gentle nudges and sniffs of the air. My eyes widen.

I snatch the coin back and scramble out of the tent scanning the air around me. Then I stick my head back in and grab Trey's hand. "Get up," I shout.

"What's wrong?" he asks.

But I don't stop to answer: I'm already out and ambling toward the edge of the heated dome. I brush through the silky perimeter and sprint across the plateau, scrabbling over rocks and our crew's debris until I reach a small peak. I close my eyes, setting my essence free to run through the breeze, hunting for anomalies, tasting the air molecules, searching for the oddity that caught my attention. There's an Imbalance. I've been feeling it for days. The strange void I told Sheridan about, only now it's bigger than before. But those times it faded, like whatever it was couldn't quite catch its breath. But this time it's different. It's solid. And it's not disappearing.

The first streaks of sunrise emerge in the distance, spraying the horizon with mustard yellows and fruity oranges. Then it appears, a sliver of maroon slicing through the sky, crisp and dark, like a bloody wound in the horizon: Imbalance. My hand clasps my mouth. The voids, the anomalies, they were all tiny growths in the fabric of Trutinor, too small to notice. But now they're bulging and ballooning like scabs, and the tiny Imbalanced bacteria have silently multiplied into a virus. Trutinor is sick.

Arms wrap around my shoulders. Trey's head slips into the space between my jaw and my shoulder. "What was all that about?" he asks, inhaling the scent of my skin and peppering me with kisses. I wriggle out from under his grasp.

"Trey, LOOK." I pull him off me and point his head at the sky.

He stiffens, blinking at the maroon.

"Trutinor is sick," I say.

"It could be Victor," he says, a tremor in his voice.

"Yeah, it could. Or Trutinor could be sick. Maybe they're linked, I don't know, but what I do know is that we need to stop whatever is going on before it destroys the whole of Trutinor."

He slides his hand into mine, gripping it tight. My heart pounds in my chest, fear prickling the back of my neck.

"How long?" Trey asks, "how long is it in your dreams before Trutinor crumbles?"

"It changes. Sometimes it's months; other times, it's years of slow deterioration. But once it starts," I say, and look up at him, "it doesn't stop."

He pulls me around to face him; his face is tight with worry, lines drawn around his eyes. He sinks his soft lips onto mine. For a brief second, I forget about the sky and about Victor and lose myself in the perfection of us, alone, standing on a mountain peak, kissing as the sun rises.

Then he lets go, his expression serious, "Eden, listen..."

"No," I say, shaking my head, my eyes instantly stinging. "Don't you dare. Sheridan said she thought the prophetic part of my dreams was about Trutinor. Not about you. I can't even... I won't..." I fall silent, my throat so thick the words stop forming.

He strokes my hair; his eyes are soft. I shake my head,

trying to make words and sounds with my mouth, but tears spill out instead of sentences.

"We all die eventually," he says, "we have to confront the possibility that if your dreams of a broken Trutinor are manifesting, there's a chance..."

"No," I snap, anger helping me find my voice. "No. There isn't."

We're both silent again for a moment, then Trey sighs.

"Just say I do. Don't spend your life like Hermia, in a futile search. Live your life, be happy." He brings my chin up so I'm looking at him.

"Promise me?"

My lips press shut as tears spill down my cheeks and I shake my head no.

"Eden, you need to promise me. It's what I want." He places his palm against my chest and lowers his barrier; a wave of his emotions flows into my body: hot lust, a yearn that reaches my bones, then the soft silk of love that touches my soul, and the knowledge that he loves me enough to let me go.

It makes my heart ache so much I gasp for breath.

"I..." I start as he takes his hand away, "I pr..."

A flash of something over his left shoulder catches my eye. I scramble away and drop to the floor, squinting in the direction I saw movement.

"What's wrong?" he asks.

"I thought I saw something. But I'm not sure wh..." It moves again, a black dot, barely visible about half a mile away on another ridge.

"Get down," I say, pulling Trey to the floor. We lie prone, squinting at the ridge.

"I could be wrong. It could be a wild mountain wolf or goat. But..."

"You think it's Victor?"

"I looked at Kato's projections last night. I'm convinced it's him."

"Keep watch; I'll get the Trackers and Arden."

Trey scrabbles backward retreating down toward the camp. I shut my eyes and let my senses drift out through the air. It must be half a mile or more to the ridge he's walking across. It's a stretch, but if I concentrate I should be able to reach him. I take a breath and send my essence out. Pushing, feeling my way as I jump through wind pockets like hopscotch. I stretch further and further until a bead of sweat trickles down my back. The change in the air is just out of reach. I can almost taste it, I know it's there, I just need to push a little harder. There's a void, dark, blistering with determination, making the breeze feel rigid and bumpy. My eyes open. Standing on the ridge is a figure, staring in my direction, and it makes my back ripple with gooseflesh. I know without needing binoculars that it's Victor. And now he knows I'm watching him.

Trey returns with Arden in tow and hands me my CogTracker.

"You found Victor?" Arden asks, crawling over the rocks next to me. Then he goes rigid. "What in Trutinor's name is that?"

"We don't know," I say, looking up at the wound in the sky, "but given the plants..."

His skin drains of color as he blinks at me. His hands race over his CogTracker firing out CogMails faster than even I can, "We can't contain it if it's in the sky. Everyone will see. This is going to cause widespread panic."

As he's typing, his screen cuts out and flicks to a CogTV channel. Then mine beeps and changes to the same channel. So does Trey's. I glance up at the mountain Victor was standing on half expecting him to have a CogTV crew there messing with the network like he did last time. But it's the First Fallon's face that appears.

"Attention, Trutinor. Do not be alarmed at the sky marks. Please be aware that the Guild of Investigations is running some ground to air defense magic. You may see some maroon staining in the future. There is no need to panic." Her eyes are ablaze, just like Trey's when he's using compulsion.

My chest tightens at the thought of millions of Keepers lapping up every word because they're under her spell. She has to be stopped. The announcement loops a few times then cuts off.

I turn to Trey, "Just me, or do you find it convenient that she was able to hack the network only a few days after Victor did?"

Trey's eyes narrow. He swipes across to the call screen and dials Kato, whose face appears.

"I'm already on it," he says, without even glancing at the screen. "And this time, thanks to the systems we set up in Hermia's spare room, I was able to hack into the network while she was live. I slapped tracer worm on that baby. I'm working my magic now."

"You really are a genius, aren't you?" I say, grinning.

This time he does look at the screen, "Obviously, darling." He hangs up.

Arden's zoomed in on Victor's location; he pushes the screen in our direction, and I wriggle over the rocks to get a closer look. All three of us stare at Arden's screen as the images blur in and out of focus. They inch closer to the rocky ridge, and as the image sharpens, Victor's face stares back at us, grinning, yellowed teeth on show, his maroon vein pulsing down his temple. He tips his head, giving us a salute. Then he runs.

"Shit," I say, jumping up and grabbing Trey. Victor sprints across the ridge plateau as if he's going to head down the mountain.

"Let's go," Trey says, grabbing my hand. Arden, Trey, and I sprint down the slope back to camp.

When we reach the camp, Bo is already shouting orders at the group, demanding beds be packed. Sorcerers are flinging their wands around, wispy green enchantments flying through the air, packing the equipment away at light speed.

Trey CogCalls Kato back, relaying our position and where we saw Victor. I can hear Hermia shouting commands in the background, barking at their new super-sized tracker to display maps and relay information to us. Trey signs off. "They're sending the best direction for us to cut him off."

I nod as Bo charges over to us, hopping on her prosthetic as she pulls her boot on. "The Six are ready. Eden, you can ride Delphine Delacroix, Trey ride Angus. It's better than trying to chase him on foot."

I hesitate, "Is Delphine okay with that?"

"Delphine will be fine," Bo snaps.

I recoil and decide that when this is over, I have to ask her if something's wrong. She was funny with me before Stratera started too. I shrug it off and decide it must be the stress of being a general. When Bo was given The Six, they were less than impressed that Israel relinquished control to a seventeen-year-old. I think Angus' exact words were 'my boss is a little stick insect brat.' Bo later found out that

Delphine, head of the Third House of the North was the ringleader of that little tryst. Apparently, Delphine had a soft spot for Israel and was less than impressed that she hadn't been given The Six. It was never a possibility, of course, because control of The Six stays with the First House of the North. But that didn't seem to matter to Delphine.

When Bo lost her leg in the battle against her brother, the rest of The Six saw the way she fought and decided to toe the line. Delphine did too, eventually.

"Delphine will be fine with what?" Delphine says, strolling through the bustling group with Angus. She's tall, taller even than Angus, who has a constant bear-like appearance about him, with shaggy brown hair and mud-colored clothes. While Delphine is thickset, she has fine creamy-white features. Her eyes, like her lips, are jet black, which I assume is her essence mark. She flicks her long cream-colored hair behind her back, then folds her arms.

"Letting Eden ride point," Bo says.

Delphine peers down at me, raising her eyebrow as if I'm an ant that needs squashing. Her lips thin into a slip, but she detaches a huge collar that was hanging from her hip and throws it at me. Her body plummets to the floor then billows up and out, making me stumble back.

"She's a polar bear?" I ask.

"Couldn't you tell?" Bo says, rolling her eyes at me, "God, the attitude alone should have been a giveaway. Cold as an iceberg that one."

Delphine grunts, the corner of her darkened lip rippling up. Bo turns and glares at Delphine. I take a nervous look back; Bo has balls of steel. Delphine bears her long thin incisors at her. Bo shifts her body forward so fast I think she's going to slap Delphine's black nose. Delphine flinches but holds her position and growls so loud it rumbles through my chest.

"Guys," I snap, "there isn't time."

The pair of them look at me then Delphine lowers her head, allowing me to slip the collar over neck and on to her shoulders. She nudges me to mount her. I clamber on, pausing to realize I've never ridden a bear before. But I figure it can't be that different to a camel. We're surrounded by desert in the East, and camel riding is compulsory for all Elementals, a throwback tradition from before the trains. I squeeze my legs into her sides and hold the two handles that stick out from the collar.

"I'll shift and go airborne," Bo says, "it's faster, and once I get a lock on Victor, we won't lose him."

"Go," I say.

The air around her body shimmers and pulses, until she disappears and reappears, flapping long sleek wings. Her slender peregrine figure shoots skywards. Her belly is speckled taupe, her back covered in a silky white strip. She circles us, squawking out what I imagine must be commands. Obert, Vega, and Markov stop what they're doing and look up. They throw their last few belonging into their kit bags and dump them in the growing pile of kit and equipment then, they too, shift.

A thread of green magic from Olivius' wand zips around us lowering the protective dome. Angus, in brown-bear form, bounds across the gravel and rock and skids to a halt in front of Trey, lowering his massive head and shoulders for Trey to climb on.

Arden reappears at my side, "Find him, bring him down, and capture him. *Alive*. I'll finish up with Olivius here, and then we'll follow the route Kato sends us. Trey, do you have the plan?"

"Yes," Trey says, flipping open his CogTracker. "Kato's trying to get a lock on him now. They couldn't track his essence because he's dead, so they've found a way to track the Imbalance he's creating, and they're narrowing the parameters. But Kato sent a proposed route of attack." He taps his Tracker and mine. Arden's beeps in response so I open it to view Kato's plan. I nod in agreement; he's suggested we ride down the mountain and split into two groups to set an ambush. He thinks Victor's going for the forest. We'll cut him off inside.

"Once we get to the forest perimeter, you take one group, and I'll lead the other."

"Okay," Trey says, tapping out coordinates on his tracker.

"Let's ride," I say, and dig my heels into Delphine's ribs. She rears up, her jowls bellowing out a roar, and she jerks forward, racing down the mountainside.

After half an hour of riding hard, we're three-quarters of the way back to the forest, and I cannot help but wonder why we didn't ride out yesterday instead of walk.

Our pack, two wolves, two bears, a panther, and a peregrine, is panting hard. The pace has slowed, and underneath me, I can feel Delphine's muscles are tired and twitching.

"Does Kato have a lock on him yet?" I shout over to Trey.

Delphine cocks her head in Trey's direction just as he shakes it 'no.' She slows to a halt and wriggles me off her back, shifting into Keeper form.

"Well, what are we doing to find him? We can't keep blindly running," she says, her cheeks pink with exertion.

Trey and the others pull up too. He takes a small water bottle out of a pouch attached to Angus' collar and throws it to Delphine who takes huge gulps before throwing it back. Above us, Bo's wings flap hard as she slices through the air, but she too slows until she's hovering above us. She lets out a shriek, and her wings fold into an arrow-like position, and she plummets down the mountainside.

"She's got him," I shout. Delphine shifts and in seconds, I'm on her back, and we're bounding over the craggy ground. Finally, I spot him too, breaking through the field at the bottom of the mountains. He's in wolf form and running straight toward the forest, just like Kato predicted.

My legs grip Delphine's belly, cramps in my thighs make my muscles scream, but I refuse to let go. My knuckles whiten as I cling harder to the handles. *He will not get away. Not this time. Not again.* I dig Delphine's ribs, spurring her on as if she were a horse. Her jaw swipes round, growling a warning at me, but it spurs her on anyway, and she runs faster over the pebbles, rocks, and sheer cliff faces toward Victor.

Our group must look like a stampede tearing down the gray Eris hills. The wind, cold and sharp, and full of snow, whips through my hair and bristles Delphine's fur. My eyes stream, and for a minute I lose sight of Victor. But I spot him entering the forest in the direction of the Pink Lake.

The lake stretches further than I can see, meandering through the Ancient Forest like a snake and off toward the North. Bo squawks and dives in his direction, chasing after him again. Our group races off the foothills, across the field between the mountains and the forest, and into the tree line after them. When we hit the edge of the Pink Lake, we pull short. Bo is back in her Fallon form, crouched behind a large trunk. Her fingers point to her eyes, then over to the north-west rim of the lake. I crouch down and spot Victor, twitching by the lake shore.

What's wrong with him?

Bo's hands form a rapid set of shapes, as she dishes out silent instructions to The Six. Obert in wolf form and Markov in panther, move off to the left. Angus and Delphine cut right and around the back. Trey and Vega, the last member of The Six, remain although they form a defensive line behind Bo and me. Bo pulls me into her crouched position. From here I get an even clearer view. The peaks and ridge lines of the Eris mountains are visible in the distance. The surface of the water is cloaked in pink water lilies and cherry blossom, detritus discarded by the perpetual flowering of the trees.

"What do you want to do?" Bo asks.

"Approach directly," I whisper. "He's going to be expecting me anyway; there's no point springing a surprise ambush if it isn't a surprise."

Bo nods in agreement. When everyone's in position, she signals for us to go, so we step out from the cover of the forest's undergrowth.

Victor's body convulses, cracking and spasming as if his bones are breaking. His eyes glaze black, as does the vein that trails from his temple. He lurches forward, then snaps back, his chest cracking open. I scream and stagger back as a dozen creatures spring from his ribs, bald purple veins crisscrossing their skin. The creatures' mouths hang low, detached hollow jowls that gape like cave mouths. They howl the sounds of death and Imbalance at us. I've seen these creatures before. They're lost soul demons infected with Alteritus. They land on the floor, scuttling and scurrying toward us like insects. Victor shakes himself down, his chest knitting back together.

Bo barks out a series of commands. The Six charge out of the bushes and into action. Biting, swiping, and attacking the creatures. I run at Victor, launching a fireball right at his torso. He laughs, batting it away with a wave of water, taunting me with his new ability to control my powers. But I now know it's not his ability; it's the Last Fallon. I close on him. Twenty feet. Ten feet. Five feet. Something slams into my back making me stumble to the floor and smack my shoulder on a stray log. I yelp as blood oozes down my top. The demon creature is on top of me, its mouth swinging just above my chin. Black drool spills over the side of its lips and drops onto my neck causing me to gag. Its head kicks back, shrieking, but I'm not sure if it's in delight or anger. I don't care. I reach up, clasp my hands around its clammy neck, and squeeze. I shove it onto its back and ignite my hands. Not with electricity but with fire. The dead burn like gasoline.

When the creature is still, and dead again, I climb off and run to Trey's side. He's battling two lost soul demons and Victor is right behind him. I skid to his side and fling fire at the creatures. I kick one in the head, and it scrambles away.

Bo's blond ponytail flies across my periphery as her body is launched skyward and lands in a bush. I freeze. Waiting. A second later her wolf form bounds out of the bush, howling, her fangs bared as she lunges for the creature that hurt her and sinks her teeth into its neck. Delphine roars and tramples on another creature, breaking its neck. Then she reaches down and tears its head off for good measure. She really is cold-hearted.

In the seconds I was distracted watching Bo, Victor's pulled his clawed hand back ready to strike Trey. I shout Trey's name, launching a fireball at the creature he's fighting and another one at Victor, but his name is lost in the chaos. He's too preoccupied attacking one of the demons and doesn't see Victor's hand as it swipes through his side, splitting his skin, spraying all of us with blood and chunks of skin and bone. Trey spins round and tumbles forward, dropping to the ground. Lying motionless.

I scream. A deep guttural cry rips through my chest as all my fears about my dreams manifesting come true.

My vault snaps open.

A maroon gloss colors over my vision, and my body fills with Imbalance. Lightning covers my hands, and feet, and spins in loops around my chest as if it's going to encase me.

Words form in my mind. *Kill him. Destroy his soul.* And I want to. I want to hurt him for everything he's done. I launch pulses of lightning at him, mindlessly firing, and with each shot, Bo bellows 'no' at me and runs full pelt toward us. My arm rises like a zombie, electricity throbbing around it, ready to stop her from getting in my way.

Angus, Obert, and Markov are all behind Victor now. He's hemmed in. A trail of demon corpses litters the forest floor. But he's surrounded. His fate is sealed, yet still, I want to end him.

The lightning builds, throbbing harder and faster until both my legs and lower body are encased. I pull back my arm ready to throw every bolt I have at him when Bo's voice cuts through me.

"Trey's still alive."

It's enough to slice through everything: the noise, the electricity: and the rage. My eyes skirt to Trey's body; he's on his back, a pained expression carving deep lines into his face.

He is alive.

In one groan from his mouth, all my energy is sapped.

Angus, Obert, and Markov all dive on top of Victor pinning him to the ground, allowing Delphine to straddle him and Bo to shove Faraday cuffs over his hands, legs, and torso. As the Faraday helmet is attached, Victor's face slackens with relief, as if whatever magic was controlling him has dissipated.

"Is Trey okay?" Bo shouts.

"He's alive, for now," I say, touching his cheek and tearing the rest of his top open to see a gash that's pumping blood out.

"I'm taking Victor straight to Datch. I'll contact Arden, but you need to get Charlie, now. He can save Trey."

I nod, and Bo, Delphine, and the rest of The Six, drag Victor into the forest. I'm left with Trey.

"It's going to be okay," I say, cradling him. But his skin is sweaty and pale. A pool of blood has stained the leaves underneath him.

"You can't die on me. I mean it, Trey. Do not die."

His hand reaches up to my cheek; he splutters out words I can't understand, which makes blood taint his lips. Then his body falls limp in my arms.

TWENTY-FIVE

'The strangeness of the Dryads is acute. Born of the soil, they evolved as the lands evolved, wielding earth magic and the raw power of Trutinor. While they are Keepers in part, they are also something more. They are also the manifestation of Trutinor itself.'

Excerpt - The Book of Balance

My hands drop to the earth; I bury them as deep as the leaves and mud will allow, my fingers pushing past twigs and pebbles as I channel power through the wet undergrowth. I push my essence through the ground until I reach a tree root. Dryads are all connected, meshed by earth and nature and a web of intertwined tree roots. But finding Charlie somewhere across thousands of acres of forest is going to be impossible. I shake the thought away. I can't give up. I have to try. He can't die in my arms. That thought makes a sob burst from my chest, and giant tears fall down my cheeks. *Get a grip, Eden, there isn't time.*

I curl my fingers around the largest root I can feel and concentrate.

Charlie? I need you. Come to the Pink Lake. Trey's dying. I funnel the message over and over again through the earth and rock and tree roots, pushing the message deep into the forest, stretching my essence until my head feels like it will crack open. Pressure builds in my head making blood ooze from my nose, but I don't care. I will not let him die. I throw even more energy through the ground, pumping everything I have until my vision speckles with static, and I think I might pass out. My essence smacks into a something hard: Charlie. The power I funneled through the earth reverses, surging back toward me. I pull my hands out, backing away from the vibrating earth, and with what little strength I have left, I drag Trey a few feet away just as the ground splinters and breaks open.

Roots twist and entwine, wrapping and knotting into a physical form. I've only ever seen this done once before. Dryads don't move like this often, it requires too much energy.

"What happened?" Charlie asks, pushing his leafy root-locks behind his ear. His brown bark-skin is paler than usual, probably a consequence of the extreme travel.

"Victor. He took Nyx. Now Trey's cut." I'm babbling, full of panic. I take a deep breath as a fresh wave of tears spill down my cheeks. "Victor's claw sliced through Trey's side, and I think it's nicked his lung." I glance down at Trey, my body trembling as I survey his injuries. His breathing is shallow, his figure limp, bubbles of red rising up and out of his mouth.

"Charlie, please," I say, gripping his barky arms, "you have to save him."

Charlie nods; he cracks his feet, severing his connection to the roots so he can move and places his hand over the ground. Several roots fly up from the earth, matting together to form a stretcher, which slides under Trey and then rises until it hovers in the air. Three roots join the stretcher to the ground, and as Charlie moves, so too, do the roots, swapping and knitting back together as new ones join and old branches part, making the stretcher appear like a flying carpet.

Charlie is the chief medical Dryad and was my parents' doctor. He's treated my family my entire life. If anyone can save Trey, it's him.

"You need to take this," Charlie says. His hand buckles and cracks as it reforms in the shape of a wooden flask. I take it, but the sound of his wrist breaking off makes me nauseous. His palm and fingers regrow in seconds, but the queasy sensation in my gut doesn't leave.

"Fill it with lake water. I hope you remember basic sorcery," he says. Gather three heads of the Icarus plant, two Farnbush stems, a dozen Izzenberries, and five Jinxbur petals. Got it?"

"Icarus, Farnbush, Izzenberries, and Jinxbur," I repeat.

"Good, there's a cabin about three hundred meters up on the right side of the lake. Meet me there."

"Okay," I say, and take one final look at Trey before tearing myself away and sprinting to the lake shore. Behind me, the snap, rustle, and whoosh of Charlie and Trey racing across the undergrowth toward the cabin urges me on. I fill the flask, pick the roots and stems, and then have a minor panic when I can't remember what Jinxbur looks like. A quick CogTracker search shows me an image, and I gather the rest of the items Charlie wanted. Once I have everything, I sprint, as hard as I can, around the waterside toward the cabin.

Memories of the nights Trey and I spent here staring up at twinkling skies, hand in hand, rush into focus. Tears prickle my eyes as I remember our first kiss. Barely able to catch my breath, I force myself to run faster, until, finally, I reach the cabin, panting and sweating. I wrench open the door, to find Charlie bent over Trey. His brow is wrinkled.

"Don't you give up on me, Charlie, don't you let him die. Do you hear me?" I shout.

"I'm trying, Eden. I'm trying. Pass me the water and the berries."

Trey is lying on a wooden bed, the fabric beneath him an alarming shade of red. Charlie's hands work fast, multiple branches twisting and undulating over Trey's body until Charlie looks more like he has six hands and not two. He waves his root-like palm over Trey's wound, a shimmering light emanating from his palm. In response, Trey's muscle and sinew knit together. Charlie takes the Izzenberries I picked and crushes them against the Jinxbur. He reaches for a silvery powder in a jar on a shelf above the bed and pours the two into the flask of lake water, adding the Farnbush and Icarus. Then he shakes it and undoes the lid pouring some of the liquid into the wound.

Trey's body jolts upright. He lets out a cry that makes my skin crawl, before he drops back again, unconscious.

"Good," Charlie says, "that's very good."

"Is it?" I wonder how any cry like that can be a good thing.

Charlie continues to wave his hand over Trey's ribs until there are three long red, weeping wounds stitched together. He chooses three root-locks on his head and plucks a selection of leaves from them, crushing some of the silver-berry powder mixture in. Once the leaves have matted into a gauze, he applies it to Trey's ribs and ushers me closer.

"Up you get," he says.

"Up?"

"Yes, up. On the bed. You need to keep pressure applied to the gauze."

"Umm, okay. Is he going to be okay?"

Charlie glances up at me, "I hope so."

"Hope?" my chest tightens. My gaze hovers between Charlie and Trey. I thought if I got Charlie here, everything would be okay. His breathing has normalized, his color is returning – I don't understand how Charlie can only 'hope so.'

"We will know more in the next hour," Charlie says, patting my forearm. "He will be unconscious for the time being so he can heal properly. When he comes to, he will be sore."

"And if he doesn't come to?"

"If an hour passes and he doesn't become conscious, then you need to summon me again. This time, use the tree lines," he says, nodding to a wooden CogTracker shaped device hanging on the cabin wall.

"Okay," I say, as I clamber up the bed and straddle Trey, placing my hands over the gauze as Charlie pulls his away.

Fear grips my entire body like a vice. Trey has to survive. He has too.

"Hey," Charlie says, frowning at me. He touches my arm, "Trey's strong. He's lucky he's a Fallon."

The vice loosens a fraction, and I lean down and pop a kiss on Charlie's cheek. "Thank you," I say, "thank you for traveling like that and saving him. I know it's dangerous for you."

He nods, and gives me a soft smile. "It was an honor," he says, and then the door clicks shut, leaving me alone straddling a half-naked, unconscious Trey.

The next hour crawls by in a slew of anxiety, tears, and occasionally relief when Trey radiates a brief wave of emotion out, and I think he might wake up this time. With each wave, I close my eyes, savoring the knowledge that he's alive and getting closer to consciousness.

He slips into a slow steady breathing pattern. I torture myself, re-running the fight in my mind over and over again, picking out my mistakes, trying to figure out how I could have stopped Victor attacking Trey, until I'm so confused and anxious I want to scream.

I take a deep breath and focus on my surroundings instead. Hanging from the ceiling is a candlelit chandelier made of antlers that seem to sparkle. The bed we're lying in is enormous, much bigger than Trey's in Siren City. Four living tree trunks make the corners of the bed; they pierce the cabin floor and impale the ceiling, then a mesh of thick branches just off to make the base frame. The cabin seems to be built around the trees themselves. The walls are woven from living branches and twigs. Like everything in the Ancient Forest, it's connected, one part of a sentient whole. Silver silk drapes hang at each corner of the bed and in the left-hand corner of the room is a door to what I assume is the bathroom. On the right is another room, which I think is to the kitchen. Despite the horrific circumstances, the cabin is seriously romantic.

Trey's bare chest rises and falls, his muscles twitching and contracting as he flits through a listless healing sleep. I tear my eyes away from the ridges and dips of his abs, choosing to look at the walls and branches instead. I don't know why I'm struggling to look at him; it's not like his string vests ever cover his body. But even though we're alone, and no one's looking, and I'm Bound to him, I still blush.

After straddling him for almost forty-five minutes, applying pressure, my back aches so much I can't take it anymore. Holding my hand on his ribs, I slump down onto his chest and roll next to him, nuzzling in under his arm. I hope the wound is almost healed now, but he's not awake, and I don't want to take the risk, so I push a little more pressure on my hand. I rest my other one against the bare skin of his stomach, which makes my cheeks glow. I scold myself for finding him so attractive at such an inappropriate moment. But my clothes are torn, bloody, and hanging half off; he's practically naked, and we're alone for miles in a beautiful cabin next to the Pink Lake…The lake where we shared our first kiss.

A hand comes up and strokes my wavy bloodied hair away from my face. "Almost déjà vu," he says, smiling. "Last time you were in the bed, and I was looking after you."

"You're awake," I say, and before I know what I'm doing, I'm crying all over again, my body shaking with relief. "Thank the Balance. Thank the Balance," I keep saying to myself.

"Eden," he says, bringing my chin up, "It's okay. I'm fine. Look at me." He frowns, "What happened to your face?"

"My face?" I let go of his gauze and wipe my hand over my cheek. Crispy flakes of blood peel away from my nose and mouth. "Oh, that. Yeah, I'm fine. It was nothing. A little overexertion is all."

"Are you sure?" he says, pulling my face this way and that to check me.

"Trey, you nearly died. I had a nosebleed. It was nothing."

"Okay, good. Because I want a shower," he says, pushing himself up.

"Careful, you still have a few minutes left before Charlie said you'd be fully healed."

"I'm already healed," he says, grimacing as he pulls the leafy gauze off his ribs, "three more scars to add to my collection." He laughs. But I don't laugh because he nearly lost his life, and I haven't quite recovered yet.

The three claw wounds have knitted back together leaving neat red scars over his ribs which, even as I stare at them, are fading to white.

"Okay. But slowly."

He leans on me as I help him down from the bed; his legs wobble at first, but he adjusts himself, and after a couple of steps, he doesn't need my arm anymore. I watch him for a few more steps, but he seems fine, so I set about removing the bloodstained covers and throwing some new blankets on the bed. When I'm done, the patter-patter-splash of the shower running fills the bedroom. I turn around realizing the bathroom door is wide open, and Trey is staring at me, "Would you like to join me?"

I glance around the room as if he's summoning someone else. "But you're injured," I say, acutely aware that we're alone, in a romantic cabin, next to the Pink Lake and that my breath is suddenly very short.

"Then I guess I need a nurse to help me shower," he says, his eyes glimmering at me. *Oh God, oh God, oh God.* I bite my lip, trying to control the explosion of butterflies in my stomach. I take two tentative steps forward, then a third, then I'm in the bathroom, and this time he shuts the door behind me. The thought of what we're about to do, and where his hands are going to touch, makes my skin tingle with electricity and my brain go into overdrive.

He peels off the remnants of my bloodstained t-shirt, leaving me in my bra. Then he stares into my eyes as if checking for permission, or perhaps he's reading my emotions. If he is, he'll know how much I want him. How much I want this. But he'll also see the conflict.

His hands reach for my fatigues and he unbuckles them, making them fall to the ground. He unfastens his trousers, and they fall away too, discarded. We stand in our underwear, our clothing abandoned in a pile by our feet. He pauses, looks at me, and I nod. So he pulls me into his arms, reaches behind me, and unhooks my bra. I slip off my underwear, and so does he. We're naked, bruised, and covered in blood, but all I can think is how beautiful his body is and how grateful I am he's alive. He steps into the shower and reaches back to pull me in with him.

The warm water soaks away the dirt and blood while we rotate in and out of the water in silence. Our eyes roam each other's skin, learning where the bumps and dips curve around our bodies, the scars that mark our skin, and exploring the parts we haven't seen yet. He pulls a loofah off the shower shelf and pours liquid soap onto it. He lathers my arms, stomach, and eventually my chest and then hands me the loofah so I can do the same.

I thought I'd feel awkward being naked. But the softness in his eyes, and the warmth he's radiating makes the anxiety wash away with the dirt.

"You're beautiful," he says, and then his lips are on mine,

our skin and bodies gliding together under the warm soapy shower. His arms slide around my waist pulling me in close so that my kiss never leaves his mouth.

I remember his wound and pull away, "Wait. Stop. Seriously, Trey, are your ribs okay? I don't want to do any more damage."

He leans into my neck, smiling and kissing me, "Does it look like they're bothering me?"

It doesn't. So I shut up and kiss him back. He gathers me into his arms and carries me out of the shower, grabbing towels and wrapping them around us, putting us in a fluffy cocoon. As he lays me on the bed, I get a pang of nerves that fill my stomach with a hundred bubbling knots.

His eyes widen. "Are you okay?" he asks, sensing my nerves.

"Of course," I nod, pressing my lips shut. *Liar.*

His eyebrows pinch. We both know I'm lying. Bloody Siren abilities.

"We don't have to..."

"No. It's not that. I want to." *Truth.*

"Then...What?"

"Just..." Pink dapples my cheeks.

"Don't leave me," I choke out. Tears sting my eyes all over again, but I force them back down. Now is not the time for tears.

"Leave you?" he's almost laughing, "Eden, we're Bound, and I'm madly in love with you. Why on earth would I..."

I reach out and touch his ribs, making him falter.

"Oh," he says.

"I thought..."

"Your dreams?"

I nod. "I thought that was it. Especially after the sky this morning. I thought... Just don't leave me."

"We all die eventually," he says.

"I know. But I've lost so many people already. I can't lose you; I've only just got you. I want to keep you for a while."

He grins and places a soft kiss on my hand, pulling me closer and dropping petal-like caresses all the way up my arm, over my shoulder, and up my neck until his forehead rests on mine, "You can keep me for all the lifetimes."

I smile, and he lays me down on the pillows, kissing me, slow, gentle, and loving. He moves down my neck and over my chest, making a soft moan escape as his lips brush over my breasts. Then his hand slides down my leg. He kisses me again, his hands brushing against my stomach and thighs, leaving warm trails of essence and energy in his wake. Somewhere in the jumble of our bodies, we end up under the covers. The remaining piece of his Siren guard drops, and I'm hit with wave after wave of his emotions; the intensity makes me gasp, the longing, the urgency. I pull him up toward my mouth, our lips skimming each other in hot wet kisses.

"I'm ready," I whisper into his ear, as my fingers thread through locks of his hair.

"I love you," he says, and then he's inside me.

I bite down on my lip. For a moment, it hurts. Not unbearable but not what I was expecting either. Eventually, our bodies move as one, the pain disappearing, replaced with sensations I've not felt before. We create a rhythm, sliding together, like the waves and the ocean: two parts of the same whole.

I smile into his kiss, feeling complete, happy, loved. He is mine, and I am his... In all our lifetimes.

TWENTY-SIX

'Long has the debate raged over the differences between Mermaids and Sirens. Let me put this debate to bed. Mermaids and Sirens are not the same, neither in physicality nor power.

Simply, Sirens can manipulate and control (emphasis mine) a single emotion (exception – a Siren Fallon). A Siren will, by force, remove a person's free will over control of said emotion.

Mermaids, however, have the power of seduction. They will call and woo the mind to them until a person is desperate to give control of themselves over to the Mermaid. Both are highly dangerous and extremely proficient in the art of manipulation and control.'

Professor Vindros, Excerpt - Essays of the Lost Race, 1908

I lie there, wrapped in Trey's strong arms, drifting in and out of fitful sleep. I'm safe, warm, loved, yet there's an unrelenting nag in my gut that something is wrong. Fear is spreading through my system like a virus. A parasite filling my cells and consuming my body. Right now, at this moment, everything is perfect, and yet outside this cabin, everything else is falling apart. Nyx is still missing, Trutinor is sick, and I'm terrified my dreams are coming true.

I know what happens when I close my eyes: Trey dies. No matter what he or Sheridan say to reassure me, I'm living with these nightmares.

I lean over and grab my CogTracker. In the mayhem of capturing Victor, I never told Arden about my dreams and the connection to the maroon streak in the sky. The time reads 2AM. I decide to send Arden a CogMail anyway.

From: Eden.East@FallonCogMail.com
Subject: We need to talk
To: Arden.Winkworth@FallonCogMail.com

Arden,
In the chaos of yesterday, I didn't get a chance to talk to you properly. But I think we have a problem. I've been having quite intense nightmares, visions if you like, of Trutinor ending up in one of two ways:

Either it dies, like literally the world crumbles and decays, or it ends up in this strange whitewashed world where

everyone's silent and zombie-like. In all my dreams,
Trey dies.

I went to see a dream Keeper. Initially, she said because I'm
not a scryer, I can't be using scrying abilities to predict or
see the future. But since then she's found a case of two
twins who predicted the Siren-Mermaid War.

I'm concerned; I've been feeling anomalies in the wind,
then there were the dead plants, and the maroon Imbalance
streak in the sky. Jacobs said eczema, but I think this is
much more serious. What if Trutinor really is dying?

Is there any news on Nyx? Has Victor been questioned? Is
he in Datch? Can you send me his prison cell information?
We'll come to Datch first thing in the morning.

E x

  I put my CogTracker down, but Trey must sense I'm
awake because he pulls me in tight. I snuggle into the crook
of his neck, listening to the soft thud of his heartbeat and the
rhythmic lull of his breathing. After a while, it pulls me into
the darkness of sleep.

We're naked, in bed, his hands caressing my skin, his mouth
moving over my neck and shoulder, electric sparks flickering
off my skin and onto his lips where our bodies meet. I let out
a soft moan as he rolls me over and on top of him. Our
bodies moving in sync together.
  The light trembles, the temperature plummets. Ice

crawls up the walls, freezing the ancient trees that make the walls of our cabin. Trey is clothed, stood with his back against the wall. My hands are around his neck. Sheridan appears, in the corner of the room. I glance at her, unable to call for help. Trey's lips turn blue. He doesn't fight. His eyes are round, sad as he touches my cheek. "One of us has to die," he says.

"No," I scream, "NO."

But no matter how much I fight to pull my hands away my grip on his neck tightens until his blue lips turn gray, and his body sinks to the floor.

I wake, panting, a pool of cold sweat at the back of my neck. There's a rich orange glow coming from the window, the sunrise flirting with the horizon. But the room is cold; morning isn't quite ready to arrive yet. The first chirps of dawn birds whistle through the canopy outside bringing the smell of dew and wet earth. I roll over and touch my hand to Trey's chest; his heart is still beating, once, twice, three times. He takes slow, deep breaths like he's thick with sleep. I kiss his forehead and roll over to reach my CogTracker. It's 4:30AM. I debate sending Sheridan a message at this time of night, but given she saw my dream, I suspect she's awake.

I saw you in my dream. Why did Trey let me kill him this time? I also don't recall him speaking in any of the others? Oh, and there's been more developments. Yesterday morning there was a streak of Imbalance in the sky, I'm sure you

**saw the First Fallon's announcement. But the
streak was like my dreams. I've had to
tell Arden.**

I re-read it quickly and send it. Then I follow it up with
a second message.

**Oh, and I have a bone to pick with you… Don't
suppose you have anything to do with me
meeting a certain Castor Jameson, do you?**

Before I even put the CogTracker down, it vibrates in
my hand.

No idea what you're talking about…

Ha. So it was her. She replies again.

**On a serious note, I am extremely concerned
that the Imbalance has now spread. Based on
the twin case, I'm inclined to think that there is
a prophetic basis to your dreams. Correct me if
I'm wrong, but in your dreams, the deterioration of Trutinor takes some time? That's a good
thing, but all the more reason to do something
now. I think we need to meet to see if we can
figure out what's causing it. Maybe we can halt
the decay, or slow it? There's a method, not
used often, but I might be able to put you into a
forced sleep state to make you dream for a
longer period. It would give us a chance to**

explore your vision. I think I can create a spell to make you lucid so you can control where you go. Give me some time. I'll investigate. S x

You're up late.

Guess you're not the only bad sleeper. Ironic, hey, Eden?

I hate that he told me one of us has to die.

I know.

You know?

No one wants to hear their Balancer say that, but honestly, Eden, I still think Trey's not the prophetic part of your dreams. You just lost your parents, it's natural to be afraid of losing the people you love.

Mmm.

Mmm?

Not convinced.

Am I going to be able to convince you before dawn?

No...

Then, I'm going to take a snooze before Felicia starts snoring again.

Ha! I hear earplugs are a winner. Night, Sheridan. x

I'll get some tomorrow. May your dreams be Balanced, Eden. x

I turn over. Then roll back again and pick up the CogTracker typing out another message to her.

You're such a liar by the way... I knew as soon as I got into the camp it was you.

No comment.

I think you know more about them than you're saying...

Possibly. Maybe. Who knows.

You're not going to tell me?

Not over CogTracker.

Okay. I think I want to know more.

In that case, I think I can tell you more. Night, Eden. X

Night. X

Trey's eyes are wide open looking at me. I jump, and yelp, "Some warning would be nice."

He laughs, then grabs me, and slides me under his body. He kisses me hard and fast, his hands gently tugging through the back of my hair as his mouth wanders over my skin.

"I want you," he whispers into my ear before kissing gently down my neck.

"I'm already yours."

His hand strokes down my thigh before pulling my leg up against his hip. I slide my ankle around his thigh, holding him in place. His eyes burn fiery blue. I reach up to his stubble and pull his head down, so his lips hover above mine.

"Let go of your guard," I say, and as I kiss him, he does. My back arches as a wave of his emotions hit me. It's intense, addictive, and consumes me; his love isn't just strong, it's ferocious.

He draws his mouth over my collarbone, leaving a trail of hot kisses in his wake. I pull him back to my lips, pushing his mouth open so our tongues can slide over each other. Then he moves inside me, and our essences and emotions flow and mingle together with bursts of static and fire I can't help releasing.

When we wake the second time, the room is warm, and light pours in through the cabin windows. I climb out of bed and grab a pile of spare clothes from a shelf and pull on a pair of loose pants and a cotton top that's far too big for me.

Trey rolls over and rubs his face. His hair is a mess, all ruffled and sticking out with stubble appearing. It's adorable.

"Why are you looking at me like that?" he says.

"Because I'm having to force myself not to get undressed and climb back into bed with you."

"Shame. I'd have made it worth your while."

I throw a pair of jeans at him, "Don't tempt me. Get dressed. Come on. We need to interrogate Victor."

Once he's dressed, we raid the kitchen area for some fruit and two quick cups of coffee. I check my CogTracker and find a message from Arden.

From: Arden.Winkworth@FallonCogMail.com
Subject: RE: We need to talk
To: Eden.East@FallonCogMail.com

We'll discuss the dreams and Trutinor's health once we've found Nyx and put a stop to Victor opening The Door of Fates. Several of the Guild Sorcerers are working on the streak. I've sent them and Jacobs back to the Guild to examine the dead plants in more detail and establish where the source is coming from. They're also going to investigate whether there have been any other cases like it in the past.

I'm heading to Datch now. Titus is already there... in a cell. Don't worry, he's fine, and it's only temporary. When he saw Victor being taken into the prison, he lost it and tried to attack him. The Datch guards locked him up for the night until he calmed down. Bo is there too. I've told the guards you're coming. But, umm... The First Fallon is there, and she intends to question Victor. I'd hurry.

See you soon

Arden

"We need to go," I say to Trey, urging us out the door. Trey contacts Magnus who agrees to meet us at the lake's station. On route, I update Trey on everything. The night I spent with Sheridan, the research she's done since, and everything Arden's said. He nods along in agreement as I tell him that the Guild is looking for the source of Imbalance, and finally, I tell him about the forced dream state Sheridan suggested. I go on to explain about last night's dream, how he let me kill him and told me one of us had to die. A flash of hesitation passes across his eyes. Up until now, he's been so dismissive, telling me everything's fine; they're just dreams. But something hovers below the surface of his eyes: fear. For the first time since I had the nightmares, Trey's afraid. And that, more than anything, terrifies me.

TWENTY-SEVEN

> *'Founded in the year 1111, Datch Prison was created to house the most criminally dangerous, insane, and demonic. Legend says the bricks were crafted from the blood of the First Fallon herself, and the doors were made from enchanted crystal wept from the tears of the Last Fallon after she was banished.'*
>
> Excerpt - Myths and Legends of Trutinor

Magnus drops us at Datch station in the early afternoon. The prison itself is on a solitary island one mile out in the Blood Ocean. It's a short walk from the station to the bridge that leads us to the prison. As we reach the edge of the Southern State the wind whips off the sea spraying our cheeks with salt and fishy smelling water. I really hate fish. A bridge looms above us, all sharp lines of crystal and silver.

Towering pillars jut into the sea and up through the sky to form the structural support for the bridge while silvery steel cables stretch like trapeze wires down to the bridge foundations. I slip my hand into Trey's.

"You need to keep control if we're going in there," he says under his breath.

"I know," I say, "of all people, I know that."

"Then why are you squeezing my hand so hard I've got pins and needles?"

"Sorry," I say, glancing down at our hands. "It's just... He nearly killed you..."

"But he didn't."

I glare at Trey, "That's not the point."

"Look," he says, waving our clasped hands, "I'm fine. We're fine, and he's in there."

"I know," I say, and step onto the bridge.

Giant crystal walls protect us on all sides while giving us a view of the ocean underneath. The water froths and spits as if a war rages beneath the surface and if I think about all the creatures lurking below us, there probably is. The Blood Ocean is only good for housing monsters that dwell in the nightmares of the murky seabed. I grip the bridge's railing harder. A shroud of mist billows out from Datch Island, spilling over the bridge and swallowing us into its cloudy cloak. The temperature drops, making me shiver.

We step onto Datch Island; it's so small that the prison complex fills the entire isle. The whole outcrop is made of dark pitted rocks, and the only signs of life are stray seagulls stained red from the ocean.

Three dark brick towers wrapped in layers of electrified barbed wire stand like stone giants in the center of the island. Tiny CogCameras fly through the air, speeding around the building watching for any stray movement. It fills the air with a drone-like hum. A small comfort to know we're safe and watched.

We enter the exterior gates and walk through another area with electrified fencing on both sides. After being searched, scanned, prodded, and rescanned, we're allowed to enter the prison itself. We stand at the base of one of the hollowed out circular towers. In the center of the tower, is a spiral staircase that, if I crane my neck, stretches all the way to the roof. Around the edges of the tower in circular rings are the cells, floor after floor of dank stone cells and crystal doors for bars. Dirty faces of Keepers and strange creatures peer out, all of their eyes straining to stare down at us. It makes my skin shiver.

On one side of the room is Arden, talking to several guards, and on the other side is Bo. She's yanking and pulling at her prosthetic leg.

"Wait here a minute," I say to Trey, "I'm just going to see if Bo's okay."

"I'll go check on Titus if you like?"

"That would be great," I say as I walk over to Bo.

She's mumbling to herself, pulling and shaking the leg. As I reach her, she punches the leg with her fist, and the whirring and clicking grind to a halt. She throws the leg down onto the damp stone flooring where it clatters and rolls to a stop at my feet. That's when I notice there's a bandage around her stump, and it's stained with a yellowy blister colored fluid.

"Are you okay?" I ask, picking up the leg. Her face is cold and hard, and she's not wearing any lipstick; her appearance takes me by surprise. "What's going on?"

"You wouldn't understand," she snaps, and snatches the leg from me.

I frown, taken aback by her sudden anger.

"You, with your perfect life and your perfect Trey. You might've got everything you want, but did you ever stop to think about what you had to take from everyone else to get it?"

What the fuck?

"Hold on a minute, Bo," I say, edging away from her. "My life is far from perfect. I lost my parents."

"Yeah, and I lost my brother because you stole my blood to kill him. Did you really think I could forgive you just like that?"

This time, it's my face that hardens. My eyes darken as the vault twitches in my subconscious. I speak very slowly so as not to mistake a single word. "You knowingly gave my parents your blood so they could commit suicide, Bo. I think that makes us even."

"Does it though? I didn't kill your parents with my bare hands. And you didn't lose a limb trying to protect your Balancer..." At that, her voice cracks and breaks, and I realize this isn't really about Victor or our parents but about how she's coping. All at once my anger disappears. My chest tightens, and I put my head in my hands, my throat thickening with all the things I should have said and done for her. I take a deep breath and look up at her.

"I am so sorry, Bo. I thought you were okay. You came out of the hospital and seemed so strong; you just got on with everything and never asked for help or support. I thought you didn't need me."

"Well, I did. And you should have been there," she spits, but her voice is softening, and the tears trickle down her cheeks. "But maybe I should have asked. And for once, agreeing not to talk about what happened between our families was a dumb idea. I'm responsible for helping to end your parents' lives, and you killed my brother. We can't keep brushing these things under the carpet."

"Please don't walk away from our friendship, Bo, I don't want to lose you too," I say, pleading with her. My voice is small, "We agreed not to talk about it because we didn't want it to affect our friendship."

"That's the thing, Eden; it has affected our friendship."

She affixes the prosthetic leg, wincing as she does, and stands up. She wobbles. I reach out to grab her, but she swats my hand away.

"I need time," she says, and walks to the center of the room, taking the lift, leaving me staring after her.

TWENTY-EIGHT

'Keep your friends close but your enemies closer.'

Michael Corleone, The Godfather II – Human film

From across the circular room, Trey spots Bo stalking off and walks over to me. "What happened?" he asks.

"It doesn't matter," I say, standing up.

"What happened to us not keeping things from each other?"

I look at him. Really? He chooses now to throw my words back at me? All I want to do is talk to Victor and get Nyx back.

"Fine. I think she's been holding on to a lot of things that we probably should have talked about a long time ago and didn't, and now she's angry, and I'm a shitty friend for not having noticed or done something about it."

"It's Bo; I'm sure she'll come around. You guys have been through everything together."

"Have we?" I ask. And when I think about it, I'm not sure if we have anymore. Sure, a lot of things have happened to us, but we haven't spent anywhere near as much time together as we used to. I should have seen how distant we were becoming.

"Of course you have," Trey says, putting his arm around my shoulder. "Are you ready to go?"

We walk half way toward Arden and come to a halt; a flash of the First Fallon's white robes circles the floor above us. She enters the spiral staircase and descends to the ground floor. Her pure white face is set hard, fury burning in her eyes, and those eyes are fixed on me. Trey moves in front of me, sliding me behind his back. As she nears us, Arden stops what he's doing and approaches from behind her, his hand slipping to his wand belt.

"You won't be needing that, Winkworth," the First Fallon says, without looking behind her. "It appears," her jaw flexes with every word, "that even with the most forceful of encouragement, Victor won't talk. In fact, you'll be delighted to know he's requested a conversation with you." She leans in and spits the last word at me, her gaze lingering on mine as an actual flame glints in her eyes.

"I'm not taking it personally, of course. My sister has control of him. Everything is expendable to her. She'd let me rip him into pieces before she let him give me an ounce of information. So I guess you're going to have all the fun torturing him instead of me." The flames burn harder, then as suddenly as they appeared, they disappear, and she moves back. "You'd better get what I need, Eden. Find out what he's done with that bloody lock and key before I tear

Trutinor apart looking. My sister cannot be allowed to return."

I shift on the spot, uncomfortable under her stare. Before I can stop myself the words come tumbling out, "What did Rozalyn do to make you hate her so much?"

Her face, if it's possible, gets even harder. There's a stillness in her cold features that penetrates through to my core. And I'm certain my heart stops beating.

She leans into my face again, her nose millimeters from mine. "Get me what I want," she says, growling, but I'm sure underneath the growl there was a tiny tremor in her voice, "before I tear you apart too."

I give her a silent nod and pray she gets out of my face. There's an explosion of navy smoke that makes me cough and splutter, but it dissipates quickly and when it does, she's gone.

"Are you okay?" Trey asks, tugging me around to face him.

"I'm fine," I say, but I can tell he doesn't believe me. "Honestly. Shall we go?"

"If you're sure," he says, and leads me to the lift, which we take to the thirteenth floor. The metal lift clatters and shakes inside the cage housing it. When we reach the thirteenth floor, I pull the metal cage doors open, and they rattle and click as they slide back. Victor is directly opposite us. We walk around the circular floor, the inmates jeering and hissing as we pass them. One inmate runs at the crystal wall-door separating him from us. He throws his body at it so hard it makes a loud crack and startles me. The Keeper behind the door is flat against it; he's dirty, covered in black stains, and wearing rags. He peels his face back from the door and head-butts it. Over, and over, and over again until the skin on his forehead splits, and blood smears the crystal door. I cover my mouth to stop myself gagging. I hurry past him, giving him one final look; he's still head-butting the crystal, and I realize the black stains aren't dirt but blood. I reach for Trey's arm.

As we reach Victor's cell, I see Bo's hand pressed flat against the glass door. Victor's hand is mirroring hers, on the other side, their foreheads leaning against the glass.

As we come to a stop behind her, she cocks her head to the side then stands straighter. "I should go," she says, "I'll tell Mom and Dad everything you said."

She lingers there, staring up at her brother, him staring down at her, their hands pressed against the crystal in silence, as if they're sharing something we're not party to. The sight of them makes my chest tight. Victor's eyes pinch, and his brow furrows as Bo's knuckles bend up like she's trying to grip his hand through the crystal.

"We can give you a moment if..." I start, my voice as small as it was when we fought. But Bo cuts me off.

"Goodbye, brother," she says, putting two fingers on her lips and pushing them against his heart on the glass. Then she walks away without so much as a backward glance. My breathing is heavy, and it takes me a minute to compose myself enough to speak.

Victor's wearing slim fitting leather trousers, a maroon red top, and a leather jacket over the top.

"Victor," I say, when I've calmed myself down.

Victor whistles, long, slow, and irritatingly loud, "Boy, you reaaaally pissed her off."

I glare at him.

"Oooh," he says, shaking himself, "I can just feel the tension. Super awkward." He practically sings the last word.

"I see you took your asshole pills."

He shrugs and juts his chin out as if he's proud of the fact.

"And to think you wanted my help."

At that, his face falls, and he holds out his hand. "Ah, well, yes," he says, "I mean, I was only joking of course."

"So you do still want my help?"

"Believe me when I tell you, it would be better for all of us if you did help me."

"Where's Nyx?"

"About that..."

"VICTOR."

"Fine, fine," he says, putting both his hands up in defense. "She's safe, I promise."

Trey moves from behind me, "How safe?"

"Safe. Swearzees."

Trey looks over the guardrail down to the ground floor, "We don't have long alone with you, so if you want something you had better spit it out and tell us exactly where Nyx is."

"I want you to get Karva out of Obex and into Trutinor," he says, giving me an intense expression.

My eyes narrow. "How are you able to talk openly now?" I say, glancing at the vein on his temple. It's still there, still maroon, still full of the Last Fallon's magic, but now it's unnaturally still.

"Because, moron, these are Faraday cages – even Rozalyn's magic can't penetrate them."

"Why would we bring Karva back when she's been dead for thousands of years?" Trey asks, frowning at Victor.

"I'm sorry, would you rather Rozalyn came back for a spot of Trutinor-shaped redecoration?" he says, with a single eyebrow raised.

"Answer the question," I snap.

"Because if you want to stand any chance of taking the First Fallon out, then you're going to need Karva."

"Karva?" Trey says, his frown deepening.

"But the First Fallon is Karva's mother. Why would she help us defeat her own flesh and blood?"

Victor places both hands on the crystal wall leaning so close his pointed nose touches the crystal.

"What kind of mother has the power to save her child and yet chooses to leave her in hell?"

At this, both Trey and I fall silent. There's an intensity to Victor's eyes, a raging darkness. I know that look; he stared at me with the same hatred before we fought, and it makes me wonder why he feels so strongly. It's not like he's ever cared about me or the prophecy or defeating the First Fallon.

"What's Karva to you?" I ask, "why are you helping her?"

He hesitates, just long enough to confirm my suspicion. He stands straight, moving a step back into his cell, and when he talks, his eyes look everywhere but at me.

"She says she can bring me back to life. If she's in Trutinor, she has access to particular magics that can give me my life back."

"No," I say, "no, that's not it. You have feelings for her, don't you?"

His jawline flexes, just once. Bingo. I've hit a nerve.

"That's irrelevant."

"Aww, Victor's in love," I say, "if it weren't necrophilia it would almost be sweet."

He glares at me, "Are you going to help or not?"

"Not," I say, folding my arms.

But Trey says, "Let's hear the guy out. What exactly do we have to do?"

"I'm glad you asked," he says, a wry smile peeling across his yellow teeth. He comes right up to the crystal wall, his eyes glinting, "First, you break me out of here."

TWENTY-NINE

'All warfare is based on deception.
Hence, when we are able to attack, we
must seem unable; when using our
forces, we must appear inactive; when we
are near, we must make the enemy
believe we are far away; when far away,
we must make him believe we are near.'

Sun Tzu - Chinese General, Strategist, Human

"Is that a joke?" I say, turning to Trey, "he's joking, right?"

Trey looks from Victor to me and gives me a grimace. *Dammit.*

"Are you out of your fucking mind, Victor? I'm not breaking you out of prison. This is Datch, not Keepers School. How the hell do you expect us to get you off the island?"

"I'll worry about getting us off the island. You just need to break me out of the cell."

"What, so the Last Fallon can own your ass again? Yeah, I don't think so."

He rolls his eyes at me, walks to the back of the cell and returns holding a pair of Faraday handcuffs, "I'll wear these. She won't be able to touch me."

"And then what? I just let you roam around Trutinor, all dead and lovesick?"

Trey pulls me closer, lifts my arm up from the elbow, and says, "I think you need to calm down."

My fist is engulfed in white-hot flames. I shake my hand until the flames extinguish.

Victor folds his arms, his expression hard and serious, "The way I see it, you have two choices: break me out and give yourself the opportunity to form an alliance with someone who is strong enough to take the First Fallon down. Or, you can leave me in here, walk away now, and let your family pet starve to death."

I see red. My fist balls, electricity pulses around my hand, and I punch the crystal wall smack where Victor's head is. He doesn't even flinch. He just smiles. Knowing he's already won. I scream a stream of profanities at him in my head before pulling my fist off the crystal and gritting my teeth.

"Fine," I spit. "But I hope you have a damn good plan."

"You're so dramatic, Eden," Victor says, "I told you, just get me out of the cell, and I'll do the rest."

"And how exactly do you propose I get you out of the cell?"

Trey whips out his CogTracker. "I have an idea," he says, and dials out. It takes four rings before the caller picks up, and when their face appears on screen, a grin appears on mine.

"Let me guess," Kato says, "you got yourself arrested, and now you need me to break you out of jail."

"How did you guess?" I say, my face now devoid of emotion.

"What? I was joking. What's going on?" Kato asks, his voice rising.

"It's not us you need to break out," Trey says, and then moves to the side so he can point the CogTracker screen at the cell door.

Victor waves. "Cooey," he says, and winks. *Dick.*

"You're joking?" Kato says.

"Not even slightly," I say.

"Let me get this straight," Kato says, shaking his blond mop. "You want me to break out the guy we L.I.T.E.R.A.L.L.Y just put in there?"

I nod.

Kato's eyes skirt down to the bottom of the screen and a message pops up. From him.

Be careful, I traced the network hacks of both the FF and Victor. It originated from the same place. What if he's playing you?

I type back quick.

We don't have a choice. He has Nyx. This is the price to get her back.

"Okay, so you want me to illegally hack into one of the most secure systems in Trutinor? Which, might I add, no one has successfully done yet, isolate a single cell door in amongst...oooh, at least three hundred, and then override the locking mechanism to release the door?"

Trey shrugs, "Basically."

"Next time lead with that. You know I can't resist a challenge. Give me a few minutes."

"A few? I thought you said no one had successfully hacked it yet," I say.

"I did. But those hackers are nothing more than rookie idiots, and I'm a genius. Your words, not mine. What cell is he in?"

"13G," Trey says.

"Consider it done," he says, winking, and the CogTracker goes black.

"Cuffs on," Trey says to Victor, as he puts his CogTracker away. Victor obliges.

"If you so much as sneeze the wrong way, I'm going to soul death you faster than you can shift into a puppy."

"Oh please," he sneers, "you have neither the skill nor the balls to soul death me."

I give him a sharp stare, "Wanna test that theory out?"

His teeth clamp shut, and instead of giving me a snarky quip, he says, "Not today."

He must have serious feelings for Karva if he's not going to argue with me. A couple of minutes later, Trey's CogTracker rings. He flips open the screen, and Kato's face appears. His expression is tight, the arrogance from earlier gone.

"There's good news and bad news," he says.

"Good first," Trey says.

"I can unlock the cell door."

"And the bad?"

"Out of curiosity, I looked at the schematics for the

Datch alarm systems. I'm glad I did. I realize now why no one else has successfully broken anyone out. The doors are rigged. You have to be in the onsite control room to release a cell door; otherwise, it triggers an alarm."

"Can you override it?" Trey asks.

"Not without planting a virus, and if I do that, it will override the whole door system, and rather than opening one door, it will open them all."

"How long do we have?" Victor says.

"The first ten seconds is a silent alarm. After that, it will ring through the prison. At most you'll have thirty seconds before a guard is on you."

"Thirty seconds?" I say. "Great. That's just fantastic. How does thirty seconds fit with your grand plan, Victor?"

"Now, now, Eden, dial down the sarcasm."

"Can you do it or not?"

"More or less."

"You're going to need to elaborate on the detail."

"Can't do that."

"Then I can't let you out."

Trey steps closer to me. "Maybe we can find Nyx without him," he says.

"Sure you're willing to take that risk?" Victor asks. "Look. You've got no reason to believe me; I get that. But you need me to help you find Nyx. And if you don't believe that I want to help you, then believe that I need you to help me escape so I can get what I want."

I falter; as much as I hate it, he has a point. The fact he's only helping us, so he gets what he wants, makes me much more comfortable that he'll deliver.

"Eden...? Just think about it..." Trey says.

But I've already made my mind up.

"Do it, Kato. Release the cell door."

"Good luck," he says. A low buzzing hum reverberates from the crystal door, then a click that sounds more like the slap of a wet hand against skin, and the door slides open.

Victor's eyes close, and his head leans back, a smile forming on his lips. For a second I think he's going to make a run for it. But he steps out, and his eyes lock onto mine. "Handcuffs," he says, holding his hands up to me.

My eyebrows knit together, "Not a chance."

"That wasn't part of the deal," Trey says.

"If we take them off, Rozalyn will know where you are and have total control of you."

"Ten seconds," Trey says.

An ear-shattering screech rings out through the tower. The piercing ring echoes around the circular tower, making me clutch my ears. In my periphery, there's a scuffle; I lean over the guardrail and spot four guards and Arden racing across the ground floor toward the stairs.

"Dammit. There's no time to argue. Give me your hands. Trey, help me."

Each of us takes one of Victor's hands; we pull them up and smash the cuffs against the railing. Victor yelps and gives me a filthy stare.

"Again," I shout.

We smash them again. Nothing. Trey's eyes latch on mine, the same panic filling them as my chest.

"Again."

This time the handcuffs click open and drop to the floor. A guard appears at the top of the stairs, followed by Arden. The guard looks from Victor to us and raises a baton. Victor grabs us both and pushes us against the railing.

"Oi," the guard bellows at us. "What the hell do you think you're doing?"

The guard stops at the top of the stairs; his body plummets to the ground and billows back upward as he reappears as an enormous brown buffalo. His head of curling horns dips. Then he charges.

My eyes widen as I grip Victor's arm, "You'd better have a plan."

"I do," he says, "climb up, both of you."

"Climb up? Onto the railing? Are you insane? We'll fall."

"Do you trust me?" Victor asks.

"No."

"Good," he says, as the three of us clamber up and hold onto each other. "Jump anyway."

The buffalo's hooves pound the floor; it sees us on the railing and makes a low grunting sound that rumbles around us.

"Eden, what are you doing?" Arden bellows from several feet behind the buffalo.

Victor, Trey, and I cling to each other. My fingers dig into Victor's waist, and even through his clothes, he's cold to touch. From behind him, enormous black wings unfurl. Boney spurs, sharpened to spikes, angle down toward me with an ominous point.

"Victor, hurry," I say, panic rising in my voice.

The buffalo is thirty feet. Twenty feet. Ten feet.

"Ready?" Victor says.

"No," Trey and I answer simultaneously.

"Excellent," he says, and we leap off the railing and plummet to the ground floor. Victor's wings wrap around us until they touch our skin, and then there's crushing darkness.

THIRTY

'Legend says that when Karva died, Rozalyn tortured her. Not the physical torture many experience at the hands of the Imbalanced. But a darker, more twisted torture, formed from the revenge that fuels Rozalyn's soul. It is said that she held the source of Karva's ability in her hands. She dug her nails into Karva's heart and squeezed. Slicing through the muscle and sinew, to feed a blackened poison into her soul, all the while whispering tales of the dead, broken, and vengeful.'

Excerpt - *Myths and Legends of Trutinor*

We plummet into a thick choking blackness that makes my body feel like it's being pulverized in a blender, and I wonder if this is what it's like to shapeshift. Despite the body compression, there are no other sensations. No sound, no touch, nothingness. I panic, my neck bristling. Are we dead? I imagine my body back in the prison lying broken and twisted, Victor standing over me laughing. As soon as I think it, there's a rushing sensation like the wind blowing through my hair and Trey, Victor, and I are spat out of the darkness and collapse onto cobblestones.

I lie there, my cheek pressing into the cold stone pavement, my body decompressing. Once my breathing returns to normal, I push myself up. As I pick my hands up off the cobbles, I notice they were in a wet patch; not rain, blood. Then I look up, and my anger bubbles through my body.

"You brought us to Obex?" I shout, "I thought you were taking us back to the mainland so we could make a plan."

"You know what they say about assumption," Victor laughs, the corner of his lip curling. "It's the mother of all f..."

I'm on my feet. I scramble over Trey and swing for Victor, punching him clean in the jaw.

He's still laughing So I punch him again, harder. The familiar rumble of my vault cracking rattles through my head. Trey's hand clasps my arm. "Not here," he says, "do not let it crack down here."

Victor spits black blood over the cobbles, then glares at me, "Are you quite finished?"

"You son of a bitch. Do those wings get us back out of here?"

"Not exactly."

"Then how the hell are we getting back to Trutinor without a train? We're here with no backup, no help, nothing. What do you expect us to do? Break Karva out with smiles and sarcasm?"

"Something like that," he says.

Obex's skyline is a fiery shade of burnt orange. Gray and black clouds streak the sky like tiger stripes. But then I notice a line in the sky, a baby blue slice that cuts through the twilight shades and makes me falter.

"It's the same as the one in Trutinor," I breathe, "like the sky is inverting."

"What do you think it means?" Trey asks.

"I have no idea."

The hue of the sky makes the street feel like a sepia photograph; to our left and right are several story high townhouses in shades of faded creams and whites. Black iron railings picket the front of the houses and the entire block is quiet, abandoned almost. Even the air is thick with inertia. Like the first time I was here, it reminds me of Victorian London, as if someone picked up half the city and dropped it into Obex.

"Are you coming?" Victor says, his black wings retracting into his back.

"Where are we going now?" Trey asks.

"To find Karva. No time like the present."

"You'd better have a plan to get us out of here, Victor," I snarl. "And as soon as we get Karva, you're taking us straight to Nyx."

"With pleasure," he says, his eyes narrowing. There's a glint of something that makes my gut clench with nerves rather than reassurance. I don't trust him.

We walk the streets of Obex, Victor in the lead, Trey and I behind. I stick close to Trey, my hand wedged inside his, my grip tightening every time the shadows move and judder with things I can't see. That's what Hermia said last time we were here; it's not the demonic creatures you can see you need to worry about but the things just out of sight that are the most dangerous.

We walk down street after street of tall townhouses with iron railings and silent pavements, curtains in ground floor windows twitching as nosy faces slide out of sight. We pass three parks, each one filled with human rocks that make me cringe. They're not rocks, of course. I just thought they were last time we were here. They're the lost soul demons that sprung out of Victor's body at the Pink Lake, all bald and jowly and veiny.

Every street looks identical. I'm convinced we're walking in circles until we pull into the next lane, and it's a dead end. It has the same rows of townhouses on either side in a mosaic of creams, but at the end is a house in the middle facing us.

"We're here," Victor says, and for the first time, there's no hint of sarcasm or hate in his voice, just happiness, and it takes me a second to process.

We approach the house facing us; it's white, milk-white like the face of the First Fallon, and something about it makes me uneasy. The wrought iron railings are higher than the other houses, and instead of balls at the tips, there are spikes. There's a strange smell lingering around the house, like the cold slick of fear tipped on a metal blade.

"I'm not sure about this," I say as Victor's hand pushes the gate open.

"Get a grip, East; I live here. It's fine."

I look over my shoulder, checking to see if we're being watched. The pit of my stomach is screaming at me like the desperate scratch of fingernails down a prison wall. Before I can protest, I'm hustled inside the house, and the door is slammed shut.

We're in a white hallway. Everything is the color of

bone and ivory. The walls, the furniture, even the photos and their frames. It reminds me of my whitewash dreams, and it sends a chill crawling down my spine like the delicate patter of a poisonous spider. I don't like this. Not one bit. My heart races in my ears, and I pull Trey close. He gives me a reassuring look, but it doesn't remove the panic in my eyes.

"This way," Victor says, and starts climbing the stairs.

Trey puts his hand on the small of my back; a single pulse of encouragement trickles into my skin – it's warm and smells like weekend mornings and fresh linen. I take a step onto the stairs and frown as I peer at the ivory staircase. My fingers skim the undulating banister pole. I recoil, stumbling back down the stairs into Trey. "It's bone..." I say, looking up at Victor, "the poles are made of bone?"

"I know," he says, grinning at me, "quite the fashion statement, aren't they?"

We climb floor after floor of stairs, and after a while, beads of sweat form on my brow, and I pull to a stop. "Haven't we been past this landing already?" I ask.

Victor sighs, "Karv, babe, stop dicking about, it's me."

Karv, babe? I glance at Trey; he's wearing the same repulsed expression I am. I'm not sure if I want to throw up or cut my ears off. I lean over the banister. Despite having climbed stairs for several minutes, we're only two floors up the bone staircase, and although I'm standing still, there's an uneasy rolling in my stomach like I'm on a boat. The harder I try to focus on the ground floor, the blurrier it seems.

"This is a trap," I say, grabbing Trey, "we need to get out."

A shuffle above me makes my head snap up. "Oh, bravo," the woman's voice says, "bravo indeed. Usually takes trespassers much longer to figure that out, if they do at all.

There was a Shifter once; he got lost in that loop for a month. I used to sit sometimes watching him and laughing as he cried, and begged, and tried to throw himself over the banister. He'd end up in a mangled pile of twisted flesh weeping. It really was delightful to watch."

She looks at me, my mouth hanging low. "Yes, well, you probably needed to be there... Anyway," she says, and gestures for us to ascend the final steps to her floor. I hesitate, unsure if I want to help bring back a Fallon that sees tricking and torturing people as fun.

I try to focus on her but I can't. It's as if I'm looking at her in my periphery vision. The sensation makes my toes curl. She must notice my apprehension because the fuzziness around her seems to soften as her face crystallizes. She smiles at me, but I'm not entirely sure if it's pleasant or horrifying.

Her skin is as smooth as her mother's, but unlike the First Fallon's milk-white skin, Karva's is much darker. Darker even than my desert-tanned skin. Her eyes are the same bright lilac mine are turning, and her hair is a mass of white curls. She's beautiful, in a terrifying kind of way. Her lips, even though they're relaxed, form a perfect pout. It's the only sharp thing about her as if she could spit venom at you at any moment. She and Victor are quite literally the perfect match.

"Can't be too careful down here," she says, pointing to the stairs, "sometimes it's hard to distinguish between friends and enemies."

I nod, still a bit awestruck by her appearance.

"Well?" she asks, "are you coming up or what?"

"Actually," Victor says, "I think we should make a move. Rozalyn will be tracking me now I'm back in Obex."

"Fine," Karva says, rolling her eyes. "We'll be boring

then. I just wanted to show our guests my collection of shrunken souls. They're super cute."

I look at Trey, and I wonder if he's thinking the same thing I am: we're about to let a certified psychopath out of Obex. I walk down the stairs shaking my head and put my hand on the front door handle. "Right, Victor, you've got what you wanted. Now tell me where Nyx is."

I open the door and freeze.

"Yes, Victor," the Last Fallon says. "Where exactly is Nyx?"

THIRTY-ONE

'We are all merely pawns in fate's game.'
Balance Proverb

"What's wrong, Victor?" the Last Fallon spits, "been hiding things from me, have you?"

She sweeps her long black coat tails around her back, revealing tight leather trousers and spiked heels. Her maroon hair is pulled back in a bun like it was last time I saw her. She wipes something dark and crusty from the corner of her mouth, and a bracelet with two crystals, one white, one maroon, catches my eye.

"I think we need a talk, don't you?" she says. But Victor's motionless behind me. "Let's go."

None of us move.

"I said, let's go." The Last Fallon grabs my wrist to pull me out the door but instinct kicks in, and Archie and Arna's lessons flood back to me. My fingers wrap around her wrist, electricity brimming at the pads. I twist her arm over, so I control the hold. My fingers squeeze her wrist, pressing the two circular crystals hanging from her bracelet into her arm. I try to let go, but I can't. Both our eyes snap up to each other, her maroon pupils as wide as my lilac ones. Then my vision blurs, and Obex dissolves.

When my vision clears, I'm confused and disoriented. It's like I'm in one of my dreams. I'm standing in the Ancient Forest outside the Council. But nothing looks the same. The five towering roots are no longer made of wood but mutilated bone. I spin around; the trees across the clearing are ash white. Instead of the billowing green canopy, their leaves are missing, and tree trunks that once held bulging branches are spindly tendrils poking out of the sea like tentacles.

In the middle of the clearing is an enormous statue of the First Fallon made of the same strange bone-white material as the Council towers behind me. Her face is serene, but even carved out of stone, the expression in her eyes makes my insides knot. It's vacant, hollow, lifeless.

An alarm rings somewhere in the distance. Keepers emerge from both the Council entrances and what's left of the forest. They too are wearing white, their hair, skin, essences all bleached of color. Every. Single. One. Of. Them. Their face are blank, devoid of any emotion like the First Fallon has drained Trutinor of life and replaced it with an army of bones. As if on command, the sea of faces all look up and stare straight at me. No. They're staring through me as if I'm nothing but a smudge that needs to be wiped clean like their surroundings. There's no recognition, no consciousness. Unease grows like a weed inside me.

A pair of Keepers stop near me so I ask, "What happened to this place?"

The one closest to me hesitates but eventually looks at

me. She's young, her eyes are the piercing blue of a Siren, but her skin doesn't look as it should. I can't see an essence scar and any essence she's giving off is so dull I can't tell what type of Keeper she is.

She smiles, but like her eyes, it's empty, and it makes the knot in my stomach tighten. "Why, it's become paradise," she says, "Trutinor is finally Balanced."

There's a tremor in her eyes. I almost miss it. But it was there as she spoke; she doesn't believe what she's saying. I frown at her. But she blinks rapidly, her smile widening, then she turns and hurries to catch her Balancer, and they disappear.

I'm aware of a presence behind me. I turn, startled to see the Last Fallon at my shoulder.

"You shouldn't be here," she says, "no one but me can access the crystal's knowledge."

"This isn't the first time I've seen this place," I say.

"Well then," she says, staring at me, "do you see? Do you see now why you need to side with me? Why we cannot allow this to happen?"

"What is this place?" I ask, shaking my head as I scan my surroundings.

"It's the future. If my sister is allowed to continue her reign unchecked. What you see before you is her greatest desire. Control. Order. Power. Fate so entrenched it saps the essence out of life itself. She will cause us to lose everything that means anything: love; curiosity; spontaneity. It's the destruction of the most powerful force in all our realms."

"Which is?"

She turns to me, her maroon eyes boring into mine. Her head tilts to the side as if she's examining me. "Hope... She will destroy hope."

This is what I've been seeing. I know that for definite now. My dreams were showing me visions of the future. But I had two dreams, two versions of the future. My eyes sweep over her wrist there are two crystals. One white, one maroon. If the white crystal is the First Fallon's greatest desire, then the maroon must be the Last Fallon's.

"Eden, don't..."

I grab the Last Fallon's wrist, my fingers slipping over the maroon bead. My vision blurs like static, and a dark cloud smothers me. I cough, choking in the thick smoke. I wave my hand trying to clear it; when it does, I'm standing on the docks of Luna City, facing the city of bungalows, and they're all on fire. Great billowing plumes of black smoke fill the sky. Sorcerers, smeared with ash and dust, run screaming through the streets. One young Sorcerer with the fiercest green eyes I've ever seen stops in the middle of the street and turns to face me. Half her face is burned and blistered, her hair still smoldering. She's carrying a baby. She holds it up to us. Its eyes are blackened, burned from its sockets. Its mouth hangs loose, and half of its arm has darkened and burnt away revealing thin bones. I turn and gag, throwing up where I stand.

"You did this," she screams. "You. Did. This." Her voice is a low growl, a single finger pointing not at me, but over my left shoulder. At the Last Fallon. Over to the right, a bungalow collapses. Once the smog and dust clears, it reveals a lost soul demon, its mouth stretching over the head of a charred carcass as it swallows the body in one like a snake.

"You think this is better?" I ask, my voice barely above a whisper. Tears sting my eyes, and I'm not sure if it's heartache or the smoke. Sheridan was right, the prophetic part of my dreams wasn't Trey but the visions of the future. When she doesn't answer, I turn to her.

"Well? Do you?"

"Chaos is always better, my dear. After all, from chaos comes Balance."

I'm shaking so hard I swear my soul is quivering. Is this it? Is this what we get? Two choices? Hermia. Arden. Rozalyn. Sheridan. Castor. My parents. Everyone tells me there are only two sides to this war, that I have no choice but to choose. But what if I don't?

Both the sisters are as bad as each other. No matter who wins this war, no matter what the prophecy says, both of them will destroy Trutinor. The First Fallon with the idea of a 'perfection' so acute, the only way she can manifest it is to wipe away everything in an oasis of whitened nothingness. The Last Fallon thinks she's going to protect us from her sister. But she's been trapped in Obex, surrounded by Imbalance for thousands of years. She's nothing more than a caged animal, imprisoned by death and decay.

In that instant, I know my parents were right – war *is* coming. But they were also very wrong. There aren't two sides to this war. There can't be, not if we want to stand any chance of salvation. The only way to survive is to make another choice. There is an ancient Balance proverb that says: *There is only light and dark. Balance and Imbalance. Right and wrong. There are only two sides to every war.*

But as I stand there, watching Trutinor melt away in flames, I decide to rewrite the proverb: *There is only light and dark. Balance and Imbalance. Right and wrong. There are only two sides to every war.*

Unless you find another path.

That's the moment I decide: I'm going to kill them both.

THIRTY-TWO

Nyx Kilburn, Private Journal
25th October, 2017

The door. It's real. I saw it. I'd forgotten the stories
Mama told me until I stood there, my hair on end,
shivering at the throb pulsing in the door's frame. It
was asking me, pleading to be opened. It was
seducing me in the same way I imagine the
Mermaids might've sung to their prey. It wanted
me, and if Eden hadn't interrupted, I would have
given myself to it. That bit wasn't in the fairytales.
The yearn to unite with the door. I can't imagine
the First Fallon wanted that, but then, dark magic
has a way of betraying you. That scares me more
than anything. Where will I go? Will I still exist?
Or is soul death my destiny?

I know she's coming. Rozalyn, I mean. The
door felt me, which means she felt me too. I've
decided I won't run. There's no point. Like the

fairytale said, it's my destiny. But what's breaking me isn't knowing I'm going to die, it's the people I'm leaving behind. It makes my heart ache like it's choking on poison. My beloved Titus, I will at least take comfort in praying I see him in the next life. But Eden, my baby girl, she's already lost so much, and all I keep thinking is who will be there for her now?

I blink, and I'm standing on the doorstep of Karva and Victor's house. I let go of the Last Fallon's arm, a glance passing between us. There's a swoosh behind me, and I'm swept into a pair of arms. A second later, black wings fill my vision and darkness descends over me.

This time, when we're thrown out of the black void, it's onto stone slabs. I land on my back, and it takes me a moment to reorient myself. We're in a set of colosseum ruins, with Ionic pillars towering above us like guards and broken slabs scattered around the area. The air is warm and brittle, crumbling like the ruins.

"Dammit, Karva," Victor shouts from behind me. "I thought you said the house was protected from her?"

"It was. It is," she says, almost whining.

"Well, clearly not well enough."

"Eden?" a quiet voice says from somewhere behind me. I sit bolt upright, searching for the voice. Then I see her.

Nyx, dirty, bloodstained, and exhausted, chained to what looks like the Door of Fates. I leap to my feet and sprint across the stone to her, scooping her into my arms and squeezing so hard she taps my back. I let go and try to examine her, but tears are blurring my vision so much I can't see.

"Oh, Eden, honey, I'm so glad I got to see you one more time."

"One more time?" I say, shaking my head, "what are you talking about? I've got you now; I'm taking you home."

She gives me a soft smile, her green cat-eyes curved with sadness.

"Don't do that, Nyx. Don't you give up on me, I'm getting you out of here."

"We both are," Trey says, appearing by my side.

"Look at you two," she says. This time the tears are in her eyes, "You'll make beautiful babies one day."

As she lifts her hand up to wipe the tears away, the chains keeping her bolted to this other Door of Fates rattle and clink.

"Is that what I think it is?" I ask.

She nods. "It's the other side of the door. My mom used to tell me a fairytale as a child. About a magical girl who bore a lock mark on her skin. She used to tell me how powerful this little girl was and that one day she would open the doors between all the worlds bringing everything that was once fractured back together. But I was just a child, and I lost her when I was so young I'd forgotten all about the stories. Until..." her voice cracks.

"Until that morning in Stratera?" I say, remembering our first day there, how frazzled she looked when she found the door.

She nods. "The stories came flooding back, and I felt the throb in my cheek. I knew then that the stories were true."

I slip my hand inside Trey's, tears welling in my eyes. He kisses my forehead and squeezes my hand.

"Aww," Victor says, staring at us, "it would almost be sweet if you hadn't had to murder me to be together."

"You've got what you want, Victor. Leave us alone."

He laughs, "I'm not even close to getting what I wanted. The deal was to get Karva back into Trutinor." He pauses, folds his arms, and glances around the stone colosseum. "By the looks of things, I'd say we were still in Obex."

There's a ripple in the air, and behind Victor, the Last Fallon materializes holding a short silver dagger, or maybe it's a key. I slide in front of Nyx, my spine tingling as I realize it *is* a key. It's *the* key. The one Victor was searching for, the one that will end Nyx's life and tear down the barrier between Obex and Trutinor. Trey must realize what it is too, as he moves next to me forming a barrier between the Last Fallon and Nyx.

She looks at us and laughs, one short sharp indignant snort. *The patronizing bitch will have to go through my cold dead body before she gets to Nyx.*

"Well, isn't this quite the little family reunion," the Last Fallon says, then she scruffs Victor by the collar and slaps him so hard on the back of his head his teeth clamp down, and he spits blood over the floor.

"You stupid fuck. You could have had everything. You had so much potential. But you had to go and fall in love with my niece of all people. Did you really think I didn't know what was happening?"

He stays silent, motionless, save for the wrinkles drawing into his forehead and the rapid rise and fall of his chest. Karva moves, circling her aunt, step by step, like a cat hunting a mouse. The Last Fallon doesn't even acknowledge her. Trey glances at me and peels back. He paces around the group, mimicking the same steps Karva takes from the opposite side of the colosseum. He hunts her, while she hunts Rozalyn.

"I know what you're doing," the Last Fallon growls at Victor. Embers of fire stream from her mouth and a flame ignites in her eyes. "You think I'd let you sneak Karva through that door to prevent me from escaping?"

The flame in her eyes burns harder, and her lips peel over her spiked silver teeth. For the first time in my life I am terrified for Victor.

"How stupid do you think I am? What is it with you anomalies? You just can't toe the line, can you? Well, you will now, boy."

The vein on Victor's forehead darkens, as do his eyes. His face contorts, stretching and pulling his skin tight over his sharp bones until it's not him anymore but the Last Fallon. Both of her faces smile, pulling his lips into a warped grin. I step forward, but Victor holds his hand out, and I freeze.

"I wouldn't do that if I were you," they both say.

"You're not killing Nyx." My hands throb where enormous electricity pulses spin around my fists.

"Hand," Victor and the Last Fallon say. Victor raises his palm out flat, and the Last Fallon places the dagger-like key in his hand. I shift my body weight, aiming my fists straight at Victor.

"Eden," Nyx gasps in a strangled voice. I spin around. For ten long seconds, Nyx's body quivers as it shifts and spasms between her cat-self and Keeper-self. Then her body convulses and stays in her Keeper form, her face crumpled, pale and sweaty, as if the rapid change drained her. All except the birthmark on her cheek, which is now black. Her face contorts, her chin and cheek dropping as pain creases her expression. *Nyx.* I take a step forward, but she shakes her head at me. "It's already too late," she says, tears brimming over her lids.

No. My chest clamps so tight I stop breathing. It can't be too late. It can't. But the skin inside the birthmark is dissolving into a hole, perfectly shaped for a key. Just like the fairytales, it was never a birthmark; it was always a lock mark.

Her eyes are wide and wet. Her body is yanked upright, her arms chained to each side of the door, stretched out. She's shaking, but like the soldier that refuses to face the final battle lying down, she looks the Last Fallon straight in the eye.

"No," I shout, and spin on my heel launching multiple bolts of electricity at both Victor and the Last Fallon.

"Victor, STOP," I shriek.

I halt, unsure of who to go to first – Nyx, Victor, or the Last Fallon. Victor is much closer than Nyx. He angles the dagger-key at Nyx, and my body lurches forward, sprinting toward him, throwing as many pulses of electricity as I can. They ricochet off pillars and crack slabs in two. For each bolt I throw, the Last Fallon counters it with five more, batting them away like I'm nothing more than an irritating wasp.

I change direction, and just like the drills Archie and Arna made me run, I throw fireball. Watercuffs to the ankle and fire wrapped in electricity to his chest. But I stumble to a halt. I'm too late. He's already released the key, which is flying through the air toward Nyx's face as if pulled by an invisible magnet. I break into a run, stretching out my fingertips trying to grab the key, but everything moves in slow motion. The key is always an inch too far away.

Nyx's eyes close, she leans her head back, and the key slams into her face, clicking into the lock mark. I land at her feet. The handle of the knife-key shunts out like it's ejecting something. A glass cylinder appears. Inside the tube is a shimmering cream liquid: blood from the Heart of Trutinor.

She glances down at me, her eyes fixed on mine, and in that silent connection, a thousand things pass between us: the love, the loss, the memories, the family she became. A tear falls down her cheek, and her arms stiffen, her body erupting in light, and the key falls to the ground.

"No," I shout. "NO."

A sharp pain fills my chest as I scream and reach out to her, but shards of light are emanating from her torso, limbs, and head as if she is her own sunrise. The shadow of her face fades into the glistening cloud of sparkles. Her body disintegrates, molecule by molecule, dissolving, floating into the air, dancing with the sunlight, until she's a swirling mass of shimmering particles. The image of her, and the sensation of my tears stinging my cheeks as I watch her drift apart, burns into my memory.

Like a newborn star, the particles rush together forming a ball, compacting, growing, and building until they're a dense throbbing mass. Then she explodes.

The force of the explosion flings me backward. A sheet of blinding light floods my eyes as a thunderous crack emanates across Obex. The ground quakes as a hole fractures the colosseum's stone slabs like an earthquake. I slam into the ground. Victor rips the electricity loop from around his chest and crawls to where Nyx was standing. He grabs the key, which now looks less like a key and more like a normal knife, and stands but freezes on the spot.

Trey's eyes are blazing blue. A trickle of blood oozes out of his nose and the Last Fallon, her expression contorted as if she's fighting some internal battle, has her hands around Karva's neck.

Trey's controlling her. Then there's an ear-splitting crack-crack-crack that sounds like gunfire, and everyone turns to the Door of Fates as threads split down the silver door, and it bursts open. On the other side, standing in Stratera Academy foyer, is the First Fallon.

THIRTY-THREE

> *'Never trust a Fallon that can't keep the Balance.'*
>
> *Lionel East – R.I.P. - 13th January 1972 - 3rd July 2017*

The First Fallon steps through The Door of Fates. A scream fueled by pain and fury explodes through the colosseum, cracking pillars, breaking stone slabs, and making me drop to my knees and cling to my ears wondering if this is what will shatter our worlds and make the walls collapse.

The Last Fallon charges at her sister, swinging electricity, and fire, and wisps of magic. A green wisp slams into a slab next to me. The stone blackens, hisses, and disintegrates. When the sisters plow into each other, the impact is like an aftershock. I'm buffeted across the floor, over and over, as they throw punches, and I struggle to gain my footing. I commando crawl over the floor toward Trey. I reach him, and we cling to each other.

"How are we going to close the door?" I ask.

Karva and Victor try to pick their way across the stones, but the Last Fallon blocks their path, using fireballs, and wind to throw stone slabs as obstructions.

"I'm going to compel them," Trey says.

"Them? Both of the sisters?" My eyes are wide, terror filling my body. The first time he tried to control the First Fallon he collapsed from the exertion, there's no way he can control them both at the same time.

"What choice do we have? Either Karva or Rozalyn has to walk through, and I know who I'd rather pick, even if that means giving Victor what he wants."

A stone slab flies above our heads and smashes into smithereens against a pillar. Trey stares into my eyes. He smiles and touches my cheek, but there, buried underneath his softness, is the fear that paralyses me.

"I love you, Eden. Only you. Always you."

"Trey. Stop," I say, "you're talking like this is the end, that this is goodbye."

"Am I not allowed to tell you how much I love you?"

"Yes. But the way you're saying it is scaring the crap out of me."

He closes his eyes and leans down until his forehead touches mine. "It's time," he says, his breath trickling over my skin. The scent of his frankincense and summer aftershave fills my nose and makes my eyes close. A nudge of his emotion presses against me, gentle and full of unconditional love. But behind it, just like his eyes, I feel the tremble of his fear. He's afraid, and so am I.

"Kiss me first," I say, gripping his shoulders till my knuckles whiten. "Kiss me like everything's going to be okay."

And he does.

In amongst the aftershocks, the flying slabs, and the crack of exploding magic, there's one blissful second of his lips on mine. One second of unity, our essences mixing and flowing together under the orange sky, surrounded by ruins. He slides his lips over mine, wrapping me in his arms. He releases a little more emotion: the wanting, the longing, the acres of love that fill my soul and complete me.

"I love you, Trey, in this lifetime and all the lifetimes to come."

He gives me one final short kiss on the lips then he's gone, hauling himself up and fighting against the aftershocks of the sisters' fight. His hands fly up, his eyes blazing with an intensity I've never seen, and his body quivers under the pressure. Both the Fallons freeze, their backs stiff, their eyes skirting left and right, trying to understand what invisible force is controlling them.

"Run, Karva," I scream.

She sprints across, reaches the door, and says, "Hurry, baby," to Victor who has made his way behind Trey. Then she walks through The Door of Fates, and a blinding white light blankets the colosseum.

"NO," the Last Fallon shrieks. She lets out a deafening roar; sharper, fiercer, and filled with frustration. She turns on Trey, breaking his compulsion. He falters, then raises his hand capturing her in his grasp again. But this time, blood trickles from his nose and eyes, and I scream for him to stop. As I do, Victor's hand slides around Trey's neck, and a glint of something silver makes my blood turn to ice.

Silence descends on the colosseum. The only sound is the drip of blood falling from Trey's nose and splashing against the floor as he tries to keep hold of both the Fallons.

"Oh, Eden," Victor says, his voice cutting through the silence like a homing missile.

He's holding the dagger he used to kill Nyx under Trey's chin; it's nestled next to his carotid artery. My heart pounds in my ears, my breathing loud, ragged, and cut with fear.

"Ironic, isn't it?" he sniffs. "You had to kill me, to be with him, and now I'm going to kill him, to be with her. We've come full circle. Kind of serendipitous for me, isn't it?"

"You don't have to do this," I plead. "Karva's already walked through the door. Let him go."

"Oh," he says, "I know I don't *have* to do it." His eyes twinkle; hatred drenches his black pupils. He leans in and inhales the scent of Trey's neck like he used to do to me, as if he's savoring the aroma of dinner. His eyes lock onto mine. "But the First Fallon asked me to, and let's be honest; I was only too happy to oblige. Any last words?"

"Victor, ple..."

"Too late," he shrugs, and plunges the dagger into Trey's neck.

THIRTY-FOUR

'I love you, Eden, for all the lifetimes.'
Trey Luchelli

They say that when you die, your life flashes in front of you. I don't know what Trey saw as he stood there bleeding out. But as the knife sliced into his neck, and bright red spurted in thick gushes down his chest, that's exactly what happened to me.

I take a breath, time slows, and in the instant it takes for his life to slip away, our life, the one we'll never have together, flashes before my eyes.

Our hands lace together as we kiss under a thousand sunsets. Glances stolen across hundreds of Council meetings. We stand on top of my home tower, me pirouetting around his arms under clouds of rain and thunder, the lightning dancing in the sky with me. Evenings spent by the Pink Lake, staring at a starlit blanket above us, blossom and petals falling from the trees and landing in our hair like confetti. Our family, two children with lilac and blue eyes, running by our feet as we smile and laugh and love. Growing so old, and wrinkled, and happy, that joy lines paint our ancient faces like smiles. Our essences age and entwine like the matt of a tree's roots as we spend our lives together.

All of that passed before my eyes in a single breath. When I exhale, it's gone.

And so is Trey.

THIRTY-FIVE

'Death of a Balancer – Once Bound, two souls are inextricably linked. Meshed together for eternity. The death of one Balancer is, in essence, the death of part of the surviving Balancer's soul. There are few words worthy to describe the agonizing pain of such a loss and is, in part, why many do not survive the loss.'

Excerpt - *The Book of Balance*

The vault doesn't just crack open, it obliterates my entire subconscious and consumes my body like liquid fire. With Trey's compulsion broken, the First Fallon swings for her sister, the crack of fist to head so loud it sounds like a bomb. Rozalyn crumples to the floor, unconscious.

When I turn back, Victor's running through the Door of Fates after Karva, and Trey's limp body is slumped on the ground, red spittle spurting like a fountain from his neck and mouth as his breathing slows, and the rise and fall of his chest shallows.

The First Fallon walks toward me, her pure white figure splattered in blood and stony dust. Her lilac eyes smile at me. "So much for the prophecy," she laughs, a glint in her eye.

"I won't just kill you," I shriek. "I'm going to destroy you."

But she laughs at me as she walks over to Trey's body.

"Don't you touch him," I scream, and run at her. She waves her wand at me without even looking in my direction, and something grabs hold of my legs and yanks, hard. I'm pulled away from her and toward the Door of Fates. A choked cry escapes my throat as my nails scratch the stones desperate to stay put. My feet, followed by my body, lift up, making me float horizontally as if an invisible rope is pulling me back into Trutinor. She leans over Trey's body, slides the dagger-key out from his neck, and licks the end. She wipes the remaining blood on her white dress and says, "It's already over, Eden. Without Trey, you're no more dangerous to me than a human infant."

She flicks her wand, and I'm flung backward through the door and into Stratera Academy. There are students running and screaming everywhere. Yells rip through the air like bullets. Professor Astra has her hands up barking orders and giving directions to clear the foyer. Professors are collaring students and hurrying people outside.

When the First Fallon walks through the door, the ground rumbles. Fragments of the exploded silver lift up from the ground and fly from Stratera and Obex to slot into the frame like puzzle pieces meshing together.

She's rebuilding the door? The final pieces slot into place, but there's a hole in the middle.

I inhale; my breath is harsh, cut with hate and rage, and it roars in my ears like the breath of a hurricane. My heart flares to life, beating a slow boom that fills my head. My eyelids blink shut, enveloping me in a fleeting darkness filled with Trey's face. The images of his death fire across my mind in rapid succession. Over and over he dies. Sheridan was wrong. The visions of Trutinor weren't the only prophetic part.

Trey. Is. Gone.

When I open my eyes, the darkness is still there, or maybe it's in my head. The whispers of encouragement echo around my head like furious commands.

Kill the First Fallon.

Kill Victor.

No. Kill. Them. All.

The vault is controlling me. And this time, I let it because Trey is gone. Forever. Heat floods my chest, my body encasing itself in electricity that throbs and pulses around me like a halo.

"He's gone because of you," I shriek.

"Yes. Wonderful, isn't it?" she says, "no more prophecy. No more stopping me. I *will* bring Balance to Trutinor."

With every pump of my heart, Imbalance courses through my veins.

"Oh, come on, darling. Dry those tears, he's not dead, yet. You haven't had the exquisite pain of your soul tearing in two - yet." She sucks in a breath, "I'd say you have at least thirty seconds before that happens."

She's right. I'm not hurting; there's no searing or burning, I still feel whole. I let myself slip under the comforting control of the Imbalance. I throw my arm up, launching a bolt of electricity out and flick my wrist so it boomerangs and loops around her neck. I draw on wind, picking up tables and yanking CogTVs off the wall to throw at her. She rolls those intense lilac eyes at me as if she's bored, "Oh, please."

She bats the electricity rope away, and it disintegrates before it hits the ground. She circles me, her white dress dragging over the checkered tiles of Stratera's foyer. We circle each other. An ominous black cloud forms above our heads. The first splashes of heavy rain fall to the floor. I glance up. Error. She launches a stream of fireballs at me. I roll out of the way just in time. The first misses me, so does the second. But the third careers into my side, knocking me to the ground. She sprints, fast, sliding across the floor. And grabs my wrist and snaps my arm, the bone piercing the skin, and blood gushes out around it. I cry out, the excruciating pain making gray smatter my vision.

I plead with myself not to pass out. From the floor, I use my other hand to shoot a patch of ice out making it grow as fast as I can. Icy spikes rear up from the floor like stalagmites. She slips and trips, dropping to the tiles and scrapes her white cheek on the sharp point of an icicle as it spears up toward the ceiling.

"Little bitch," she says, regaining her composure and wiping the smear of red off her face. Pain-tears sting my eyes, the strength of the Imbalance abandoning me right when I need it. She laughs as she uses my broken arm to haul me to my feet. But she doesn't notice me breaking another icicle off with my other hand. I slam it into her gut.

She rolls forward, before staggering back. First, she laughs, the light giggle of shock. Then her face grows hard as she examines the deep claret stain spreading down her dress and the drip, drip, drip of her blood pooling on the tiles.

"You got me. You actually got me," she says, and this time her voice cracks. It's the first real sign of weakness, and it tells me exactly what I need to know: she isn't infallible. She can be defeated.

I blink. I'm hoisted into the air by my neck, her hands around my throat, squeezing so hard that the last of the Imbalance that filled my vision spots and dissolves along with any remaining strength I had. As my legs dangle off the floor, my arm bleeds, and she chokes the air out of my lungs.

She lowers me until I am level with her face. Her lips pull into a sneer.

"Do it," I cough out. "Squeeze the life out of me." *You'd be giving me exactly what I want anyway.*

She cocks her head at me, narrowing her eyes as if she's reading my thoughts.

"Do you think I'm an idiot?" She laughs and spins me around to face the door.

In the hole in the center of the door is a single maroon eye glancing from me to the First Fallon. *Rozalyn.* A sharp sear follows as the First Fallon slashes the knife that killed Trey over my cheek. Warmth oozes down my jaw. She wipes her fingers over my face and smears my blood on the door. Then she throws me backward, and the wind is knocked from my lungs as I hit a piece of broken furniture and slump to the tiles.

The door shudders in its frame as if the Last Fallon is banging her fists against it. The First Fallon lifts her wand, and the hole in the door fills, sealing Trey and the Last Fallon inside Obex. A white thread drifts from where the hole was and floats across the foyer toward me.

"You're not going to win," I manage to splutter out. As

the thread wraps around my arm, it fizzes and sizzles burning a mark on my skin. A mark just like Nyx's. She's making me the new lock.

She crouches down to my level. Staring. Waiting. Silent. *What the hell is she waiting for?*

Then I realize. *Trey.*

I scream, my eyes full of fear as a heat that feels like lava coats my heart then shifts direction and streams like a fountain into my lungs. I scream and tear at my chest with my good hand trying to stop the burning, but it's in me. It's a part of me. I drop onto my back, the blistering heat unbearable. Sweat trickles down my temples and drops to the tiles.

"Is that so, Eden?"

My back arches as my chest is yanked upward by an invisible force. My body is intact, but it feels as though I'm being unbuttoned from the inside out. Like I'm a rag doll made of flimsy fabric and stitches, and they're being snipped and pulled until the thread and fabric unwinds. Pieces of me that I didn't even know existed fall away. I want to reach out, grab hold of them, but there's nothing there. More and more of me shrivels and desiccates until there is an expanse of emptiness inside me. A void of nothingness that gouges scars into my soul like a canyon.

"Looks like you've already lost to me," she says, but pauses, her mouth dropping. She coughs, blood spilling over her lips, and the hesitation reminds me she can be killed. Even lying there half conscious, I know with every cell in my body that I will end her. She vanishes in a puff of navy blue smoke.

I lie still on the checkered tiles of Stratera foyer. Tears that burn like acid stream down my cheeks mixing with the blood and dirt and pain covering my body. I am broken in body, heart, and soul.

There's screaming and sobbing and shrieking that sounds like the infinite torture of hell. The screams slice through my eardrums, but it's not until I'm aware of people creeping closer, staring down at me, that I realize the harrowing noises are mine. My world tilts and bends, the life I thought I would have splintering into a million pieces and flinging me into a realm of pain I didn't know was possible.

Bo hates me. My parents are gone. Nyx has been murdered.

Blood from my arm and face seeps across the tiles, making me dizzy and nauseous. In that moment of pain and vomit and blood, I am the kind of weak that only has two outcomes: survive or die. I wish for a quick death so I can be reunited with my soulmate. But death doesn't come. My heart continues to cry and twist and seize, but it never quits. As I slip into a shivery unconsciousness, I am left with one resounding thought:

Trey is dead.

THANK YOU

EDEN WILL BE BACK...

Thank you for reading Victor. I hope you love the second part of Eden's story as much as I do. If you did, and you can spare a few minutes, I'd be really grateful if you left a short review on the site you purchased your copy.

You can be the first to hear about the next sequel and rest of the Eden East series in **CogMail** by clicking/following the **eepurl** link below.

www.sachablackbooks.com
eepurl.com/cqA2B5
sachablack@sachablack.co.uk

ACKNOWLEDGMENTS

At this point, I usually thank coffee, chocolate, and all the bad stuff your mom tells you not to eat. Without them I'd have crashed and burned in a pile of unfinished Victor-like sentences. But more important than the sugary, caffeinated delights, I need to thank the people around me for their relentless support even when I was in various pits of despair.

My wife first, thank you for being so patient, for letting me follow my dream, and for giving up endless evenings together so I can write another book. I promise you, one day, I'll give you back our evenings. My son, who is a constant inspiration to me, may you grow up knowing you can follow your dreams no matter what.

To Mum and Dad, thank you for giving me books that filled my brain with fairies and vampires and imaginary worlds.

To Bryony Toop, for your endless support, beautiful Instagram photos, and general legendaryness. You're the kind of reader and friend that makes me feel like a real author.

To my accountability partner, Allie Potts, thank you for continuing to pepper my life with equal doses of back rubbing encouragement and threats of eternal shame and remorse for failing to meet goals. And thank you for not abandoning me during those three dark weeks when I didn't think I could make it to the end of Victor.

Helen Jones, thank you for being that beacon of constant positivity and support, for making me feel better about my writing when I'm full of doubt, and for being an amazing and super-fast beta reader, and for teaching me how to bring emotion into my writing. You're heart is my emotional muse.

Suzie, thank you for being my personal asshole, I love you endlessly, your banter, animal puns and cut throat truths keep me straight.

Lucy, thank you for talking and listening to me on a daily basis and coaxing me off various cliff edges.

Thank you to Geoff for opening his home and providing a beautiful retreat that helped me reach the final hurdle drafting Victor.

To Esther, I'm indebted, always. Thank you for being with me on this writing journey and for taking my rough diamonds and polishing them to perfection.

Thank you to Joseph Salter for his amazing Latin talents.

Adam Croft, thank you for the sprints, unconditionally sharing your wealth of knowledge, and for your occasional banter.

Karli Cook, thank you for your positivity, always spreading joy, for sprinting with me and making me both motivated and accountable.

Last, and most importantly, thank you to you, the readers, without you, I can't make my dream of writing books as a living come true. So thank you for taking the time to buy and read Victor. I hope you've enjoyed the second install-ment in Eden's story and want to continue on her journey with me.

ABOUT THE AUTHOR

Sacha Black has five obsessions; words, expensive shoes, conspiracy theories, self-improvement, and breaking the rules. She also has the mind of a perpetual sixteen-year-old, only with slightly less drama and slightly more bills.

Sacha writes books about people with magical powers and other books about the art of writing. She lives in Hertfordshire, England, with her wife and genius, giant of a son.

When she's not writing, she can be found laughing inappropriately loud, blogging, sniffing musty old books, fangirling film and TV soundtracks, or thinking up new ways to break the rules.

Keepers - The First Book in the Eden East novels

Seventeen-year-old Eden East lives in a world ruled by fate.

A fact she accepted, until her soul was bound to her enemy. Now, accepting her fate is impossible, especially when Trey Luchelli appears. There's something strangely familiar about him. Something Eden really ought to ignore. But the more she tries, the more she's drawn to him. Eden is determined to find out what he's hiding, no matter the cost, even if it's her heart.

Then her parents are brutally murdered, and everyone's a suspect, including her best friend.

Murder. Secrets. Destiny.

They're all connected.

But the path to answers is fraught with betrayal and danger. And the closer Eden gets, the more she unravels a dark history that will force her to question everything she's ever known.

Keepers will transport fans of _The Red Queen_, _The Young Elites_ and _The Lunar Chronicles_ to a world unlike any other...

The Eden East Novels:

- Book 0 - Sirens (early 2019)
- Book 1 - Keepers
- Book 2 - Victor
- Book 3 - Trey (Late 2018)

13 Steps To Evil - How To Craft A Superbad Villain (and Workbook) For Writers

Your hero is not the most important character in your book. Your villain is.

If you're fed up of drowning in two-dimensional villains and frustrated with creating clichés, this book is for you.

In 13 Steps to Evil, you'll discover:

- How to develop a villain's mindset
- A step-by-step guide to creating your villain from the ground up

- Why getting to the core of a villain's personality is essential to make them credible
- What pitfalls and clichés to avoid as well as the tropes your story needs

Finally, there is a comprehensive writing guide to help you create superbad villains. Whether you're just starting out or are a seasoned writer, this book will help power up your bad guy and give them that extra edge.

If you like dark humour, learning through examples and want to create the best villains you can, then you'll love Sacha Black's guide to crafting superbad villains. Read 13 Steps to Evil and the companion workbook today and start creating kick-ass villains.

GLOSSARY

Balance - *The fundamental rightness of fate; the result of a met destiny; the correctness that comes from following the right path. Peace, unity, clarity and light must be strived for in order to achieve Balance.*

Balancer – *The Keeper or Fallon Bound to another; the one true soulmate.*

Balance Scriptures - *The Balance Scriptures are a powerful fate reading device capable of being read only by the First Fallon.*

Barrier – *The fabric of the universe that separates each world and realm.*

Binding - *The moment two perfectly Balanced souls are joined for eternity.*

Binding Scar – *The physical mark of a Binding. Usually in the form of string-like scars in the state colour of both Balancers in the Binding. The scar resides on the right forearm stretching from wrist to elbow.*

Bound – *When a Keeper or Fallon has been through their Binding Ceremony and has a Balancer.*

CogTracker – *A handheld cog-like computer device that has multiple functions: a communications mechanism for CogMail and CogCalls and it's also a Balance scanner.*

Double Binding - *Double Binding – Myth, a Binding that occurs between three Keepers.*

Dryad - *A form of Keeper closely related to the trees in the Ancient Forest. They have particular abilities to heal others, to aid in the keeping of fate.*

Dust – *A magical particle used in funerals that can Bind to the essence of a Fallon and subsequently forms a protective barrier over their city for a short period of time.*

Dusting - *The funeral ceremony of a Fallon.*

Dustoria - *The momentary euphoria a Keeper feels when a particle of Dust makes contact with their skin.*

Elemental – *A form of Keeper with particular abilities to control one element – their essence trace, to aid in the keeping of fate.*

Essence – *The core of a person; the sum of the soul. The essence is the manifestation of the heart and spirit of who and what a person is.*

Essence heads – *Physical and immortal representations of a pair of Keepers or Fallons that manifest during a Binding. The essence heads are the record of a Binding's life and a physical representation of the Binding and the unbreakable bond it forms.*

Fallon – *A royal Keeper who is able to control all of the powers of their state.*

First and Last Fallon - *During the creation of Trutinor, the First and Last Fallons were born. Sisters of Balance, they were created to bring peace to the worlds they preside over.*

Imbalance - *A fundamental wrongness that must be eradicated. A darkness that infects the soul, leaving damage, destruction and chaos in its wake. It must always be eradicated.*

Inheritance - *A mythical occurrence when two Fallons (parents) die simultaneously; part of their essence is transferred to their eldest heir. There are no official recorded instances of this happening.*

Jugo - *Unlike a Binding, which seals souls and magic, a Jugo connects two lives. If one lives, so does the other. If one perishes, they both do.*

Keeper – *A being from Trutinor, whose purpose in life is to keep the Balance of fate.*

Obex – *The world between all worlds. Nestled inside the fabric of the universe where time no longer exists.*

Potential - *the most likely candidate fated to be Bound to a Keeper or Fallon, as decreed by the First Fallon.*

Shifter – *A form of Keeper with particular abilities to shift into one animal – their essence trace, to aid in the keeping of fate.*

Simulator – *An augmented reality machine used to recreate Earth-like situations in order to examine Keeper students.*

Siren – *A form of Keeper with particular abilities to control one emotion – their essence trace, to aid in the keeping of fate.*

Sorcerer - *A form of Keeper with particular abilities to control one form of sorcery magic – their essence trace, to aid in the keeping of fate.*

Steampunk Transporter - *A Steampunk Transporter has the duty to protect, serve and ensure the safe passage of their state's Fallons, using whatever magical means necessary.*

The Six – *Trutinor's six highest ranking generals.*

Trace – *The physical mark of magic left on a body.*

Unbound Baby - *The birth of a highly Imbalanced baby caused by the lack of Bound parents.*

CPSIA information can be obtained
at www.ICGtesting.com
Printed in the USA
LVHW092341061118
596263LV00001B/125/P